JOURNEY OF LIFE AND DEATH

A COLLECTION OF ECLECTIC SHORT FICTION

LINDA MARIE

Journey of Life and Death: A Collection of Eclectic Short Fiction

FICTION / Mystery & Detective / Collections & Anthologies

Paperback ISBN: 978-1-7341737-4-1

Hardcover ISBN: 978-1-7341737-5-8

Library of Congress control number: 1-11941477571

Ref #1-5HHNX6Z

First printing edition, 2023

Cover art by Mike Oyenarte

*For my many dedicated teammates and colleagues in law enforcement and on the DMORT and DMORT WMD teams with whom I worked for so many years.
Together, we witnessed a fair amount of the vagaries of life and death in our chosen professions.
Thank you all for our journey together.*

As always, I thank my family, friends, and consultants who read and advise on my works in progress. Special thanks to Sheila and Randy Russell, Nancy Nichols, Dee Loran-Parker, and Rhonda Landers. I am truly grateful.

Gather ye rosebuds while ye may
Old time is still a-flying:
And this same flower that smiles today
Tomorrow will be dying

— ROBERT HERRICK

The last enemy that shall be destroyed is death

— 1 CORINTHIANS 15.26

We all sojourn to our final destination
I will see you when our time comes

— LINDA MARIE

CONTENTS

1

THE COLD HARD EVIDENCE

Sometimes, life zaps us with a real shocker – a flat-out zinger. When it hits a small, sleepy little town, it makes the thing all the more shocking. In our dot-on-the-map town of Egret Beach, Florida, we got that zinger in spades – an undeniable bombshell.

When you're a cop, you expect you'll get a case or two in your career that'll confound you – that's a given, I suppose. So you just work all the harder to solve it. If it lingers unsolved through the years, you pull out the case file year after year and take another look. If they're still alive, you call those old contacts to see if their story has changed. Did they see more than they initially revealed? Can the liars remember their lies and avoid detection? Have the guilty carried the burden of their crime for too long and need to unload? You check out the evidence again, spread it all on the table, and work it through every scenario in your mind until some smidgen of evidence or some piece of the puzzle grabs you in a new way and alters your perspective. Sometimes, you're lucky, and that baffling case is solved.

Sometimes, it lies dead in the water, or, in our case, it's solved – dead in the water.

The case we had to deal with in Egret Beach was one of those unsolved, tough-as-nails cases. See, the thing was that Violet was not a violent person. It threw *even me* for a loop. And everyone knows how cynical I am. As a police detective in a small town, you might think that cynicism wouldn't be part of the territory. You might think... how much hard crime actually happens in small towns? I'd say most people would be surprised. It happens. However, nobody could have anticipated a crime anything like what we experienced here – as I said – not even me.

The thing is, before I signed on with Egret Beach Police Department, I'd already done six rough, soul-hardening years in the worst areas of Los Angeles. That skewed vision of life and crime had already become part of me forever. So, I thought I'd seen every possible thing and nothing – I was absolutely sure – nothing could shock me anymore. I'd still have been in L.A., but two big life-changers happened almost simultaneously.

First, I lost Lorene. She was the reason I'd stayed in California, to begin with. We met and immediately fell for each other right after I was discharged from the Navy in San Diego. She was heading back to her home in Los Angeles, so I followed and got on with L.A.P.D. Life was good. Lorene and I never married, and things were great until they weren't. Then she was gone. Six years, and done. Better for both of us. Then, when my father died a few weeks later, my mom needed help. So, in the end, my family obligation sent me, lock, stock, and barrel, back to my old hometown in Florida.

So there I was at Egret Beach, Detective Stone Coulter. "Stoney" to my friends and "Stone Cold" behind my back. A small-town cop suddenly shocked out of my mind by a crazy, convoluted crime. It happened in a way I had never experienced in big-time Los Angeles. But you see, what threw me off is that it was too unbelievable. In every sense of the word. Even for stone-cold me.

This crime was such an unbelievable zinger because Violet was so meek and mild. She wasn't a cop, but one of our own, nevertheless. The woman seemed to take with grace every awful thing thrown her way and believe me, she got hit with a lot. Besides taking things gracefully, top that off with the fact that she was a non-intrusive person. Not a "most likely to kill" type.

"Sweet Violet," we used to call her. We'd tease her by singing that old Mitch Miller tune. "Sweet Vi-o-let!" We'd sing. "Sweeter ... da da da da da." Crazy that I can't remember the words because we teased her so much with that song. Been too long, I guess. Anyway, she'd stand there, blushing and avoiding our eyes like a Sunday school teacher caught with a beer. She was so slim, and quiet, and so nearly non-descript that it seemed she existed virtually invisible. She loved country music and a Chihuahua named Tyson. We knew that about her, but if someone asked you to describe her, it couldn't help but cross your lips that she was "just average." And that's coming from a guy trained to observe and gather information on people. In fact, though she had brown eyes and brown hair and was petite of stature, the only truly remarkable physical thing that stood out that I could recall about Violet was that blush. The most innocuous comment of appreciation could set her to blushing. It was as if she was embarrassed that she was taking up space. It was a part of her and remained so even after she'd lost her innocence, as we'd discover long after the fact.

No one would ever suspect violence from Violet. She was

just so stoic and so easygoing. Too easy, I guess. Must be why she stayed seventeen years with her husband, Marvin. I never met the guy, but they say that he abused her pretty regularly and pretty severely. She'd come in with bumps and bruises and black eyes, but always claimed that clumsiness was the culprit. But, of course, people didn't believe it. People swore it was Marvin. Violet swore it wasn't. That guy was bad news, though. He was so bad, in fact, that nobody thought she'd ever get married again after he ran off with some low-class woman from his high school reunion.

The whole issue of abuse was a sad situation. But, in those days, familial abuse was still an accepted fact of life. Some people just thought it was a husband's right, and some actually thought it was a man's duty to keep his wife and kids in line. Those who found that kind of attitude appalling still just figured that what happened within a person's home and family… well, it was their own business, and outsiders shouldn't interfere. Blind eyes everywhere. Unless it turned deadly, of course, and that's when us cops would come into the picture. Sadly, we rarely got called to intervene, and our participation often came just a little too late.

Ol' Marvin was before my time, but I heard enough stories so that I was a little surprised when Violet got married again. As I remember, it was in the fall of 1969, just under a year before Lois – the terror of our department – left on her eternal vacation. Violet met some ol' cowboy wanna-be who worked his charms on her. Some people just never learn. Sad to say, but that marriage was almost as bad as the first one. At least Violet lucked out after six months with James Willoughby and didn't have to serve another sixteen years of hard time like she did with ol' Marvin. Willoughby took off precipitously just a few months before Lois did. That ol' cowboy went back to Cincinnati, some said. Good riddance for our fair city, I said. But, of course, we found out much later where James actually went.

When Lois disappeared into the sunset, the ever-philosophical Violet just said, "You know what, Stoney? With James and Lois gone, darned if I don't feel like I've done had boots and high-heels surgically removed from my spine all in the same year."

I remember that she kind of chuckled and shook her head at the thought, and I said to her, "All good news and fresh starts for you, Kiddo. Time to enjoy your new-found freedom."

And she said to me, "I plan to do exactly that."

Privately I still thought, *ah...Violet. Perpetual victim if I ever saw one. Kind that just naturally draws in the abusive creeps of the world. Poor Vi.*

Violet became quieter than before, but she stayed sweet. Maybe that quiet should have been a red flag of some sort, but it raised no hackles on me. I've often wondered if there was some clue that I missed, but I just took it as part of Violet.

The fact is, police work makes some of us cynical. It makes some of us hardened, tough, distant, detached, alienated – you name it. Not all of us, obviously. Each person, over time, develops their own way of handling things. But, stay in this line of work long enough, see enough of the truth of humanity, and one of those adjectives will eventually fit some of us. We see the worst, and we're human.

Violet wasn't out there in the field seeing what we saw, of course, but she'd lived and suffered the hell of Marvin, Willoughby, and Lois, yet she had endured. She remained sweet, Violet. Quiet Violet. But, of course, it's the quiet ones that you really gotta watch out for. That's what I heard at the very beginning of my career as a police officer, and it sure held true for Violet. I guess I sort of got lulled into a false sense of ease regarding Vi. She was so unassuming that I disregarded the quiet in her.

None of us thought about that when Lois came up missing, however. Detective Tim French was assigned to the case, and I was partnered with him. I'd been in the department for just over a year then. I'd started out on the road. Even though I'd come from a big city department and probably had more hands-on experience from my years in L.A. than all of the Egret Beach force combined, the Chief had initially put me on hold. I imagine he had planned to knock out any big-city ideas that I'd brought along and have me learn the Florida statutes *and* the Egret Beach way of doing things. Still, Chief was smart enough to realize I could be an asset in the detective unit and assigned me there after eight months when he found out French was having health problems and talking early retirement. From the beginning, I tried hard to keep my mouth shut when I saw things I'd have done differently. I mostly succeeded, I think. Only when my silence would detrimentally impact the case did I speak out and loud. Even then, I'd hear a few stray remarks about my "big city, know-it-all ways." So, I'd been taking a firm back seat whenever it made no difference to the outcome of a case but would undoubtedly foster resentment.

So, at the time Lois went missing, I was a detective in a four-man unit. Initially, I was assigned to and played tag-along with Tim French. Treated as an interested observer. That's how it was when Lois went missing in the late summer of 1970. Shortly after that mess, French decided I could contribute without ego, and we worked as full partners until he retired.

I remember the Lois fiasco well. It was the talk of the department for a good many months before it began to be slowly replaced with new issues. After the way it went down with Lois, I think the chief wanted it to disappear. Through the years, it was occasionally referred to jokingly by one disgruntled officer or another threatening to "pull a Lois Crully." The case resurfaced from tips received here and there for fragments of time. Sightings and such. But all those tips came to nothing. For me, though, the case never ended. After French retired, I continued to follow the leads and possible sightings that trickled in here and there. For a detective, unsolved homicides or missing persons cases like Lois' are never over till they're solved.

Looking back, I guess I'd have to say we were blindsided by the way it all happened. Maybe a greater investigator would have entertained more possibilities. Unfortunately, French and I have to take that hit. Not one glance did we give Violet. Damn – not *Violet*. If it had been anyone else, we might have said, "Well now, wait a minute, and let's look at this person over here who took so much Lois abuse." But Violet? No way. The thought just never occurred.

When it all went down, I was still on "hold," watching and listening, of course. I was privy to all the information being gathered, though. Old-timer, French, was the lead investigator. I knew everything about the case that French knew, so I've got no excuse there. I admit it. It's just that it all seemed so plausible. Not one clue or thought led us in anybody's direction except straight to Lois. The evidence fit. No squirrely bits to gnaw at your brain. It was so cut and dry: Lois Crully "took the money and run."

Ah… Lois. How do you describe a "Lois?" I'll bet that most working people have seen her personality type on the job. The complete opposite of Violet, that's for sure. Her hair was either prematurely white, or she bleached it out that way. I never knew which. She was a large woman – not fat. I don't mean that. She was one of those big-boned women with an ample bosom and hips to match, but in a tightly packed package. Lois was one of those you'd see walking down a hallway and know for sure that you could bounce a quarter off her anywhere, and there wouldn't be an inch of give. Very tightly packed. She wore form-fitting clothing that confirmed the details, and when she marched down the halls with her heels click-click-clicking on the polished tiles, there wasn't a bit of bounce to her. It was the same with her personality. Not a bit of bounce. All trounce.

Lois once reamed out little Susie Pine for a minor typo that had no real significance. She did her reaming in front of two other detectives and me. When Lois finished her tirade, she clicked off down the hallway. Susie, thoroughly embarrassed but feeling the need to say something, looked each of us in the eye slowly, one by one. Then, out of the blue, just like it was normal conversation, she said, "Lois Crully sounds like a horse pissin' when she pees." We nearly fell on the floor laughing. For long minutes, we couldn't stop. That picture just would not leave our minds. Well, it just fit Lois to a T, is all I can say.

When Lois Crully disappeared, she was vested in our meager retirement fund as a twelve-year employee in the Egret Beach Police Department. She got hired on at a time when there were few women in law enforcement, and those who got appointed filled the menial and clerical positions. Lois was different. Her brother Robert was chief at the time, so she got a pass on everything and easily worked her way around the department. Lois gathered no moss but plenty of dirt along the way. She eventually became Robert's secretary. Now, being the secretary for the Chief of police in some big departments was a good job and paid better than most other jobs women could get in those Neanderthal days, but our department was small. It surely wasn't big enough or lucrative enough for Lois. She wanted to *run* something.

When Lois disappeared, we'd had our new Chief, Bill Watson, for just over six months, and still, the hateful woman had dug up nothing on him. It was true that he was the cousin of one of the county commissioners, but he was well-qualified for the job, nonetheless. Watson had retired out of Jacksonville, which was a little beyond Lois' reach for scandal and gossip. Chief Watson was a real upstanding guy and a family man from all I could see. I think Lois finally realized she was never going to get much on him. He saw the good in people, appreciated their work, and didn't seem to buy into her type of mentality even a little bit. I imagine Lois probably realized the chief would eventually see her ruthlessness and send her packing. I think she was smart enough to anticipate that. If the truth was known, she probably got herself out of his office before he could see what she was really about and toss her out with her coffee mug and pocketbook.

Anyway, from the beginning and over the years, as Lois had moved from job to job within the police department, she was able to try out things to see what she liked best. She had a knack for causing problems everywhere she went, eventually wiggling her way into better-paying positions. Some of those positions had traditionally gone to men. By the time her brother, Chief Robert Crully, had his stroke and died, Lois had gathered enough dirt on enough people to secure choice positions for herself for a lifetime. The dirt she gathered was rarely the crooked stuff, though there were rumors of a little of that, too, way back when. I suppose there are unscrupulous people in every profession and every walk of life. But no doubt, Lois, though, had all the dope on who was sleeping with whom, whose marriage was on the rocks, and who was hitting the juice or the dog track... or the wife – that kind of stuff. There was even a rumor that Lois kept a journal documenting all of the goings-on within the department. She carried a little book around with her, but nobody ever claimed to have actually seen what was written in it. It could have been just a scare tactic. I know that there were enough people afraid of what Lois knew or could do, that half of them just stayed out of her way, and the other half gave her anything she wanted.

When Lois began to see that her days were numbered as secretary to Chief Watson, she decided that it was time for a move again. It just so happened that there was a position open in the Property and Evidence Section—P&E, as we called it. She got in and soon overpowered the supervisor there. After working her machinations on the man, he retired early. That gave Lois the most seniority in that department, and she stepped right into the supervisory position. It surely gave her the most power and control outside of being a certified officer and moving up through the ranks. For women, becoming an officer was just about unheard of in the South at that time and certainly unheard of in our little department.

Once established in P&E, Lois ran her section with a fist as tight as her body. Nobody, but nobody, would question her authority. Now, some outside observer might look at her, watch her a little, and say, "She seems nice enough. Pleasant." But let me tell you, those nice words coming out of her mouth had an edge and an intent to them, and if the words were directed toward you – well, you knew you'd better watch your step. Some people have that kind of ability. Their words seem okay on the surface, but they hold a much deeper meaning. A bite. An implied threat. An excellent example of that threat is what I once overheard Lois tell a rookie officer. Tom Wilson wasn't long out of the academy when she stomped his confidence and showed him whom he should fear. She didn't see me standing by the lockers, hearing her in action.

Tom turned in some evidence from a burglary scene, which he listed as four items when there were only three. Lois says to him, "Uh-oh! Your evidence sheet says two Coca-Cola cans, a screwdriver, and a cigar box.... You got only one can here... What," she says this in a sweet sing-songy, accusatory voice, "What in the world have you done with the other can?" Says she. "Oooh-ooh, someone might construe this as tampering with evidence. Not good. Not good at all!" Poor Tom stumbled and bumbled, shuffling his feet and shuffling his report papers.

"Now, what did I...Oh, wait. Sorry! I remember now," he says. "See... this here can's got Coke spilt on it. Wet. I dusted the other one at the scene. Got prints and left it there... like they taught me. Just brought this sticky one. So... so processed one an' collected one. That's the two. Figured Buddy over in the crime lab could work the sticky one better'n me and...so... yes... so it's just the one can I'm turning in here. See... I just forgot that cause I had two barking-dog calls out on Yeller Toad Road an' then right after, see... had that fender bender out by the Baptist Church when ol' lady... I mean, Miz Swift from the flower shop run her big ol' Buick into the side of Whitley Brampton's pick-up... an' him hauling four of his hogs that broke loose an' we had to chase 'em down...an'...." He went on and on.

That poor guy. I thought about butting in but waited to see how far Lois would take it. Poor rookie. But already aware of Lois's reputation. He was so nervous facing her that his words ran together all rapid-fire, and if he'd gone on much longer, I do believe he might have confessed to killing

President Kennedy. But Lois was already tired of toying with him and interrupted: "Ohhhhh…" she says. "I see! Well… we'll just change this evidence receipt to list *one* can, then. I can fix that for you. Yes. I'll do that for you." Then she quickly made a notation in a little book she pulled from her pocket. Tom couldn't see that notation, but the implication was clear. Then Lois says in this low, confidential voice, "Now… no one has to know about this screw-up. It's just between you and me." And just as I walk up, she gives him a little conspiratorial wink. Later, I told Tom that was just Lois B.S., but I don't know if he believed me.

Scare tactics. That was Lois's way most of the time. She'd save little innocuous tidbits that didn't amount to a hill of beans. Later, she'd embellish her version of what happened. Later, when it would better serve her purposes. But she could be openly vicious, too. Some said it was like a game she played, and some said she was just downright mean and rotten to the core. No one ever challenged her that I knew of. Not even the new Chief. Of course, with all his duties and fighting with city hall to update our department, maybe he'd not had time enough to get wind of her antics. Some said that if there were dirt to be had on Chief Watson, Lois would eventually find it, but who knows?

I had Lois figured a little differently than most. I think there was a more fundamental principle at work there. My theory was that she was just one of those insecure control freaks. You've seen the type. We've all seen them. Whatever job they're in, they push and finagle and eventually carve out a niche for themselves while destroying others along the way. It starts off with simple, insignificant things. That person gets away with those small acts time after time because, *at the time,* it seems not worth challenging someone for something so petty. After a while, though, that Lois-type person has escalated to more significant issues. Finds they have cultivated a great deal of power from the many small victories. Makes 'em feel heady. In control and indispensable, one way or another, if you know what I mean. Then, they dig their heels in for the long haul. Once built, can't anyone touch their little kingdom, and God help anyone dumb enough to try. I think it's all based on fear and underlying insecurity. Others disagreed, of course. My lieutenant, Wylie Zorce, said I was wrong. Said Lois was just full of plain ol' meanness and power lust. Could be that he was right. Who knows? Only Lois knew for sure, I guess.

I bet that Lois caused the firing of a dozen employees over the years. Most were employees she supervised or worked with directly. Their biggest mistakes? They either showed too much interest or too much aptitude in their job, and that made them a threat to her. Others ticked her off, or she just didn't like their looks. Crazy as it sounds, one girl was booted for some flimsy reason, and Lois later admitted that she just couldn't stand to look at the girl. She made it so miserable for some that they left voluntarily because they simply couldn't take it anymore. Lois often acted as though she sacrificed people for the good of the department, but inevitably, her little, accompanying, sly smile gave away her thrill in the power. In the Lois years, many people in the department had valid reasons to dislike or even fear her. Violet was one of those people.

Violet had only been working as a trainee in P&E for a month when Lois took over as supervisor. She'd transferred from Chief's secretary to payroll, then, to make more money, Lois had moved on to P&E. That move sure made poor Violet earn her pay. I heard that Lois made the woman's life a living hell from the get-go. I couldn't figure out how Vi could stand it. Lois gave the woman lousy evaluations for not knowing her job, but she literally refused to let poor Vi learn anything that might ever threaten Lois's position. That woman made Violet into a whipping post, and Violet took the abuse. I'm sure Vi put up with it because she feared losing her job. She was actually the ideal employee for Lois to hang onto, and I think Lois knew that. Violet couldn't afford to quit, and she wouldn't or couldn't stand up for herself. I guess that Vi's experience with two lousy husbands had taught her to just keep her mouth shut and follow directions. I say you teach people how to treat you, and Vi was an experienced victim. She was the perfect victim for a dictatorial boss because, with Violet, Lois barely had to work at keeping the upper hand. Depending on her mood, she could toy with Vi, vent her frustrations, or ignore her entirely. Violet never fought back.

It was a rather sad and embarrassing thing to witness when Lois was on a rampage. First, she'd ream Violet out in front of anyone. Lois called her stupid, inept, lazy. You name it. She bad-mouthed Violet pretty consistently. Then, behind Violet's back, she'd tell others how kindhearted she was to allow Vi to keep her job. Poor Violet wouldn't even try to defend herself and stopped me once when I tried to step in to defend her. She'd just say, "Sorry, Miz Crully, I'll try to do better." I saw a lot of others crumble under Lois's pressure and persistence over the years, but I never saw Violet get ticked or flustered or even cry. She just took it and persevered. I guess when you really think about it, that kind of extreme self-restraint must indicate a deep inner strength. I know that I sure couldn't withhold the wrath of hell from someone who'd speak to me as Lois did to Violet.

Shortly before Lois went missing, I asked Vi, "How do you take that crap from her?" She looked me square in the eye and said, "I didn't cry for Marvin, no matter how danged bad it got in seventeen years... and it got pretty bad. Didn't let James get the best of me... so I don't think the likes of Lois Crully will crush me either." Then her eyes got this faraway look in them for a few seconds before she turned her focus back on me. She smiled this real funny smile. It looked like she might be gritting her teeth or something, but it was hard to tell. I waited for her to continue, and finally, she said, "Sometimes, Stoney... I've learned that sometimes it's smartest not to let your smarts show." Guess I found out that was true.

I don't know if it was insightful or cautious or an uncanny ability to read people, but though Lois did mistreat many others, there were some she left alone. I was one of a handful of those she approached with more caution or simply decided not to tangle with at all. It was as if she could sense a potential danger in people. Lois seemed to know who would knuckle under and who might bite back with a vicious fury. I'm sure she still looked for dirt on the ones she left alone because if she found something significant, *then* they'd belong to her. For most, though, the wrath of Lois could come crashing down at any time when they crossed her path. It was just so much worse for Violet, who was stuck in that evidence storage area with the old witch – day in, day out.

As you might expect with this kind of history, when Lois left for her two-week vacation to the Bahamas in September of 1970 and didn't return, the people in personnel and administration had some mild concern. They called her house but got no answer. They sent an officer there to check on her welfare, but everything appeared normal. Her house was secure. The officer peeked into her windows and saw that nothing seemed out of place. The ones aware of the situation decided to wait a bit longer to pursue the issue further. They figured that as pushy as Lois was, she might be inclined to take an extra week without asking. Like it was her due. Who would dare question her? The ladies in personnel were certainly not going to take that on. Nor Violet. And whoever alerted the chief was in for it when Lois returned.

When Lois was finally two weeks overdue, they began to take it more seriously. It might seem odd for them to wait that long, but it would not have been out of character for Lois to extend her vacation without previous approval. She'd done it before. So anyway, at the two-week vacation plus two-weeks-late point, personnel began looking for Lois in earnest.

The chief was advised, and employees in personnel made numerous phone calls trying to locate Lois through family members and even neighbors. It turns out that her few remaining family members and neighbors disliked her just about as much as the rest of us, and they had kept no regular contact with her. That was when Det. French and I were handed the missing person case, and a full investigation started. French and I made more calls and discovered that Lois had never checked in at the fancy hotel in Nassau that she'd bragged about getting a great deal on. When we told the Chief about the hotel, he started to get pretty nervous about the situation. He ordered Violet to open the safe in the evidence room. The safe held money from several cases and should have included ninety-six thousand dollars from our first, really major marijuana drug bust. That case made headlines all over Florida. It was a big haul for such a small department, but it had really just fallen into our laps because of bungling, drug-addled criminals.

The Chief's concern increased exponentially. He knew that the press would be all over it, and if Lois had pulled one over on the department... well, it wasn't going to paint a pretty picture. Years before, after a series of botched cases and Keystone Cops style blunders due to lack of training, Egret Beach P.D. had attained the moniker of "Barney Fife P.D." Unfortunately, it had taken years for that Fife-ism to wear off, and Chief didn't want that slapped on us again.

A sigh of relief was audible from all of us when Violet opened the door to the safe, and we saw the envelopes inside. There was one big fat envelope sealed with evidence tape and a couple of smaller ones, so at first glance, all seemed well. "Open them," the Chief had said. We all stood by and watched as Violet pulled on a pair of gloves and began to open those envelopes. She picked up the first one, cut through the seal, and pulled out a stack... of paper. She then fanned out and flipped through the pieces of newspaper cut to currency size. We were all momentarily speechless. I heard the chief suck in air, and it felt like he sucked every bit of oxygen out of the evidence room in that one breath. I let out a low whistle as French snatched the worthless papers from Vi, fanned, and flipped through them on his own. He rapidly tore open the remaining envelopes, and the newspaper money rained down everywhere. The Chief stood in frozen silence. French continued scattering the papers across the floor as if he thought his actions might somehow turn them into real money.

When news about the fake money circulated through the department, we all thought it was a shame that Det. French had not worn gloves before handling the papers. It was thoughtless, but a gut reaction by a genuinely disturbed detective. He just wasn't thinking, and quite honestly, we were all stunned to silence. We were expecting money in those envelopes, and with each one opened, the situation just got worse. Later, French had the lab check for prints, just in case – but Lois would have known to keep 'em clean anyway. She was too smart to mess that up. In the end, the only prints that turned up were those of French. No help there. In all, over a hundred and sixteen thousand dollars was missing. That was big money back then before the really big trafficking problems had overwhelmed Egret Beach and the rest of Florida.

With the money gone, Chief Watson had just about everybody in the department working on some bit of the investigation in one way or another. It was a real scandal in our little town. Hell... it went beyond. Made the papers as far as Tampa and even Ft. Myers. All points in between, too, I imagine.

French and I got a warrant and went to Lois's small house. We found her suitcases packed, stacked, and ready to go when we went inside. We figured that she'd somehow gotten spooked. Maybe she thought somebody was on to her, and she'd taken off in a hurry. Her purse, tickets, passport, and everything else was gone, including her car. Even though a passport wasn't needed for the Bahamas, Lois had bragged for weeks about receiving her passport and about her future plans to travel "abroad." We figured she'd used it and gone someplace where one was needed. We checked to see if the passport had been used. We checked all the airlines and cruise lines but got nowhere. We wondered if she had fake papers and went out under another name. Or maybe the bragging about a passport was to throw us off. We considered that, too. We just got nowhere on the case. Dead-ends at every turn. Her car was never found. Except for our "hasty retreat" theory, the left-behind bags remained a mystery. The real reason for finding those suitcases became clear later. Much later.

At the time it happened, though, aside from the black eye

for the department and the state's investigation, everyone was glad Lois was gone. She'd been such a nasty person around the station for so long that I don't know of one soul who genuinely missed her. I'm sure some people were more worried that she'd actually be located, go on trial for the grand theft, and possibly spill her guts on other stuff in the process. But, I can tell you one thing – the whole police department ran just plain smooth and easy after Lois departed.

Violet handled everything in P&E after Lois disappeared. The administration people saw that, in reality, she did know property and evidence procedures quite well despite evaluations to the contrary. So she was given the department and ran it alone for a while. Violet would be called to come in if important, oversized, or perishable evidence came in during the night. She never complained once and never got on-call pay for it. We all thought, *what a trooper that gal is*. A few years later, they finally hired an assistant for her, and Vi became the supervisor. It took a while, but eventually, the crime rate increased, the department grew, and they hired a couple more people to cover evening and night shifts.

Violet gained an air of confidence and contentment. I always thought that was because it was pretty apparent that Lois would never be returning to the P.D. Violet made her own mark over the years. She got commendations and such for excellence, professionalism, and service. The woman had smartened up in her personal life, too. She never married again after James Willoughby left her. Violet said she finally found out what true contentment was and how to get it. She told me that her version of happiness was reading, walking on the beach, the companionship of her dog, Tyson, and a new cat named Carson – named for McCullers, not Johnny – and, of course, dad-burn peace and quiet. Now that I think back, she never did say what the recipe was for obtaining that last part. I just assumed it meant living the single life because she sure did seem at peace. You know what they say when you "assume," though. I should have looked deeper, I suppose, but over the next twenty-one years, I never knew Violet to raise her voice or speak unkindly to or about anyone. But like I said, it's the quiet ones that fool you.

So now I get to the zinger: The case of the century for Egret Beach. In case you think I just told the story about the zinger case – missing woman, missing money – no, indeed. Not by a long shot. Lois and the missing money was not the biggest shocker – just part of the story.

It all started several months after Violet retired. Or maybe I should say it all ended then. We'd had an excellent twenty-five-year retirement party for her, and she went on her way. She'd talked for years about the little retirement house she'd been paying on down in Key West. Showed us pictures, even. Said she'd gotten a great deal on the place and rented it to weekenders. But said she still had to scrimp and save to afford it. Once, one of the sergeants asked her about renting it for a week-long fishing trip. Violet seemed a bit uncomfortable with the request. She hem-hawed and stuttered a little before she explained how she had rented it out full-time to help pay the mortgage.

When she retired, Violet stayed around town long enough to receive her retirement money in one lump sum. Trying to be of financial help to her, I had advised her against taking the lump sum. I showed her the figures. Told her that with her excellent health, she'd likely have a long life and make much more over time by electing to take monthly payments. She listened and seemed to take the advice to heart, but in the end, she went with the lump sum. Violet sold off most of her belongings and then moved on down there to the Keys... or so we thought.

We had no reason to think otherwise until the Property and Evidence freezer broke down. The freezer was old. And maybe this is a crude comparison, but it wheezed and rattled and struggled to hang on like a dying old man in his last days on earth. The thing was long past any reasonable expectation you might consider for a freezer.

It was one of those oversized walk-ins, and in its day, it was top-of-the-line. Lois had insisted on the equipment, and it was purchased just months before she disappeared. She constantly complained and threatened the loss of evidence until they finally budgeted for it and got the big, new, walk-in model.

That freezer *was* a needed item. I'll say that. We also kept a lot of evidence for Fish & Game officers and Marine Patrol. There was always seized property from illegal netting, undersized fish, out-of-season, and illegal game – that kind of stuff. Egret Beach had an ongoing problem with some of the commercial and sports fishermen. So we were kind of proud of that big freezer. For a long time, it could nearly out-do Ft. Myers. In the last two years before Violet retired, though, the freezer had become as cantankerous as the woman who'd fought so hard for its purchase. It was just worn out. With budget issues prohibiting the purchase of a new one, the P&E people were used to checking it hourly to make sure the thermostat was reading out properly.

One night, the dying freezer finally kicked the bucket. Unfortunately – or fortunately, as it turns out – Duke Tanner was the night shift evidence man on duty when the freezer finally fizzled. Duke was narcoleptic. He could literally fall asleep right in the middle of a conversation. It was kind of a funny thing to watch, but Duke couldn't help it, and it was probably a little embarrassing for him when other officers or personnel would have to holler to wake him. We all sort of suspected – *ex*pected, actually – that when things were slow, old Duke would grab a catnap or ten during the night. So if we came to the evidence window and rang the bell, sometimes it would take two or three rings, some hollering or a fist banging on the grated window to rouse him. A bad case of the bed-head would give him away if there were any doubt, but no one ever complained. The guy just couldn't help it and couldn't afford to lose the job. Everybody knew that.

Anyhow, on the night of the freezer breakdown, it was a particularly slow shift. Gus, from Marine patrol, brought in some confiscated, out-of-season snook or redfish or something. That was right when Duke came on duty at eleven that evening. Somehow, Duke failed to close the freezer door properly, and that was the beginning of the end for the freezer. No other evidence was brought into P&E that night, and Duke likely slept all through his shift undisturbed. Duke made Zs, and the freezer wheezed – and died. By morning, water was pooled up in and outside the freezer. They called a repairman who pretty quickly declared the appliance DOA.

Everyone pitched in, trying to round up some coolers for temporary storage, and P&E filled them up. By mid-day, however, it was clear that we'd have to transport evidence to the state lab way down in Tampa. You can imagine the smell coming out of that freezer by then. They brought in three floor fans and a rinky-dink pump from somebody's boat that couldn't bail out a small bucket. It was pretty bad. Even upstairs in the detective unit, the smell of dead fish had begun to take hold, and everyone started finding lots of people to track down and cases to investigate out in the field.

They were literally fleeing the station like rats abandoning a sinking ship. Everyone avoided P&E unless they absolutely had to be nearby. I had some phone calls to make before I could get out, so I bit the bullet and was the last remaining detective upstairs in the office.

I felt real sorry for Duke. I could hear Chief Watson in his office down the hall giving the guy what for when I got a phone call from Shelly. She was the rookie evidence clerk and had only been with the department for about three months. Frankly, she was still a little unsure of herself about all the report procedures, but she knew the basics of the chain of custody and packaging and such. She spoke so quietly that I had to ask her to repeat.

"I said," she says nervously, "There's some weird stuff down here in this freezer. Ya'll had any dismembered body cases I ort to know about? Something Duke and them maybe forgot to tell me about?"

I says, "We never had a dismemberment case here in Egret Beach. Heck, not even a run-of-the-mill murder, for that matter." I told her, "Probably still got that hit-and-run panther in the freezer… and Shelly… you do know, don't you… that any murder victim – dismembered or not – would be in the district morgue? Not in our freezer, for Pete's sake. Why would you think or ask that?"

"Well, Stoney, I tell you what…I seen a leg, and…" she hesitated for a long moment. "I just think some'a ya'll better come on down here and take a look at this stuff."

I told her I'd be right there, but I figured the smell of all that thawed-out fish and game had gotten the best of her and given her the willies or sent her on some flight of fantasy.

When I got downstairs, she was all nervous and fidgety. She stepped from foot to foot in very oversized rubber boots that squished and squeaked in watery disharmony with each movement she made. She let me in through the security door and handed me a pair of rubber boots to slip on. While I struggled with the too-tight boots, I began explaining to her how a skinned-out deer leg could possibly look human at first glance. I asked her, "You ever seen a skinned deer?" She shook her head. I told her how a deer hunter out of season would sometimes skin 'em at the scene. She listened politely, with a few 'uh huhs' thrown in here and there. All the while, she was staring at me through round, thick-lensed eyeglasses that made her eyes appear huge and somewhat like a young doe herself. Well, no. Maybe more like an owl. I continued my explanation while she nodded some degree of understanding and twisted the straggly, blonde hair that had fallen loose from her ponytail and scattered loosely about her face.

I kept talking, and finally, as I stood up, she interrupted me.

"Sir... sir," she said.

I realized she'd probably not been focusing on much of anything I'd been saying about the deer leg.

"I... I... d-didn't mean to drop it... it's all slippery, kinda, is what happened," she stammered.

I started to reassure her, but she cut me off and began rattling off a steady stream of details.

"I was just gonna carry the box to the back door... stack it for the truck... that truck that's gonna take the evidence down yonder to Tampa. Weren't my fault... I just... it was slippery. Fallin' apart and wet. All them boxes at the back of the freezer... they're soaked. Just plain soaked. That box was just so dang wet it fell right through! I tried to pick it up, but it kept slippin' outta my hands. Tried to wait for Duke to help me... I did... but the water's done got us by several hours, and they're sendin' that 'frigerated truck over here pretty quick to pick this stuff up, and what was I gonna do? Couldn't wait no more for Duke, you know? It's only me down here to get it ready… I ain't got any help, and… and…"

I grabbed her arm to stop her rambling, nervous explanation.

"Shelly… just calm down. It's ok. Now, slowly…what fell through?"

"I… I…" She says, and she's looking at me then with those hugely magnified, blinking brown eyes and was suddenly at a loss for words. "Just come 'ere," she says. She lets out a big, loud, frustrated sigh. "Come 'ere and see."

I sloshed behind her through the stinking, standing water. She moved much more carefully than I – sliding as I was – like a skater toward the broken-down freezer. I grabbed onto a shelf full of evidence packages to keep from going down.

Shelly stopped several feet outside the wide-open freezer door. She jabbed her index finger in the general direction of the freezer, but not daring to look where she was pointing and making no move to venture closer to the door.

"Yonder," she said.

I eased forward a couple of more steps and looked inside. The original freezer light was long since dead, and now the light in use was a bare bulb at the end of a brown extension cord. A rigged-up affair that looked ripe to electrocute someone and offered wholly inadequate illumination. The bulb, swinging in the breeze from the fans, cast constantly moving shadows in the stinking freezer. I have to admit, it was quite an eerie feeling. That light swaying slightly, casting those shadows and the water dripping plunk… plunk… plunk, from the ceiling into the inches-deep pool of water on the floor. Each drop echoed off the walls of the freezer chamber, and an involuntary shiver ran up my spine. I think

I knew something was very wrong there before I saw it: we shouldn't have had *that* much frozen evidence.

The stench was incredible, and I was kicking myself for staying to make those phone calls. Still, I scanned the area around me and finally stepped gingerly toward what looked like part of a mannequin's leg. It wore a black high-heel shoe, textured stockings, and there was a gold bracelet with double hearts attached around the ankle. As soon as I saw that gold bracelet, some vague memory scratched at my subconscious, but at that moment, it wouldn't work loose and clue me in.

Obviously, the thing before me was no part of a deer, and I could think of no reason why a piece of evidence such as a mannequin would be kept in the freezer, but I still had in mind an actual mannequin. My brain just couldn't wrap around it being human. Of course, I knew that an actual human leg would be kept in the county morgue until identification was made *if* we'd had a dismemberment case, *which* we hadn't.

Then, I moved closer. I wondered if it could have been an elaborately contrived Halloween prop. Closer still, I realized that the textured stocking wasn't a stocking at all but appeared to be freezer burn mixed with the mottled markings of defrosting veins and capillaries beneath pale skin. From what I could see, the leg – if it was real – seemed to have been severed rather crudely, several inches above the knee. I wanted to be one hundred percent sure before I notified Chief Watson. He was ticked off already, and if I alerted him and the leg turned out to be something from a Halloween prank, he'd be livid. I needed a better light – and gloves. I would have asked for a mask as well, but I knew the flimsy things we had would be useless against the stench. I turned back to Shelly and told her what I needed.

She stepped away, and I scanned the several dozen boxes

thawing and dripping in the far back corner of the freezer. Even in the dim light, I could see that the case numbers on the sides showed twenty-plus-year-old dates. Most evidence was usually destroyed after the conclusion of a trial or past the statute of limitations. I knew that there was no way we should still be holding perishable evidence that old. Something was very wrong with that scene. I think I began to slowly collect nagging, fragmented puzzle pieces right at that very moment. Somehow, I began to know.

"Here..." Shelly managed to step inside long enough to hand me two pairs of vinyl gloves and a flashlight before retreating outside the confines of the freezer again.

I put on one pair of gloves, placed the extras in my shirt pocket, then squatted down and played the light slowly across the leg. I pressed my index finger against the leg. It was still mostly frozen, but there was enough give in it to show me that it wasn't plastic or plaster. It was no Halloween trick. I was trying to wrap my head around a body stored in that freezer. I splayed the beam of light across the length of the leg. I saw that the texturing or mottled appearance was what I'd thought: veins and freezer burn. I took a pen out of my shirt pocket and used it to turn the leg to better see the hearts on the bracelet. When my light hit the golden hearts, the name engraved on them flashed out at me like a ghost from the distant past. I sucked in a sudden, deep breath that I'd been sporadically holding off against the stench, and I jerked backward so quickly that I nearly fell over.

"LOIS," the engraving declared. Lois. And I knew exactly what it meant and exactly what had been stuck too deep within my memory to retrieve earlier.

I let out a long, low whistle. My heart was racing, and my mind was whirling around the possibilities. Even through my absolute shock and horror, I couldn't believe the ingenuity of it. The thought behind it. Sounds crazy, but that's what I was thinking – the ingenuity of it. What better place to hide evidence than the evidence room at the police station?

"Damn, Violet," I whispered. "I'll be damned!"

Over the next few days, we worked that scene. It was the biggest shock and biggest case we ever had at Egret Beach. Right there inside the police department. The Property and Evidence room became a crime scene. The state lab sent people to help with the investigation, and the medical examiner was there to collect the evidence. Still, crime scenes take time to process, and procedures and chain of custody are everything to a case. Violet had assigned different case numbers to each boxed body part, so we couldn't find and assemble them quickly. She'd thought of everything. It was, therefore, two and a half days later before we had waded through every thawing package and found all of Lois along with Violet's second husband, James Willoughby. At the end of the third day, he and Lois lay in reassembled pieces over at the medical examiner's office. I was there as the doctor did complete autopsies on both. I thought about James and Lois lying there side by side. They had been packed away for all those years. The two people who had so tortured Violet had been made quiet by their victim. We all wondered about the first husband, Marvin. Maybe he'd also been made silent, for later investigations failed to locate him. I figured that only Violet would know the answer to that one. By then, however, I think most of us knew that we'd not find Violet in the Florida Keys. I think I knew that we'd not find Violet at all. I pictured her lying in a lounge chair on some remote South American or South Pacific beach, sun hat shading her eyes, a sweet, cold drink in one hand and a book in the other, and likely with some pup lying by her side.

Sweet Violet. I remembered her telling me that sometimes it's best not to let your smarts show. I knew that some detective would probably spend the rest of his or her professional life searching for signs of Violet, but at that point, I only had two months left until retirement, and I'd finally found Lois.

- the end -

2

THRESHOLD OF DEATH

Janus backed her new, green Pontiac into the driveway and parked as close to the front door as possible. Since the rain had gone so quickly from a slight drizzle to a steady downpour, she'd been caught completely unprepared.

"So much for weather reports and, of course, perfect timing," she moaned. "Story of my life."

Mentally configuring her next steps, Janus unclicked her seatbelt, pulled the strap of her purse over her shoulder, and picked up a grocery bag containing a dozen eggs. She reached for the door handle but, rethinking that option, stopped short of opening the door.

Janus couldn't articulate but thought it weird that the whole day, since awakening, had seemed somehow peculiar – not in proper alignment. She had dropped things repeatedly, forgotten why she'd entered or left a room much more than usual, and even lost her grocery list. Janus knew Dan would be thoroughly annoyed about the overlooked ketchup – the main thing on her lost list. She sighed deeply and suddenly felt more tired than usual.

Janus sat in the car motionless while her mind wandered. She became momentarily mesmerized by the intricate patterns of rain flowing down the windshield. A sudden flash of light, followed seconds later by a violent cracking sound, broke the spell, and an involuntary shudder moved through her body. The inner windshield had become fogged over, and for a brief moment, Janus thought she saw her mother standing on the walkway in her funeral attire. Her heart beat frantically while she quickly rubbed her hand across the glass. No one was there.

"Of course," she whispered. "Of course, Mama's not there. Pull yourself together, Janus. Good grief. What is wrong with you, girl?"

Janus recovered quickly and fell back into a dragging and weary state. She lifted the door handle, hesitated again, and ran her fingers through her short, curly hair, uplifting the mass that was rapidly going limp.

"And, yep… here goes my twenty-dollar cut-n-style."

Janus sighed again and used her fingers to wipe the damp fogginess from the rearview mirror.

"Gosh… just look at that gray! I should have just let Tanya go ahead and dye it. Thirty-seven next week, and you look… forty-five at least! When did you get to be so old? Crept right up on ya. Gotta fix that, Jan. Lots of things to fix. Gotta get with the program. Ugh."

Unable to look at her reflection any longer, she quickly twisted the mirror toward the passenger side of the car. Janus focused again on the rivers of rain on the windshield before her. Once again, she sighed deeply and pushed her hair back, well aware that she was weary and stalling. *Guess it's not gonna let up any time soon,* she thought. *Better get these groceries in before everything thaws out. Now or never.*

Janus secured the fallen purse strap over her shoulder,

cradled the eggs to her chest, and grabbed two other bags from the front passenger seat. Finally, she opened the car door and had to squeeze past the steering wheel with her packages. Once outside the car, she hipped the door closed and ran up the walkway to the covered entry.

It took two more trips to get everything inside the house, but finally, Janus had all the bags piled haphazardly on the kitchen counter. Rainwater from the wet bags left a trail from the door and pooled on the countertop. She quickly removed a box of saltines and two boxes of cookies and dried them off before she did anything else. Her clothes were soaked, however, and she added her own dripping trail all over the kitchen floor. Shivering, she struggled out of the clinging, wet jeans, T-shirt, and underclothes and threw them into the washing machine in the laundry room off the kitchen. The cat that had avoided her wet jeans now circled her legs in a figure-eight pattern.

Janus caught a quick glimpse of her reflection in a mirror stored beside the washer and, ignoring the cat grabbed a terry bathrobe from the dryer. She rushed to pull it on as if observers were present, but she and the cat were the only witnesses. Even though she was only about ten pounds overweight, Janus avoided mirrors. When her body was hidden in the bathrobe, she pulled a towel from the dryer and wrapped it around her wet hair. The hair, she decided, was a lost cause – beyond redemption. She couldn't help thinking about the twenty dollars down the drain. Dan would be irritated about the wasted money if she mentioned it.

Half an hour later, everything was mopped up, groceries put away, and Janus sat at the kitchen table, eating two leftover egg rolls and a bag of potato chips. With each bite, she handed a morsel to the needy gray cat still circling her legs.

"Grocery shopping always makes me hungry, Frodo. But I have *got* to stop eating like this. Getting too darn fat. You heard Dan's rude comments about my weight yesterday. And the day before and... well, you know. And constantly reminding me to get on that darn exercise bike. Geez. And what do I do? Sit here eating junk. Why do I keep doing this to myself, Frodo? Tell me, little dude."

Janus remembered the year before her marriage and how fit she'd been. Then, just as quickly, she diverted her thoughts away with another bite of food. She offered the last bit of egg roll to the waiting cat and then allowed him to lick the crumbs from her fingers.

"That's it, Frody. Next week for sure, me and you... we're gonna start a diet and get on that darn Christmas present exercise bike. Geez. Romantic gift, right? All my hints about that ruby ring went right over his head. How did I let my life get away from me?" Janus questioned the cat as if he might actually answer.

"Best laid plans. Yep... best-laid plans, Frodo. Question is... when did it happen? I can't even look back and say when. I just wasn't even looking, I guess. That's my whole problem. Just walking through life on somebody else's path. Not even paying a bit of attention to where I'm walking. Just staying on that path and letting ol' time get away from me."

The cat jumped into her lap and surveyed the stray crumbs on the table while Janus scratched his head. She paid no attention as he began eating the bits within his reach. Instead, her mind wandered back over the years to the various significant and innocuous events that had led to her present-day life. It was a trip she took frequently, but like an inexperienced traveler in a foreign city, Janus often got lost and missed some of the more important connections.

Another loud crash from the storm outside brought her back into the moment. The rain suddenly came down in more furious cascades, and Janus thought how much it sounded like bacon frying. She closed her eyes to listen more intently. Yes, there was that hissing quality of frying bacon.

"Bacon," she sighed. "There I go, thinking about food again."

She pushed Frodo brusquely from her lap and pulled the robe tighter around her. The cat looked up at her, and Janus knew he was wounded – insulted by his sudden banishment. She smiled and reached down to stroke his back.

"Sorry, Buddy. Not thinking right today. So sorry." Janus focused a few moments on soothing the cat when he jumped back into her lap.

"Now… for sure, we gotta do it, Frody. You're too fat, too, ya know! Yep. Time to diet. Straighten up and get a new lease on life. Maybe I'll even start to do some of the things I always planned on doing."

Janus slowly smoothed Frodo's fur down his back, and he purred in appreciation and burrowed his nose into the palm of her hand.

"I don't even know how I let all those plans get away from me. Can't blame it all on Dan. He wanted a wife waiting at home. Like his mom. I knew that. Why did I… Well… Frodo… I let him lead me right where he wanted me, so it's my own fault. Yep. Didn't even protest traveling on the pathway he laid out for me. Sounded good after working in the hardware store all through high school. Seemed a little luxurious at first. What on earth made me turn my life over to someone else so easily?" Janus' voice trailed off to silence, and she sat there, momentarily transfixed by the cat, who now lay still but for soft clawing against the fabric of her robe.

"But, hey… it's never too late to begin anew, right? And… and… first thing I'll do is get this gray hair taken care of. I'm gonna call Tanya. Tell her she was right. It's time to color. And that will be my new start… and I'll go from there. But don't worry, you can keep your gray, and I promise I won't make your diet as harsh as mine. Just no more goodies. You'll get used to it."

Janus finished the last few chips, though. *No sense wasting two or three bits*, she thought. She flattened and smoothed the chip bag, then laid it aside.

After a moment, the cat jumped down, and Janus slid the chair back from the table. She remained seated, staring out the window at the rain. It hadn't let up at all and didn't look as if it would anytime soon. A deep lethargy so overtook her that when she stretched her arms over her head, intertwined her fingers, and yawned, she could not summon the energy to untangle and return her arms to her lap. She found that it was too much effort. Finally, the arms drifted back down to her lap of their own accord without a conscious thought from Janus.

"Geez, I'm so sleepy. What a day to rain. So many things I needed to do in the garden. Oh well… there's always tomorrow, as Miz Scarlett would say."

Janus loosened the towel wrapped around her head. She slowly patted and rubbed it against her damp hair, then threw it onto the table. After squeezing handfuls of hair to get the sagging curls to tighten up again, her arms fell limply back to her lap, and she stared languorously at the kitchen clock. Its rhythmic, humming motor blended with the rain and the refrigerator's intermittent purring to create a lazy symphony. The combined sounds, along with the sizzling rain, were hypnotic and made her even more sluggish.

Frodo flexed his claws lightly against Janus' ankle to remind her of his presence. As always, he seemed to know just how much pressure to apply without causing his human any harm. Janus reached down, absently rubbed his head, and gently pushed him away. He cocked his head to the side as if confused by the recurring rudeness in one so ordinarily loving.

Janus started calculating as the cat walked a few paces away from her, sat down, and stared.

It's almost two-thirty, she thought. *I could lie down til four and still have time to vacuum, straighten up the living room, and fix the chops before Dan gets home.*

"God knows," she pointed a finger at Frodo. "God knows... we can't let Dan's dinner be late. Or have magazines in disarray... or have kids, for that matter. Kids who might be messy or annoy Dan. Why... that might actually break us out of this nice little rut we live in, and we certainly couldn't have that, now could we? Well... no sir, we could not."

Janus let out a deep sigh and looked back to the kitchen window once more. The rain fell in a steady stream from the eaves.

"Perfect day for sleeping. No doubt about it."

With great effort, Janus lifted herself from the kitchen chair and started down the hallway toward the bedroom.

"Come on, Frody, we'll have us a nice nap."

As Janus walked through the living room and down the long hallway, she made a mental note to dust the coffee table before Dan went into another tirade about her housekeeping skills.

In the bedroom, Janus opened the French doors to the enclosed porch. The downpour continued, but she left the sheer, beige curtains closed, and a breeze animated them to a billowing rhythm. She folded the bedspread down to the footboard, removed her robe, and eased onto the bed, pulling just the top sheet over her. The ceiling fan rotated slowly overhead, pulling the rain-cooled air in from the open French doors.

Frodo paced the length of the bed. He paused now and again at her feet and cocked his ears toward the bedroom door. His tail whipped spasmodically as if his feline radar picked up silent signals from the air. Then, finally, he curled up and lay down at Janus's feet, but he continued to watch the door, and the end portion of his tail tapped in nervous repetition against the sheet.

Janus lay first on her side and then on her back. Suddenly chilled, she reached for a light blanket from the nightstand shelf. She shook it out and spread it over the sheet. Frodo held vigil on the door. The digital clock on the nightstand proclaimed 2:35 p.m. in bright red numbers. Janus set her own uncanny internal clock to wake her at four. She turned onto her side again, drifted off to sleep, and soon slipped into a dream state.

In one dream, she and Dan were driving over the Skyway Bridge, and the fog was so dense they could barely see the road ahead. She couldn't remember how they got there or where they were going, but she begged Dan to stop. He told her, "Settle down... I know what I'm doing." Then, somehow, the fog was swirling inside the car, and Janus could barely see Dan anymore. As the fog separating them became more opaque, the situation began to feel quite natural to her, and she did settle down and no longer paid it any mind. It didn't seem to bother Dan either, for he kept driving. By some conscious thread, Janus perceived that the dream of traveling in the fog dragged on far too long. The bridge seemed endless, the fog relentless, and the drive pointless. She and Dan never did reach the end of the bridge, and the dream slowly evaporated into nothingness.

When another dream began, Janus was exercising in an aerobic dance class with a group of young, vibrant, slender women. She struggled to match their movements and keep pace, but the music became more and more frenetic, and finally, Janus's legs gave way beneath her, and she slid to the floor. The women continued with the exercise routine until suddenly, the music stopped. The other women seemed bewildered at first, but then they noticed Janus lying on the floor. None of them made any move to help her, and all of them looked at her with disgust. The music started up again just as suddenly as it had stopped. Each of the thin women turned away from Janus and began to exercise again as if nothing had happened.

One dream blended into another with all the wild and implausible mixtures that an altered state can bring, and then Janus dreamed of Eddie.

It was the summer Janus turned eleven. She and her brother Eddie were riding bikes in the neighborhood where they grew up south of Tampa. It was just south enough and just rural enough that Tampa seemed like a city a million miles away to them. Their shorts and T-shirts flowed easily over thin, tan bodies as the cotton fabric intermingled with the light Gulf breezes. They left their sparse neighborhood, and finally, after just over a mile, they reached the point where the palmetto-lined dirt road to their house intersected with Highway 41 to the east. It was long before Interstate 75 was completed, so the two-lane 41 was the closest north/south road, and traffic could often be heavy.

In the dream, they wanted to cross over the highway to Bannon's Quick Stop. Eddie had saved lawnmowing money to get more baseball cards. He'd been trying for a Joe DiMaggio for a long time, and Janus knew she'd get some of the gum from the card purchase.

They sat on their bikes at the highway, but each time there was an opening in the traffic flow, another car or truck would appear from out of nowhere. They couldn't seem to get a break in the traffic, and Eddie was getting frustrated and madder by the minute. He was athletic, and Janus knew he could make the crossing by himself, but he was stuck with her. She lacked his speed and agility, so she was holding him back.

"I'm fifteen, dammit," he yelled over the noise of the traffic whizzing by. "I'm tired of being your babysitter!"

Janus was about to protest his implied reference to her as a baby, but the exasperated Eddie suddenly made a quick dash through the traffic. The horn blast of an oncoming tractor-trailer bellowed a warning, and Eddie's tires slid sideways, spewing pebbles into the air. Still, he managed to reach the other side of the road safely, but without Janus.

The dream continued with the cool gulf breeze suddenly turning into a dry, hot wind from the speeding trucks and automobiles. It whipped Janus's long brown hair into violent, whirling tentacles that lashed out to sting her face. She stood straddle of her bike on her side of the road, watching Eddie. He stared back at her, and she thought he looked suddenly sorry that he'd left her behind.

A large truck – a rock hauler – roared past, and its wash nearly knocked her down. The vehicle spewed gravel, dirt, and debris as it passed Janus. She held her face in the crook of her arm, trying to deflect the debris from her eyes. When the truck passed, she wiped grimy hands across her face, leaving streaks of dirt behind. She spit dirt from her mouth as well, but she could still feel the grit on her teeth. Finally,

Janus pushed aside the stinging hairs that still flew around her face, and she could see Eddie again. She blinked away sand. It *was* Eddie, but it confused her. He wasn't fifteen anymore. He was grown and tall. Her brother was no longer a boy on a bicycle but was suddenly a man wearing fatigues and boots. He had a rifle slung over his shoulder and stood at attention with his hand by his brow, rigid in a military salute. Bannon's store was gone, and on Eddie's side of the road was a small clearing with a palm-thatched hut in front of a dense jungle. One by one, several other soldiers were climbing aboard a helicopter in the clearing. The others called out to him, and just before Eddie boarded, he looked back past the speeding traffic to where Janus stood with tears streaming down her face. She tried to call out to warn him not to get on the helicopter, but it seemed as if sand had choked off her vocal cords. Then it was too late. She blinked and wiped tears away, and suddenly, he was wearing Marine dress blues, just like the ones they buried him in. Eddie started to wave, half raising his hand. He seemed to have second thoughts about waving to her as if it was pointless. Her brother then lowered his hand dejectedly and, without looking back again, he turned and climbed into the helicopter that Janus knew would take him to his death in a crash in Vietnam.

That dream had touched a slender thread within her conscious mind and had been deeply disturbing. Usually, such a dream would have been enough to awaken Janus, but her subconscious reined her back in, and Janus remained in a deep sleep. More dreams came and continued, each intense and disturbing, until her sixth sense told Janus it was time to wake up.

Janus tried to open her eyes but could not. She could feel herself hovering somewhere just below the point of full consciousness as she struggled to awaken. Her physical body seemed unwilling to be roused, yet her mind became fully conscious and aware of the effort she was making. It was as if her physical body and her conscious mind had disconnected from each other.

After trying urgently, Janus found that she still could not move – not a finger, a toe, or any part of her body. No matter how much she focused her wakened mind on different areas, her body would not respond to the commands given. She tried again to concentrate exclusively on opening her eyes. For what seemed like several minutes, Janus strained every mental muscle to achieve that one act, yet nothing happened. She began to feel severe panic rising within and was aware her heart was racing. She silently urged herself to calm down and felt her heartbeat begin to respond. That gave Janus some hope that her body was, at least to some degree, listening to her mind. She resumed focusing on her eyes, and after some time, she managed to open them a mere fraction of an inch. As they fluttered with her struggle, her eyelids opened enough to catch a glimpse of the red lights on the digital clock but not long enough to comprehend the numbers. Then her eyes closed, and she could not force them open again. Her paralysis was complete.

Her panic returned in full force and overwhelmed her. Thoughts were flying through Janus's mind like a newsreel running out of control and without end. Though her voice was inaudible, inside, she was screaming, panic-stricken.

Why is this happening? What's wrong? God, please help me... what is wrong with me? She tried to regain control of the thing that was overtaking her and inducing her panic. *Come on, Jan... get up. Get up,* she silently screamed. Janus could not, however, alter the thing that had engulfed her. She could not rise against it, and her heart continued pounding, but much more violently. It seemed to rail against her chest, erratic – somehow off-kilter. She knew it was not beating in a regular rhythm. It was all the more obvious because no other muscle in her body would move. Still, she could think. Her brain was working, and that mystified her. Janus felt as if her mind was entombed in a sarcophagus that was her own body. She was desperate to get out of that tomb.

Just move one toe! One finger! The words exploded in Janus's head. *Just make a beginning... move, dammit! Break out!*

Struggling to overcome the heart-pounding panic, she tried once more to calmly concentrate on one small movement – a finger – any little twitch to break the paralysis. Nothing happened. Janus's body would not move. Her breathing became labored, and she screamed inside her head. *Please, God. I don't understand. What's happening to me?*

Suddenly, Janus lost all consciousness of her wildly beating heart. Then, hundreds of tiny black specks appeared before her closed eyes, and just as the blackness completely enveloped her, it quickly dissipated. In its wake, Janus saw a bright light. She became focused on the brilliance, and instantly, the remnants of her panic disappeared, and her breathing slowed. The light was radiant, beautiful beyond description. Some small, offset part of her psyche still tried to direct her body to move, but her heart was not in it, and her will had evaporated. Finally, she gave herself entirely to the warm, white radiance.

A pure calmness came over Janus like nothing she'd ever experienced before. Her breathing became slower, shallow to near-nothingness, as she was captivated by the brightness before her. She watched as a figure seemed to flow or float out of the brilliance of the light and began to move almost like a fluid toward her. Janus watched as it came closer. Something seemed very familiar about it – him. She recognized something about him, but not precisely, as he was just too bright for her to see clearly. He flowed closer still, and then, almost in slow motion, he held his hand out to her, beckoning. With eyes still shut, Janus could finally see his features clearly. His eyes were wondrous, filled with love, such as she had never seen nor felt before. His body was translucent, fluid, and seemed weightless, yet his form was three-dimensional. His movements appeared effortless and graceful – ethereal. Janus was entranced by the strange, radiant beauty. She felt irresistibly drawn to him, and from somewhere – attached, yet somehow above her body – a part of Janus pulled free and separated from the useless body lying on the bed. She was no longer paralyzed and suddenly felt light and unrestricted as she reached out and took hold of his hand. Together, they turned and began moving back toward the source of the brilliant light – she moving now, as effortlessly as he in the slim body of her youth. Janus hesitated once, turning for a last look at the lifeless form under the blanket. She hesitated only a fleeting moment before she turned back, squeezed Eddie's hand, and walked with him into the light.

- the end -

3

A RECIPE FOR DEATH

Nancy Matthews didn't know she was living the last day of her life. Being in great shape and assuming there were many years ahead of her, it would never have occurred to her. She was the most healthy and fit of all her friends. They each had various medical issues and complaints, and Nancy had only minor allergies. At seventy-two years of age, she felt blessed to have lived a busy and productive life and believed that had contributed to her excellent health. She and her husband had traveled extensively across America and had been members of an active hiking club. Nancy had always been on the go, and after retirement as secretary to the owner of a large car dealership, she found she couldn't slow down. She and her high school best friends lived in a small retirement village near Miami. They were all widows. Vickie, Martha, and Carolyn had settled into more sedentary lives than she, but they still got together often.

Nancy thought it was unfortunate that Vickie and Martha had taken to their recliners even before their husbands passed. However, they worked at keeping their telephones and televisions busy. Carolyn kept a part-time hostess job at her sister's restaurant, but that was just two half days each week, and she mall-walked with her friends from church on Monday mornings. When those activities ended, she joined the recliner set. While it was true that they all participated in the senior's morning bowling league on Thursdays and bingo on Wednesday nights, that was just about the extent of their retreat from recliners.

A year after her husband died, Nancy found other activities to keep her busy. She just found herself unable to sit for long periods, so she went line dancing on Fridays, played tennis on Tuesday mornings, and volunteered at the Veteran's Hospital on Thursday afternoons. In addition, Nancy worked in her beautiful flower and vegetable garden outside her back door every day. This small plot was her pride and joy, where she spent many hours outside weeding and planting.

Though they were familiar with her habits, sometimes the other women would get a bit aggravated when they couldn't reach Nancy until late in the afternoon. She not only stayed busy, but it was a bit of an open joke that Nancy disliked and avoided talking on the phone. Still, she always enjoyed actual time spent with the girls and was ready to go when they wanted to get out a little. The four had maintained a close connection since high school and supported each other in the good and bad times. They all looked forward to their monthly get-togethers at each other's homes, where they'd enjoy a meal, play records, and talk about old times. Carolyn had dubbed this monthly get-together "Ridin' the old time machine."

Since her husband's death, Nancy had become more of a listener and observer, and most of the "girl" talk centered around family, books, news stories, just a smidgen of town gossip, and their youthful years. She particularly appreciated the walks down memory lane when their conversations turned to the antics of their high school years at Miami Central. The girls – as they still thought of themselves – considered their teen capers funny and fun, though, now, in 2019, they figured younger generations would surely disagree. The women had witnessed technology taking over the world. They saw how much of the face-to-face human interactions had become irrelevant. Each remembered and spoke of times spent with their mothers and grandmothers, eagerly listening to stories of their growing-up years. Now, the tales of their journeys through life seemed so diminished that their grandchildren could find no humor in them – let alone interest. The world had changed too dramatically.

Though she loved her friends like sisters, if pressed for the truth, Nancy would have said she didn't particularly like what she thought of as "frivolous" chitchat. Sometimes, Martha would get on a roll comparing prices on grocery items in different stores and bragging about the "great deals" she'd secured. Other times, Martha would drone on about who insulted whom in some housewives show in some city or another. Nancy would listen, and though she found it terribly tedious, after so many years of friendship, she'd never say so and hurt her friend's feelings. Martha loved a good sale and those housewives. The others accepted that.

Nancy hadn't always been a more quiet and reflective type of person. She'd been quite the talker in her teens and was considered the witty one among her friends. In her senior year of 1965, that personality trait had attracted Craig Matthews, who was a talker himself and very much a cutup. She never forgot the movie date in downtown Miami, when afterward, he performed a crazy dance in the middle of

Biscayne Boulevard. He wasn't at all shy about drawing attention to himself.

Nancy married Craig in 1967, two years out of high school. She'd just gotten her AA degree at the community college, and he worked for his father's construction company. They thought themselves off to a great start. Unfortunately, Craig's number came up, and he was in Vietnam a year later. When he returned, he was no longer the same guy. He was quiet and often withdrawn. Craig would only tell Nancy he'd lost too much and seen things he couldn't un-see. She suspected part of his reason for not sharing those experiences was to save her from things she couldn't un-hear. Nancy loved him and would take him under any circumstances. Their marriage lasted for forty-two years when he had a brain aneurysm and died in his sleep in 2009. They never had children, and it took Nancy a long time to get over losing Craig, but with the help of her friends, she slowly returned to life. Though she dated occasionally, she'd never found another man with whom she felt a strong connection.

On Nancy's final day on earth, it was her turn to host, and she'd planned an evening of dinner and games with the girls. She was engaged in light house cleaning before starting dinner and had music playing, as she usually did. She still had an old-fashioned, oversized console record player and stacked it with albums from the 1960s. It made the chores go faster when Nancy could dance with the vacuum cleaner and sing to the music. The girls would be arriving at 6:30 p.m. They'd eat dinner, play a few rounds of Yahtzee, and have coffee and the chocolate cake she had baking in the oven. Nancy expected there would be lively conversation all evening, as always, and then everyone would leave and prepare for a new day.

With cleaning chores done, Nancy finished the cake and began preparing the meal. Vickie always raved about her potato salad, so she began to work on that after she had placed the small ham into the oven. The broccoli would be cooked at the last minute.

Nancy used her mother's Southern potato salad recipe that her friends all loved. It was good served cold, but best when it was still warm. It called for small chunks of potato with chopped boiled eggs, finely diced dill pickles, mayo, a little yellow mustard, salt, and pepper – no onions and no celery, as some recipes required. Nancy's aunt, by marriage, was from Vermont, and she never put pickles in her potato salads. Nancy thought it just wasn't potato salad without the pickles. Her mother had made the best potato salad, and her recipe deserved all the raves it got. For this meal, Nancy had just enough pickles left in the jar to complete the recipe and made a mental note to pick up a jar at the grocery store on her next trip. Finally, she poured the pickle juice down the sink and placed the jar inside the plastic bag in the kitchen garbage pail.

Soon, the girls were arriving. Vicki and Martha came together, and Carolyn followed a few minutes behind. Then, after pouring Sangria for all – Martha's favorite – Nancy flipped the stack of records, and they all sat down to eat.

It was Martha's night to be on fire, and Nancy suspected she'd perhaps imbibed a bit before arrival.

Martha took off, "I'm gonna tell ya'll now... I got so mad today! Oh, my Lord! I was going through pictures and saw one of us all posing by Nancy's car in our bikinis. That old faded yellow car you had sophomore year, Nancy. Remember that?"

"Never forget it. It was a good ol' car – my first. Of course, I remember! My Goodness! That car gave me a life.

Loved 'ol Mustard!" Nancy laughed and shook her head. "We had so much fun with her."

"Right! 'Ol Mustard!" Carolyn snapped her fingers and sipped her Sangria.

Nancy instantly thought of the time she and her sister had to search the car for gas money. She recalled they could only find a dime and had to put in ten cents worth of gas to get to school.

"Well, okay. You loved it, and I loved our bikini bodies, but let me get to the point. The picture of that car brought up a little irritating memory for me. Ya'll remember how we used to go off campus for lunch? Hop on I-95 and race down to Nathan's hot dogs? Ya'll always said we could make it but damn! Late back to class *every* damn time. And... and who always got caught?" Martha asked.

"You and me," Vickie cut in. "How could we forget?"

"Damn right... me and you." Martha pointed back and forth between herself and Vickie with a ham-filled fork. "And I would be flaming fuming mad when we passed your typing class, Nancy. I'd see you sitting there typing away. Little Miss Innocent! Not a problem in the world. Clickity-Clack. Honest to God. I'd be fuming. Me and Vickie always got referred for detention, and *your* flaming teacher was later than us by a long shot! Sitting her butt over in cosmetology, getting her gaudy red hair done! Old Miss What's-her-name. So unfair! So unfair! Girl... you skated on that deal. We got raked over the coals, and Miss Liester near about wore out her hand writing up so many detentions. Almost lost the right to leave campus."

"Well, ya'll know I had no control over that," Nancy said. "I watched for ya'll out the window. I knew you were bound to get caught. And I saw you giving me the evil eye, Martha! 'Bout burned a hole in my skull. Coupl'a times, I got to my seat and paper in the typewriter 30 seconds before Mrs. Carey... that was her name. Skin of my teeth. I lucked out, is all. Pure luck."

"And... girls... Martha... Come on, now. I lucked out, too," Carolyn chimed in. "I never got caught sneaking in the back door for algebra. Mr. Dorn passed an attendance sheet around, so I was there by the time it got back to my desk. I think he knew. How could he not notice? He just let it slide. Didn't care. And you didn't ride me about it... you just picked on Nancy."

"Well, she bitched about both of you guys to me," Vickie laughed. "Ya'll got a free pass, and I got an earful every time! And look... here we are getting an earful again, 55 years later!"

Carolyn patted both Martha and Vickie's hands and laughed. "Well, whatever made us think we could get to Nathan's, order, eat, and get back to class on time? Shoot. It wasn't our fault our teachers were lax, Honey. And the bottom line is... it was all great times, anyway. So worth it and so much fun back then, wasn't it? Remember? Just breathe in that memory... and you wouldn't change a thing, Martha. Wouldn't have missed Nathan's and cutting up on the interstate for all the detentions. You wouldn't. So here's to a great past." She lifted her glass, and the others followed her lead to toast to good times.

Carolyn continued. "That's the whole fun of the memories. Great times to look back on. And we were quite a crew... detentions or not."

They all laughed as Carolyn pushed at Martha's shoulder, teasing her friend for her reaction to a less wonderful side of the memory.

"Okay. I know ya'll are right. We were a fun group. Yes. Just that darn picture got me going, is all," Martha said.

"Exactly! But just think about those bikini bodies and not the detentions!" Vickie pressed Martha's hand and continued. "And we're still having fun. I know we had good times with our husbands and kids and all. Great times. But that's a whole different part of life. Our teen years were something else entirely. Just think about it, girls ... what on earth could compare to the real freedom we had before we took on adult worries of marriage, family, and responsibilities?"

"So true," Nancy said.

Vickie continued. "You know... we had a certain kind of ignorance. I mean... what did Home Ec really teach us? A little cooking, a little sewing, and, honest to God, little else! We were true innocents in a sense. Back then, our youth kept us ignorant of life, really. And that was a good thing. Kids nowadays are thrust into an adult world way too fast. Our time allowed most of us a longer season of fun and freedom before we were hit with some of life's harsh, untaught realities. Yeah. We were still innocent, in a sense, and I'm grateful for that."

The others all nodded or spoke their agreement as Vickie continued with a laugh.

"What could beat riding down that interstate to Nathan's? And remember when we got the water guns and were shooting water at other cars? Oh... Martha... you were literally hanging out the window to shoot! Your big butt practically knocked Carolyn out the other window! I was cracking up. All in good fun, then... not a chance kids could do that now, of course. Not a chance. And it's sad, really. We lived in the best time for a teenager. No doubt about it."

The girls continued to laugh and discuss the times and how, on late return to school, they'd opened the hood of the car to smear burnt oil on their hands to claim an auto breakdown as a late "excuse." Of course, it hadn't worked, but they all laughed as they discussed each one's version of events.

The music played on. Nancy played The Beatles, Rolling Stones, Beach Boys, The Animals, Sir Douglas Quintet, and many bands long-forgotten by so many. The girls kept the conversation going as they all laughed and sang along with some of the songs.

Happy about the lighter mood, Carolyn started talking about the sock hops, and Vickie and Martha soon chimed in. Nancy was smiling but quiet. She sipped her wine and watched their interaction. She kept reflecting on Vickie's words as she gazed at each of the aging faces and saw the teen girls they'd been. She couldn't help thinking... *If I could give one gift to the younger generations, I would give them a parallel universe in which they could all experience life in the 60s. Surfing songs and car and teen love songs. No hateful songs with disrespect and cursing. With few exceptions, no destructive songs. A time of more innocence. When there were so few crazies to worry about that, it likely made freedom easier for a generation. I wouldn't give them the Mansons,* she thought. *I wouldn't give them assassinations or Vietnam with young boys having no choice and dying for nothing. And poor, damaged boys returning just to be treated so horribly. I would give the younger generations the good parts to experience and barely let them see the bad. But I guess a parallel universe wouldn't let you pick and choose the good and evil. For us, though, even with the bad, there's no doubt it was the greatest time to grow up. God, I'm so thankful to have lived my youth then.*

"Nancy... Nancy?... you ok? You checked out there for a minute." Carolyn shook her friend's arm. "I was saying, do you remember that first sock hop when Eddie Martinez drove his new pickup into the fence after the dance?"

Nancy was pulled out of her reverie and rejoined the conversation.

After dinner, the girls helped clear the table, and they quickly moved on to a game of Yahtzee. Then, The Beach Boys came on with their song "Fun Fun Fun," and Carolyn laughed and threw the dice for her Yahtzee play.

"Oh... Oh... I bet you remember this, too. Well, Martha, you weren't there that time. You were married to Stan by then and off in your own little Suzy Homemaker world. You missed a lot. Married too early, I think, but Nancy was driving that new Chevy she had, and...."

"Chevelle... '66. It had a 396 cubic inch engine with 360 horse. Way more powerful than the Mustangs. They only had a 289 with 200 horse. That Chevelle could flat-out move. Most powerful car I ever had. Loved it. Lemonwood Yellow with a black vinyl top. A real beauty!" Nancy felt compelled to fill in the details about her favorite car.

Carolyn continued. "Listen to that girl go! Well, yes! Nancy can still recite all those numbers! Heck... I didn't know what they meant then. Barely do now... but Martha, listen to this. This was so fun. We three were out tooling around. Heading out to the Hialeah Pizza Palace, as I remember it. So anyway, we pull up to a red light on Red Road, and this car full of guys pulls up next to us in a... well, I don't remember their car, but nothing special. Nothing fast. And they start asking something like... 'Hey, what's under the hood, and what'll she do?' or something like that. And Nancy, she just starts rattling off all this stuff about car motors, and those guys were practically drooling. It was crazy."

"When they asked what I had under the hood, I told 'em, the 396 with 360 and added I've got a fuel-injected engine and dual quads, with four on the floor... which I really did have that. But I only had a four-barrel carburetor. I said it had a positraction rear end, but I don't think it did. So it was just stuff I heard in car songs... like... remember the Beach Boys with their song "409" and "Shut Down," and ... oh yeah... Ronny and the Daytonas singing "GTO"?

"Great music. Great, great music." Martha poured more Sangria into her glass and sipped a bit before offering it to the others, who all declined.

"Also, it was some car stuff my brothers talked about. But, really... I was just funnin' with 'em," Nancy shook her head, thinking of her teen confidence back then.

"And those boys bought it 100%," Nancy continued. "So right then, I suspected they didn't know what all those car terms meant. It was funny, really."

"Oh yeah! But they looked mighty impressed anyway... and also," Carolyn snapped her fingers repeatedly as she tried to remember something. "Oh yeah... pulling this out of my brain here... another good one was, I think... Little Cobra."

"Right. Hey Little Cobra. That was the Rip Chords," Nancy said.

"Well, ya'll remember all those car songs," Vickie said. I was always more into the love songs."

"Oh, we know that, Honey," Martha chimed in with just a touch of a slur to her words. "Oh, man... Vickie, I remember you playing... Uhm... "Will You Still Love Me Tomorrow?" And, oh yeah... "Soldier Boy" and "Navy Blue." I remember those three playing over and over that last time you had a slumber party."

"Because I loved those songs! Come on! I'm allowed to love those songs the most. And... and ya'll remember I had something like seven... eight pen pals in the military. Damn draft took those boys," Vickie said. "I wasn't so much into the car stuff… or car songs, either, but it was pretty cool that night showing those guys what Nancy's Chevelle could do."

"It was so cool. Finish telling Martha about racing down the street, Nancy." Carolyn nudged Nancy's shoulder. "It was so much fun, Martha. I wish you'd been with us."

Nancy threw the dice. "Well, ok… I'll tell you Martha, but hey… for the record… no pun intended… I liked those love songs, too. And surfing songs… Geez… we had the best rock & roll music, didn't we? Anyway… ok… back to the story. So… those guys wanted me to show 'em what that Chevelle would do off the line, and it was late. We'd all just gotten off work at Kwik Chek after counting those darn Top Value stamps. Y'all remember those? Haven't thought about those things in years. Remember those saving stamps for gifts, Martha?"

"Yes. Took me forever to fill enough books to get a toaster. Ooh, look. Got my three of a kind." Martha passed the dice to Carolyn, and Nancy continued.

"Well, anyway, it was probably close to ten before we changed clothes, fixed makeup, and got out of the store. Hardly any cars on Red Road. No cops I could see. So it looked safe to show 'em whenever the light turned green. So I'm in first gear… playing with the clutch and the gas pedal to make 'er growl and lunge… just waiting for that light. It turned green, and I floored it. Man, I can remember how that motor sounded. Well, I shot off the line and flew down that street, shifting into all four gears, then slowed down for them to catch up. Burned a little rubber, too." Nancy smiled as she remembered that night.

The girls continued the game and remembrances, and afterward, Nancy served dessert. She sipped her coffee, barely touched the cake, and thought how lucky she was to have these women in her life. She thoroughly enjoyed the time spent with her old friends.

When the evening had ended, Nancy saw her friends out. They offered to help with the dishes as always, but it was a wind-down chore that she preferred to do alone. When they were gone, she went to clean the kitchen. The music continued from the record player, and she sang along. She didn't know why, but Craig had been on her mind all day, yet she hadn't mentioned his name once all evening. That was quite unusual for her. Even while the girls were there, she'd had several quick flashbacks of good times spent with Craig. She guessed it was the music, the talk, the nostalgic tidbits of life lived – time travel of the mind. Nancy couldn't help but smile at the memories as she washed and dried the dishes. It was a good life, she thought. Wholly, a good, satisfying life.

When the kitchen work was done, Nancy went to her bedroom and changed into her nightgown. She sat on the edge of the bed and was about to lie down when she remembered the garbage pickup. The truck was due early in the morning. She got back up, put on her slippers and a thin robe, and returned to the kitchen. Nancy struggled but finally pulled the plastic bag out of the bin and tied the top. It was a bit heavy but not unmanageable. She turned on the back porch light, unlocked the door, and started down the three cement steps. On the last step, her foot twisted. Nancy lost her balance and dropped the bag. She held onto the railing and avoided falling but heard glass break. She adjusted her slipper and tested her weight on the ankle. It felt alright. She inspected the thin plastic bag and saw the tie had come undone, and pieces of pickle jar were on the walkway. After carefully picking up the broken glass, Nancy tied the bag again. She worried about the weight, so she picked it up but wrapped one arm around it and held the bottom with the opposite hand. When she reached the alleyway where garbage was collected, Nancy dropped the bag into the larger bin and turned toward the house. She stood still for a moment – confused – then moved slowly, suddenly feeling a little dizzy. She picked up her pace but noticed some liquid had gotten onto her upper nightgown. It was too dim to see what it was. She kept going, but the back door suddenly seemed so far away. Nancy didn't make it back up the steps into the house. Instead, she fell into the flower bed near the back door, not far from a piece of broken glass labeled 'Dill Pickles.'

———

When the girls couldn't reach Nancy by phone for two days, Vickie went to check on her. She knocked at the door and, when she got no answer, entered the garden and found her friend. She was horrified to see a pool of blood around Nancy and a blood trail on the walkway. Vickie thought her friend had been attacked in the alley and had made it back to the house before falling into the garden. However, the medical examiner found bits of glass in Nancy's wound, and the crime scene unit found the piece of glass in the garden. The doctor concluded that a broken pickle jar had sliced into an artery in her upper arm, and Nancy bled out where she fell.

- the end -

4

ENCOUNTER WITH DEATH

Gina Grant was on her way to the morgue. It was a routine trip, but lately, she'd thought it had become a little too often. However, as the lead crime scene investigator in the homicide unit at the City of Bay Haven Police Department, she knew the deal. Since childhood, listening to her father's law enforcement stories, she'd wanted to help solve crimes. Now, Gina had been at the job for close to twelve years. As with most investigators, she had become accustomed to the face of death. Working crime scenes, one either learned it early or moved on to gentler careers. It took determination, but Gina quickly adapted as required. She had discovered early on that with total concentration on death's technical and forensic aspects, she was more productive as an investigator. It helped her avoid most of the emotional effects of the death itself. Gina had also learned to compartmentalize the worst, violent scenes. Out of sight, out of mind could have been her motto.

Once a case had been resolved in court or went

completely cold, Gina didn't want to think about it again unless new evidence was found or other theories were proposed. Then, she eagerly jumped on the case again. Still, time constraints due to constant incoming crimes made it easier to put unsolved cases out of mind – to put failure out of mind. When Gina filed unsolved cases in the major crimes cabinet, she also packed them away in that remote compartment in her brain. Her ability to do that was something of which she was secretly proud. That tactic certainly contributed to her effectiveness at brutal scenes. She remained professional all the way. Gina loved her job; she loved forensics. Helping victims and their families and helping to solve cases was her goal.

Though Gina had become the most requested CSI on the team, her original job interview had been a little sketchy and not ordinarily indicative of a good investigator. She had desperately wanted the crime scene job but knew she'd be required to look at some gruesome pictures. At that time, she had never actually seen a dead person in real life. When her father had been killed in the line of duty years before, Gina had been unable to approach the casket. She'd avoided confronting the issue until she was forced to face death in crime photographs to get into forensics. Since she knew the photo review was required, she secretly planned a way to handle it. When the pictures were handed to her, Gina focused on the upper left-hand corner of each photo. She gave cool, calm facial expressions as she turned over each picture and never saw the actual crime scene images. She knew instinctively that if they hired her, she would adjust to everything eventually. Gina figured that time was on her side. She would adapt to everything as she learned the ropes. In the meantime, she decided to do whatever it took to convince her superiors that she could perform the job objectively and dispassionately.

Gina never told anyone about the photograph trick she'd used to get through that part of the job interview. During her tenth anniversary as a CSI, Major Cases, There was laughter and sharing quirky incidents with her coworkers. She briefly considered telling, but the moment passed, and she kept it to herself. Gina felt it was no longer relevant to anything. However, a deeper inspection of her compartmentalizing technique might have given her a clue otherwise. Only later did the superficiality of that technique throw her into a pit.

Some of her early days were tough, but it was fortunate, and Gina was grateful that for her first assignment to the morgue, her primary trainer, Earl Dawes, was the one who accompanied her. She'd felt lightheaded when they first entered the autopsy room. The smell hit her immediately, and it was very different. Gina couldn't distinguish the odor at first. It wasn't the smell of decomposition. She knew that smell from hiking trips with her father. It was something more akin to the odor of uncooked, sitting-in-the-fridge-too-long meat. She had not expected that, and it sickened her. Gina felt woozy. Two bodies were laid out besides the one they were to work on. Earl sensed her faintness and took her arm. That gave her a moment to adjust and somehow calmed her a bit. He held on while introducing her to the two doctors prepping for autopsies. Their assignment was to photograph tattoos on an unidentified female. Another crime scene investigator had already taken fingerprints and photographs but unfortunately neglected to take close-ups of the tattoos. They put on gloves, and Gina had to hold the woman's body in several positions as Earl photographed each tattoo.

Touching the cold, clammy, and stiff body was difficult. It was the first time she'd felt death – but Gina steeled herself against the initial shock she felt. She forced herself to examine the body, horrified to see bloodied paper towels wadded against the deceased girl's face. Without realizing it, Gina was already analyzing a crime. She wondered if the perpetrator hid the face out of their own horror at what they'd done... or by someone who'd found her in the street.

Once done with her first murder victim, Gina felt relief and was more assured of her ability to withstand the morgue and handle death assignments. She'd gotten through her first test by fire.

Though Gina still found it very difficult to handle each body in the early months of her career, over time, she adjusted, just as she'd thought. It all boiled down to necessity. To endure such a challenging career, Gina had to become hard against the face of death. She did exactly that. While filing the rough cases in the back of her mind, Gina became so successfully stoic that her childhood friend, Deborah, teased and called her Gina Granite. Deborah had moved to Ireland, but when Gina spoke to her about cases, she revealed little but did so with a quiet lack of emotion. Just the facts, ma'am.

One day, after nearly twelve years on the job, Gina's stoic attitude would take a dramatic turn. On that November day, she would face something she'd so carefully shoved to the back of her mind. It was a thing she kept locked away. Gina Grant would face mortality – her mortality – and she would be sucked into a swirling vortex that would lead to her very own encounter with death.

For the scene that was about to be, the wheels were set in motion much earlier in her life. Gina didn't just fall into law enforcement the way some others did. It was a thing she'd wanted to do for as long as she could remember. It was something she had worked so hard toward that desire had picked up a momentum of its own.

Her father became a detective in Miami after thirty years in the army. Her parents had Gina later in life after he'd served in France and Korea and before he went to Vietnam in 1970, near the end of his career. She adored her father but was saddened when he discouraged her interest in law enforcement. He and her mother tried to convince Gina that being five foot nine at fifteen with her blonde, classic look, she could become a model after high school and make loads of money. She was relentless even though her father tried his best to convince Gina that there was no money in law enforcement and told her it was often a thankless job.

"Police officers see people at their very worst," he told Gina. "When people are being helped, they're grateful. They sometimes even call you a hero... but when those same people are caught for something they've done wrong... even something as simple as speeding... they can be hateful and even violent. They don't stop and think or maybe even care that an officer is doing a job for public safety and has a family to go home to. They only think about their anger at that moment, and it can get real bad. Real bad. And that happens too often, Darlin'. "

He told Gina how tough it was to deal with physically or mentally sick people. He said he witnessed grim and gruesome things. Some as bad or worse than things he saw in war. He repeatedly told her that while he chose police work to help people, he had to sacrifice much of his personal life to do the job. Gina never forgot the time her father had come home after a difficult day and slunk down in his recliner with his head in his hands. It happened just a few months before his death, but it was something he had rarely done. Her mother was still at work, and Gina needed some help with her homework, but she couldn't bring herself to ask for assistance. He was too quiet during dinner, but later that evening, they all sat on the porch, and he told them about an investigation that had taken him to the hospital earlier that day. He said he had to arrest a man who had slammed his eight-week-old baby boy against a wall because it cried. As a result, the baby would be blind and possibly mentally disabled for the rest of its life.

Gina and her mother had simultaneously sucked in a loud breath and said nothing. They all sat quietly for a long while afterward. Her father was the one who finally broke the silence.

He said, "Some things I just can't wrap my head around. Just can't."

Gina remembered that her mother placed her hand over her father's, but she and her mother remained mute. Her dad continued.

"Sometimes I feel just like that Jackson Browne song, *Running on Empty.* Even after the wars... where soldiers expect the worst, I didn't expect... well, I was still too naive about what police work entailed. But... tell you what... I lost my innocence pretty damn fast in the true face of human depravity with no war as an excuse. I feel like I've been runnin' on empty for a long time."

He often told Gina that he didn't want her to see how evil and depraved humans could be. He didn't want her to sacrifice so much of herself for a job. She thought a lot about his comments when he was shot and killed in a traffic stop in early May of 1985 – six months after her sixteenth birthday. In the months following, however, Gina became more determined than ever to pursue that career. She knew in her heart that no matter how often he had warned her, deep down, he would have approved of her choice because it was *her* choice and because through it all, her father would have again chosen law enforcement. He felt compelled to help others.

As determined as her father, Gina chose law enforcement. She studied forensics but couldn't face working in Miami, where he had been killed. In her younger years, as they had driven through the city, her father pointed out where this crime happened and that crime happened. The whole city seemed somehow tainted, touched by blood, sweat, and, likely, the tears of her father. It had been his city, but it could not be her own. So Gina accepted a position over a hundred miles north on the Gulf coast in Bay Haven – a town about a third the size of Miami. Less pay, but still the work that twenty-year-old Gina wanted to do.

Gina loved her work and never regretted her decision. From the beginning, she'd taken great pains to learn all the procedures and techniques required for evaluating and processing crime scenes. Though she had also learned from others during the training year, Earl had taught her how to handle scenes the right way – not the shortcut ways to get you back to the office quickly, which seemed to be the training method favored by some other crime scene investigators. Earl was old-school, a stickler for details, and Gina became the same. Some of the others criticized her for being "ate up with it." It was true that she spent every spare moment experimenting with and learning the latest techniques as well as trying things that she thought might work in retrieving latent fingerprints and other evidence. Some claimed and complained that Gina was "making the rest of us look bad," but that was never her intention. She simply wanted every tool and every chance to solve the crime; minor or major crime made no difference in the effort she put forth. It was undoubtedly an advantage that Gina also seemed to possess an innate ability to piece the evidence together to understand how a crime had likely occurred. Her tenacity, skill, and expertise soon earned her a place on the Major Case Squad, where she had remained for the last ten years.

As her father had warned, however, Gina's job did take a toll on her personal life. The problem with being on the squad was that Gina mostly handled only the most serious crimes and was on call twenty-four hours – not a good formula for maintaining relationships. Her mother's mind had been failing for a long time, and though she tried to care for her, Gina was finally forced to place her in a facility. Her relationships in both love and friendship were mostly superficial. Though she tried, she couldn't fit it all in. The love interests usually faded after a few months as the men became disenchanted with her work and the hours involved – or she became bored or tired of them. Visits with her mother were sad, short, and disappointing as Gina watched her mind and body fail.

When Bay Haven's population exploded, so did the drug epidemic and the crime rate. The situation became constant, and Gina faced death much more often. A weekly major crime scene had become practically the norm. Eventually, it had to take a toll, and she occasionally sensed that it was doing just that. Still, she would push it from her mind when that reality gnawed at her. She'd witnessed others become burned out. It happened. They either transferred to other departments or sometimes became ineffective or less interested in doing the job well. She was determined that she would be different. Gina decided she'd always push herself to be her best or leave law enforcement altogether. She vowed never to let the work suffer. To maintain that high level of functioning, Gina had compartmentalized and tucked away scenes of death, violence, and her personal feelings for a very long time, and she'd done it successfully. So she thought.

In her eleventh year as an investigator, everything changed – and Gina's life with it. It was two days before Thanksgiving. People gathered, feasted, and put family first, but Gina hadn't enjoyed real family time since her father's death. Though they were unaware at the time, her mother already had symptoms of early-onset dementia. Six years later, she had a mild stroke and had recently become less responsive. Shortly after her mother's stroke, Gina ended her engagement with Jack, her fiancé of one year. Jack had been her longest-lasting relationship, and though she dated occasionally, she'd never really had a serious romance since. It was times like the upcoming Thanksgiving that made her reflect on that. Having just turned thirty-one, Gina had pretty much given up on any possibility of finding the right man and having a family. She felt too much of a loner to make a relationship work. If she could have seen what was to come, perhaps Gina would have seen that particular life outcome as fortunate.

Gina Grant's life was altered forever that day in November. It was an unusually deathly day. The calls came in almost one after the other. It had been so busy that it seemed as though death had a quota to fill as it barreled down the highways of life.

First, there was a traffic fatality; a motorcyclist was decapitated. Next, an industrial accident killed an eighteen-year-old boy when a load of lumber fell from a forklift, crushing him. Finally, an accidental drowning took a first-year med student who had just arrived home for the holidays.

Just as Gina completed that scene and her shift was almost ending, she was called to a homicide that sent her into overtime. This victim was found in the Auto Graveyard on the outskirts of Bay Haven. The female victim had been burned alive in the trunk of a junked car. With two squad members on vacation time and another out sick, Gina was assigned to handle the new homicide as well.

Gina left the homicide scene after nearly three hours of photographing and collecting evidence. When she got to the morgue, Susan Dean, a junior investigator, was there working a different case.

"God... another one?" Gina asked. "I didn't hear that one come in."

"Yep. Way it goes. 'Nother traffic. People are just driving like maniacs out there." Susan sounded exasperated. "I'm 'bout done. Just finishing the fingerprints. Yours is over there." She pointed to Gina's left. "They brought her in a little while ago, and the doc already looked at her. Said he's done a prelim and released her to you."

Gina loaded film into her camera and walked over to the charred body. She stood still at the gurney, staring off into space. Her mind was transfixed into some nothingness void. She remained that way for nearly two minutes. Finally, Susan broke into the mental space Gina occupied.

"You alright, Gina? Hey. Gina? Did you hear what I said? Doc released her to you, so you can go ahead. He said, do whatever you need."

"Oh. What? Man... yeah. Thanks. I'm practically sleeping on my feet, I guess. Tired." Gina knew full well that was not the case, but she didn't know what had hypnotized her.

"It's just... well, this has been one helluva day, I tell ya."

Gina added a paper ruler with a case number to the gurney beside the blackened body. Then, moving the ruler as she went, she walked around the stainless steel body cart and flashed off several shots at different angles.

"Mind giving me a hand over here a minute before you take your gloves off, Susan?"

"Sure thing... whatcha need me to do?" The young woman wiped her gloved hands and lowered her mask for a quick breath. Her grimace gave away her true feelings about the request.

"If you can just hold the fingers out a little bit so I can get a couple of close-ups of these rings... I've stretched 'em best I can."

Susan restored the mask and then pried open the victim's burned and blackened fingers even further. Then, using a wet towel, she wiped away debris from a wedding band and a red stone set in gold on the next finger.

"That's perfect. Yeah... you've got it. Right... just hold the ruler there. That's good. Right there."

"Think you'll get any prints here, Gina? She's pretty bad." Susan could not disguise her disgust.

"No. I looked before they took her from the scene. Completely burned off. You'd think when the tendons retract like that, it would protect the finger pads a bit. Rarely does with intense heat." Gina loved to share her knowledge with junior investigators as Earl had done with her. She turned the hand over and pulled the fingers back so that Susan could observe the damaged digits.

"See that? Down to bone. Maybe the perp soaked these hands in accelerant, but in that trunk... that heat. Dr. Luzinsky did a quick inspection at the scene and released her to me right there actually. I was hoping to get a rapid I.D., but no cigar. I'll take the rings back... clean 'em up, look for inscriptions, and get good photos for publication. Hope someone will recognize them. No one's reported a missing yet. If rings don't help, maybe the doc will get dental charts done today. Likely, he will. DNA's gonna take a while, but the rings could put us quickly in the right direction."

Gina flashed off two more shots.

"Thanks a lot. I appreciate the help."

"Yeah. Sure." Susan quickly changed the subject. "You ever see Jack anymore, Gina?"

"No. Been a really long time, actually. We're still friends, you know. Just weren't meant to be married. Not on the same page at all."

Susan hurried over to the sink, removed her gloves, and began washing up. "Way it goes sometimes," she said. "Is your mom any better?"

"No. Motor skills are gone... can't walk. They say the stroke affected what was left of her memory. She doesn't know me or anyone else. They tell me it's surprising that she's still hanging on. She'll never leave Sunset Convalescent. Well, looks like I'm gonna have to take these fingers off to get the rings." Gina picked up the cutters.

"Yeah? Too bad. Way it goes."

Gina wasn't sure if Susan meant that comment for her mother or the homicide victim or if she really wasn't listening but merely spewing out a standard response that had almost become her trademark. Gina watched the young woman's quick, nervous movements. Susan had been on the job for over a year but still remained a little jittery about morgue assignments. *Maybe she'll get used to it all eventually,* Gina thought. But, just as quickly as she thought it, Gina realized that was probably not so. Susan came on the job thinking it was "cool," but she was the type who looked at the deceased as something eerie, something ghostly to be afraid of, or, in this victim's case, something disgusting. The girl was probably waiting for a better position to open up.

Susan dried her hands and grabbed her camera equipment. As she headed toward the door, she turned and said, "Listen… I'm outta here. 'Less you need anything else."

"No. You go on. Just a few more photos. Nothing else here until they need me to photograph the autopsy. Probably tomorrow. I'll finish everything else at the office. Thanks for helping." Gina turned to look up and wave, but the door was already hissing to a close, and Susan was gone.

Gina worked at the fingers for a few minutes and finally retrieved the rings. She heard the door again and turned as Dr. Luzinsky entered the autopsy room and quickly surveyed the work that lay ahead.

"Hello, Gina." His accent was thick and Yugoslavian. "How it's going for you?"

"Okay, Doc. Busy day, though." She wiped each ring with a towel, dropped them into baggies, and began marking the labels.

"It is, unfortunately… crazy world, you could not believe," he said with real resignation in his voice. "Crazy world."

"That's a fact, Doc, and getting worse all the time."

Gina was sure she couldn't begin to imagine all the horrors he'd experienced. She'd heard some of his stories about what happened in his war-torn home country. He'd even been twice to Washington D.C. to appeal for help.

The phone rang, and the doctor walked toward a desk in the corner. "The burned one," he called back to Gina. "I have three ahead of her. I'll call you when I can get to her tomorrow."

"Just call when you're ready, and I'll be here."

When Gina placed the used snips and scalpel into the sink, she sliced through her glove and into her index finger. She'd never made such a clumsy mistake before, and it caught her off-guard. She washed up quickly and used several paper towels to stop the blood flow. Gina, embarrassed, looked around to see if the doctor had noticed, but he was engaged in his phone conversation. She was relieved and, in a few minutes, had her equipment packed and was outside in the sunshine again. However, when the bright, white sunlight hit her, she felt a little odd – dizzy. She placed her bags on the back seat and sat for a moment behind the wheel with her eyes closed. Her heart seemed to be racing a bit, and she was lightheaded. Gina saw the paper towels were holding the blood flow from the cut.

Just too tired. Too overworked, she thought. *I need a break. Vacation.*

On her way back to the office, full-blown panic hit Gina. She couldn't seem to focus her mind correctly. She started thinking about something that had hovered in the background of her consciousness for a while: *Death – he's out there waiting. He chooses who will live and who dies – just watching and waiting. Sly – tricky. Coming for the most innocent and the most monstrous.* Suddenly, Death had a face, and Gina had caught a glimpse. She could see some shadow of his face.

Gina was utterly overwhelmed and began shaking. She was sweating but felt cold at the same time. Her heart beat wildly in her chest. She couldn't get enough air into her lungs, and a massive lump in her throat refused the passage of saliva.

Still having some slivered presence of mind, Gina maneuvered the car to the side of the road and leaned back. She tried to catch her breath but realized that she was actually breathing in too much. Gina tried to concentrate on getting one normal breath past her lips and down into her lungs. Over and over, the voice inside her head told her –

calm down. This will pass. You're hyperventilating – too much oxygen. Breathe easy... easy.

After several minutes, the panicked symptoms gradually subsided so that Gina could drive back to the station, but she was never the same after that. She had given personality to death – animate Death. That personality would not recede from her conscious thoughts. The almost twelve years of dealing with death had piled up on her without Gina ever realizing it. Her long-retired mentor, Earl, had told her to slow down a bit that first year she was on the job, "You'll burn out," he'd warned. "Absolutely give your best at every scene, but also give yourself respite. Your mind and your soul... they need time away from the job. It can become too much to handle." She had assured Earl that she would take heed. In the end, however, Gina rarely took time off. She felt a need to work and never seemed to find the time to slow herself down. Suddenly, it was all catching up to her in an unexpected way.

No one knows nor can predict another's breaking point, and none could have guessed how that would manifest for Gina. Her practice of holding it in had been so perfected and complete that not one person could see her descent, and Gina shared nothing.

At first, Gina thought, rationally, that the panic and the strange thoughts she continued to experience might be the burnout of which Earl spoke. She fought to put it out of her mind for three weeks – to condemn the bad thoughts and images to the recesses as she had always done. It was a fight, but she consciously worked to keep the thoughts out. Gina continued on the job with no one noticing or suspecting that something was slightly off. She kept trying to bury the strange ideas and images that would come to her like a flash of insight. Gina feared they would lead to another panic attack. She feared losing control.

Though she worked hard to suppress the disturbing thoughts, they infiltrated every part of Gina's daily life – and then they invaded her dreams.

In one dream, Gina was in a vast, cavernous ballroom decorated with hundreds of helium balloons. They had very long strings of ribbon attached. The balloons floated up near the ceiling, but the ribbons hung down to shoulder level, and a light breeze kept them animated in perpetual lazy motion. There was no music, no people. The only sound was the hollow tapping of Gina's shoes on the tiled floor and the rustling of her taffeta ball gown as she stepped slowly toward the center of the room. Suddenly, an almost deafening crackling of static electricity filled the room. Gina pressed her palms tightly over her ears and squeezed her eyes shut. Then, just as suddenly, the noise was gone. She slowly opened her eyes and dropped her hands to her sides.

Gina stared. All around her, in various stages of undress and disarray, were dead people. They were all the victims in cases she had handled over the last eleven years. There were many. They were dancing or swaying, arms by their sides. Each danced alone, each in slow motion. Off to Gina's left danced the man who shot his wife, her lover, and then himself at her job site. Each of them was there with large gaping wounds. Beside Gina was the man who had committed suicide by stepping out in front of a tractor/trailer truck. Most of his head and chest were missing. Over to one side was the little girl who'd found a gun in her mother's purse. She looked confused. The unfortunate-little-mistake accident victims were there. The elderly man, whose sexual preferences included ropes, and caused a fatal heart attack. The teen boy trapped under his car while repairing a tire. The construction worker who fell six stories. The overdose victims – so many. The homicides, traffic fatalities, boating accidents, and on and on.

In the dream, Gina was calm and curious as these people somehow beckoned her with their deathly dance. She moved toward the center of the room and saw her first victim with the bloody paper towels still sticking to her face. All of the bodies swayed among the dangling ribbons. As the dead moved around, they began to close in on her in a semi-circle. Their movements urged her toward a hulking, darkly-clad figure at the far end of the room. He was not someone that she had ever encountered as a deceased victim.

Gina couldn't remember how the dream ended. It seemed to dissipate as she approached the figure. Then, she awakened, unafraid and resolved. She felt in control again. She knew what the deal was.

Death is inevitable. That's the reality, she thought. *We all have to die sometime. But it's the meanness of it—the uncertainty of the methods that is so disturbing. Death lurks in the corners and the darkness. In a broken mind or heart. In the wrath of a husband cuckolded. In the light of day with everyone watching. Death the deceiver. It tricks the young, speeding driver, who sees only her immortality, unaware. Death comes on its terms and by its own rules, and you ignore his whims at your own risk.*

Suddenly feeling awakened, in control, and armed with newly acquired knowledge, Gina whispered, "I have an advantage now. Because I see death for what it is. I've got years of experience."

In that moment, Gina made a deliberate decision to cheat Death. She decided to rob Death of the right to choose her time, place, and method. Without grasping the folly in this decision, a plan began to evolve.

Some possibilities for the "how" Gina rejected outright.

Of others, she reserved bits and pieces. She selected a few feasible locations and, over several days, physically inspected each location for suitability. A calmness enveloped her when Gina had narrowed the sites down to the one. She was in no hurry, for she knew she had the upper hand with Death. Finally, after years of watching Death sneak up on people, a plan was set in Gina's mind.

On the morning of December 15th, Gina Grant laid out the new dress she'd bought for the annual Christmas party with her co-workers. Her date, Det. Brad Watterson was set to pick her up at seven that evening. He could never have guessed he was part of a plan to fit a scenario.

She had tried to make all aspects of her life appear as regular Gina Grant routine. Everything in her apartment looked normal. Her grocery list lay on the dining room table with her checkbook. The water and phone bills and a dry cleaning ticket lay there, too.

She called Brad at 10:15 A.M.

"Hi. They working ya hard today?" She asked.

"Not a chance, Babe. You know me. Can't believe *you're* calling *me!* Wow... that's never happened! My lucky day. Whatcha up to?"

"I've got to run up to the mall in a few minutes, but actually... I wanted to see if you'd mind bringing the McMillan case file out of my desk when you pick me up tonight. Just tell whoever's on duty... Jill, I think. She'll know where to look. It's that narcotics/homicide thing from August. I forgot I've got deposition first thing Monday morning."

Gina tried to sound as normal as possible even though she could detect a quivering excitement in her voice.

"Sure thing, Sweetheart. Anything for you."

"I do appreciate that." She cringed at the "Sweetheart"

endearment. Gina considered him a great guy, but that's as far as it went. Brad had been trying unsuccessfully for a year to get her to go out with him, and he'd suddenly become the handy date to help carry out her plan.

"Gotta run now," she said. "See ya tonight."

Gina put the receiver down and checked herself in the full-length mirror. She wore loose-fitting jeans, a gray T-shirt, a light-weight gray hoodie, and sneakers. Satisfied that the look would not draw attention, Gina grabbed her phone, red purse, keys, and a small blue backpack. Then, after one last look around the apartment, she locked the door, got into her black Beretta, and headed north on the main highway out of town.

After traveling two hours, Gina pulled into a small rest stop south of Colleyville. The only other car in the rest area was at the far end of the parking lot, with no driver in sight. She took a shoulder-length, brown wig and a pink, long-sleeved shirt from the backpack. She also pulled out one of two vials containing the A-positive blood taken from her cut finger. Gina had collected the blood and kept it refrigerated when the wound proved slow to heal. That fit right in with the plan she had finally decided on. As she waited in the car, Gina thought about how well she'd covered all bases.

When she saw a man exiting the restroom, she quickly ducked down in the seat until she heard his car leaving the parking lot. Afterward, Gina sat back up and listened to traffic passing by. She quickly twisted and tucked her long blonde hair into the wig, making sure that no strands were exposed. Next, she placed a towel on the passenger side seat. That would protect the area where the "victim" would have been sitting. Gina then carefully arranged the shirt against the backrest and opened the vial of blood. She hesitated for a moment. A movie reel of instantaneous thoughts rushed at her. Gina blinked and cut them off.

"No," she whispered. "Just do it."

A few seconds later, she poured some blood into her right hand. Then, she flicked her fingers downward over the front of the shirt and upward into the passenger-side headliner and window. Next, Gina dripped blood onto the collar from the vial. She added some down the shirt front and more on the cuffs. The blood spatters, she thought, would be at least somewhat consistent with a violent blow to the head, and tested, would reveal her own DNA.

Gina ripped two buttons from the shirt. She threw one in the backseat and the other onto the floor in front. She put a little blood onto the fingers of her left hand, and the remaining blood in the vial was splashed onto the black upholstery, door padding, and dash. She grabbed the passenger dashboard with her bloodied fingers, sliding them sideways to simulate an attempt to remain inside the car while being dragged out of the passenger seat.

She surveyed her work on this part of the "crime scene." Gina decided it was insufficient, so she took a second vial and spattered, poured, and smeared the contents onto the headrest and some on the passenger floor. She wiped her bloody hands on the shirt before shoving it underneath the front seat. Finally, confident that the scene was adequate, Gina placed the towel and vials back into the backpack along with the purse. She wiped the drying blood off her hands with wet wipes and threw them into the pack as well. Satisfied with the work, she drove on.

On the far northern outskirts of Colleyville was one of Florida's large and popular flea markets. It was pretty busy on this warm Friday, ten days before Christmas, and Gina felt sure she wouldn't be noticed as she parked her car at the eastern end of the crowded lot. She left the vehicle unlocked, took the backpack and keys, and walked into the market aisle closest to the car.

As Gina continued down the closest row of tables, she casually glanced at the items on display in the stalls. She pretended to shop but made no eye contact with anyone as she walked calmly through the crowd. People were busy and paid no attention to the woman who shopped alone. She felt sure nothing was outstanding about her looks or demeanor.

Gina came out on the far end of the market and briskly walked half a mile farther down the highway. Traffic continuously passed her, but there were no cat-calls or indications that anyone took notice of her. When she reached Stover Road, which led to the small town of Stover, she turned and walked east. It was a lightly traveled road surrounded by sparsely wooded fields, with islands of trees here and there.

As Gina kept up her steady pace, several cars passed her by, headed most likely to the flea market. She kept her head tilted down and trusted the plan. She knew that when they started to search for a missing blonde back in Bay Haven, no one would make the connection to the possible brunette – hair mostly hidden by a hoodie – walking along Stover Road.

"It's all so perfect. I'll cheat you, Bastard. *I* will pick and choose for myself." Gina spoke to her unseen adversary, Death, as if he stood before her. She felt giddy. *She* was in control, ahead of the game. *She* would not be caught unaware like so many.

I will be just one more unsolved homicide, and Mom will get double on the insurance. She'll have everything she needs for the rest of her life, Gina thought for the hundredth time since finalizing her plan; *it's so perfect, Just so perfect.*

Gina walked at a rapid clip, head down, when vehicles

approached. Time passed quickly. She was lost again in the details of her self-described, brilliant plan when she found the place she'd previously staked out to dispose of evidence and unnecessary items. Gina waited for the road to clear of traffic, then turned and followed tire ruts running off to the right of Stover Road. She trudged through the overgrown field for sixty yards or so. The trail was long since used, and the ruts were barely visible through the overgrown weeds and vines. When Gina reached a large patch of palmettos, she removed a gardening spade from the backpack and dug a hole large enough to accommodate her discards. The ground was hard and tightly bound with tenacious weeds. Gina was equally determined but cursed the hardened earth.

Kneeling behind the bushes, Gina pulled a .38 caliber Smith & Wesson revolver, the towel, and two super-sized heavy-duty rubber bands from the backpack. She also removed her purse containing her wallet, I.D., assorted papers, and makeup. She laid these aside and put the empty blood vials and credit cards into the hole. Next, Gina threw in the wig and backpack. Finally, she pushed dirt into the hole, packed it down tightly, and covered the disturbed soil by arranging a tangle of dead branches and weeds over the area.

Gina tucked the gun into the top of her jeans, and the rubber bands and spade went into her pocket. She tucked her purse underneath the front of the hoodie and tied the hood to hide her hair. Again, Gina made her way through the weedy tire ruts toward Stover, staying well off the highway this time. She quickly got into a pine forest, and the undergrowth was minimal due to pine needles carpeting the ground. Gina watched the traffic and easily hid when she needed to. She had nearly two miles to go and didn't want to risk being seen.

With plenty of time to think as she made her way through the brush, Gina began to methodically consider the path she'd already covered. She was satisfied that she'd hidden her tracks well and gave no one reason to notice her. She began going over the scenario that lay ahead and thought... *ok, now I just get past the pines, watch for the speed limit sign, then a little farther into the overgrown woods... no... no... don't forget... you've got to toss the purse near the roadway so it won't take them too long to find the body. No body... no insurance for Mom. Gotta make sure she's well taken care of for however long her life may last. Then... let's see... am I forgetting anything? No. No. Original assault wounds hidden by a gunshot to the back of the head. When I get to the big oak, I'm home free. God, nobody would think of this in a million years. Bloody car. Some kind of assault. Abduction and then... murder. The purse will put them in an area to search and find the body. They'll never find the gun. No gun... no possible suicide.*

If Gina had been in a clear state of mind, perhaps she would have considered the other side of the investigation. She had always been careful not to jump to conclusions regarding suspects in crimes. Instead, she urged trainees to "let the evidence tell the story" as they considered the surrounding circumstances of a crime, and she practiced the same. However, Gina maintained too narrow a focus on the crime scene and evidential aspects of her own planned suicide. Of course, she hadn't fully conceded that it would be a suicide but rather had focused on taking control from the entity she conceived of as "Death." Had her thought process not been impaired, she would have considered that an innocent "suspect" might go through some kind of hell due to her actions, but Gina's mind had become entirely obstructed by her obsession with death.

She had run through several plans and scenarios to throw

the authorities off the idea of suicide. The trickiest problem Gina had faced was what weapon to use and how to dispose of it. She'd ruled out any overdose for obvious reasons. She would have preferred that but could think of nothing to make that into a believable homicide scene. It happened from time to time that poisons were utilized, but that usually involved a much longer process, and she couldn't think of a time that it had been used in a quick, all-at-once poisoning situation except with the pain reliever tampering cases back in the mid-80s.

Gina considered traffic accidents too unpredictable. She didn't want to end up paralyzed or brain dead, and there was always the possibility of severely injuring or causing the same for an innocent victim. Gina knew it had to be something that would give her total control of the situation and in no way convey the impression of suicide because homicide would double her insurance and take care of her mother's needs. She hadn't the nerve to use a knife. She'd tried a test of that and barely broke the skin. Gina was sure she couldn't plunge a knife into her chest and decided it had to be a gun. Quick and easy. Few people even knew she had the weapon, and it could be reasonably assumed that she'd sold it if some of the few remembered. A long-ago boyfriend had given it to her, and it wasn't registered to anyone. With her clever plan, no weapon would be recovered anyway, so the gun ownership issue would quickly fade if someone remembered.

From training and independent studies, Gina knew that women rarely commit suicide with a gun, but those who did usually aimed for the chest rather than the head. She believed it wouldn't be too difficult to put the barrel against the back of her head, close her eyes, and pull the trigger – mind over matter. If, by some unlikely twist of fate, she missed her exact mark, or the bullet ricocheted and didn't kill her instantly, at least she would be unconscious and bleed to death or die from exposure before she was found. She figured there would be only momentary pain involved, if any.

Gina thought the most brilliant part of the plan was how she decided to get rid of the weapon. Murderers do not usually leave weapons at the scenes of their crimes – not intentionally, anyway. Gina pictured the scene as she thought, *I'm nude, I climb halfway up the oak tree, connect the giant rubber bands, and fasten one end around that thick branch above. I attach the other end of the band to the gun's trigger guard. Stretch it out. Stand on that slightly lower limb, clear of lower branches, so I fall freely to the ground. The towel around my hands will protect me from gunshot residue. Carefully place the barrel against the base of my skull and pull the trigger. Voila... the job is done. My body and towel fall into the weeds below, but the gun retracts, pulled into the tree by the heavy-duty rubber bands.*

Gina smiled as she thought of the end scene. *They'll be searching the ground and surrounding area, but not for long. They'll realize the perp took the gun with him. No reason to search a lot. If, by some wild chance, they glance up, the bands will have pulled the gun to the opposite side of the thick branch. It will be hidden by foliage as well. If they find the body before decomposition begins, any injuries received in the fall could be attributed to the "beating" received while still in the car.*

Gina had seriously considered a traffic accident scenario. It would have been quick with fewer moving parts, but she couldn't get past the idea that it could result in life-altering injuries instead of death. Ultimately, she'd given the abduction plan much forethought and believed it was simply ingenious.

Knowing that multiple agencies would be involved in a

search for her, Gina figured there was a good chance she'd be found quickly. The possibility of decomposing had bothered her the most, so she'd tried to leave enough of a trail to be found within a day or two. She believed that since she wouldn't be there for her date, Brad would start asking questions of her co-workers. The search would begin.

If flea market security found her abandoned car with blood evidence before closing, they'd call law enforcement. The vehicle would come back to her, and her office would be contacted. If that happened before the date, a serious search would start. Since Stover was the closest town to the flea market, police units would be sent down Stover Road. She'd make the red purse easily spotted. Her forensic and other identification would be found with her cell phone nearby. The phone could be traced and give them a good lead, too. Gina had removed all the credit cards because, of course, the attacker would have stolen them. She tore the other cards, I.D., and receipts out of the wallet and threw them into the purse to make it look riffled through. She left no money and nothing valuable inside – no reason for some driver-by-finder to keep the bag. Those items would raise questions about that area. They'd see it would be a good place to dump a body. By then, the pieces of the puzzle would be overwhelming, and the final search – likely with dogs – would begin. If it didn't happen as she expected, and her body wasn't found quickly, decomposition was a reality. Gina finally came to terms with that possibility and decided it was okay. She was *not* her body.

After burying the unnecessary items, Gina continued her trek back toward Stover Road. She was exhilarated when the 'SPEED LIMIT 55' sign came into view. She watched for traffic as she made her way through the tangle of weeds, vines, and trees, and twice had to duck down and wait as cars passed. It was unlikely that she would be noticed at about twenty feet off the roadway, in the woods, but she would take no chances.

Gina took the keys from her purse and threw them as far as she could into the thick brush off to her right. She worked her way through the tangle just a little closer to the road, looked through her purse once more, snapped it closed, and hurled it into a stand of reeds less than ten feet from the roadway. The red purse would be easily seen, but only if someone was purposely looking. The phone landed about ten feet beyond. Gina figured they'd start searching the whole area when they found the handbag. The identification inside would make the law enforcement's job easier and get the body identified more quickly – another good idea, she was sure. Gina credited herself for having really thought through every course of action.

After tossing the items, Gina started picking her way back through the woods. She could see the giant oak tree about two hundred yards ahead. It stood nearly alone in a field of high weeds. It was time to get rid of the T-shirt and bra. She pulled the spade from her pocket, dug another hole – deep – and buried the clothes again, disguising the dig location with debris.

As she trudged through tall weeds toward the oak, Gina would listen for traffic and duck down when cars passed. Finally, about halfway to the oak, she threw the spade off to the right as far as she could. Once Gina got to the tree, she kicked off her shoes and removed the gun from her waistband. She took the rubber bands and towel from her pockets. She laid them in the crook of a low branch, removed her jeans, and scrubbed the knee areas in the dirt before tossing them aside. Gina ripped her bikini panties off but heard a siren and ducked. The police vehicle sped past, heading west, and she wondered if her car had been found already. *That could be a good thing*, she thought. *I'll be done here in a minute or two.*

Gina watched the flashing lights until they were out of sight. She looked back toward the road, saw all was clear, and threw the panties haphazardly into the weeds. Her heart was now beating wildly, but she was no less determined to follow the plan. She picked up the Smith & Wesson, popped open the cylinder, spun it almost hypnotically, snapped it shut, and looked up at the tree.

"It's time," she said.

Gina retrieved the rubber bands and connected them by looping one into the other. Next, she looped one end of the band through the trigger guard and pulled the other over her head. Finally, she hung the towel over them to completely free her hands for climbing.

Gina scaled the tree without difficulty and pulled the free end of the rubber band around the trunk about twenty feet up. Next, she pulled the gun through the tree band twice to secure it, then carefully held onto the gun-end of the band, moved downward, and reached her pre-selected spot. That put her standing about fifteen feet up with her feet resting on two slightly smaller branches that forked from a more substantial branch. She bounced lightly to ensure their stability even though she'd already checked that out the day she'd surveyed this location.

With her feet securely in place, Gina tested the tension of the bands by pulling the gun toward her – each time, it held with no indication of slipping or breaking. The weapon would be secure and well-hidden when it snapped back after firing the fatal shot. She felt sure that the rubber bands would hold the gun for a long time before they rotted and released the weapon. With luck and certainly with all the clues she'd left behind – even if that police vehicle wasn't about her car – Gina fully believed that her body would be found long before the gun fell. She just knew that she had devised the perfect plan.

"Okay," she took a deep breath. "I'm ready now."

Gina took one last look around her. From her vantage point, she could see the road. There were three cars within her span of vision – Christmas traffic. She would wait.

A faint breeze was blowing, and she watched it play through the trees. Above the trees, she could see the movement of the clouds. They were pale pink and stretched like cotton candy pulled between a child's fingers. On the northern horizon was a buildup of darker storm clouds.

"I guess I'm gonna miss the rainstorms," she whispered hoarsely.

The sound of her own scratchy voice startled Gina. She quickly pressed her fingers against her lips as if to stop what had already been spoken.

Gina suddenly felt a little confused. She tried to focus on the passing cars, but for a moment, she couldn't think why. Her mind traveled instantly to the times when, as a child, she would sit cross-legged in the bay window with the curtains drawn around her, encapsulated in a world of her own. She'd enjoyed the storms and was never afraid. Instead, she loved to watch the rain come down. Sometimes, Gina would imagine the droplets racing down the window pane. She'd trace her finger along the raindrop, following the one she decided would win.

"Sad little girl," she whispered – barely audible to herself. "A pastime so arbitrary. Choosing who would win."

Who... would... win?

"My God," Gina's voice was suddenly strong and panicked. "My God, who wins if I do this? Who is *really* orchestrating this? Me? Or Death? Death is the ultimate victor, no matter how it happens. What could I have been thinking all this time? I was almost tricked! What's wrong with me? Did I walk into his trap? I almost made it easier for him. Maybe his plan all along! And maybe... maybe I was about to make it easier for him. I won't do it! No. By God, I won't freely give myself to Death. No win."

Gina looked toward the highway. One large truck was half a mile distant.

"I've got to go home."

She waited for the truck to pass and thought, *I can put his whole scheme in reverse. I can. I will... I've got to get back. If I hurry, I can... I can be back to the car before dark. But the cops... and how do I explain it all? I can do it. I'll think of something. I have to. Gotta find my keys... my clothes. Oh, God! My clothes!*

Gina attempted to untie the rubber band from the gun. Her knots had been good, for she found it difficult to release the bands. The weight of the firearm and the tautness of the bands were defeating her. Finally, she realized she'd have to stretch the rubber bands to the breaking point to release the gun.

She grasped the rubber bands near the looped knots with both hands and pulled away from the center. She watched closely to see when the bands might show signs of weakening, but her mind was still on Death.

Gina kept whispering, "What was I thinking? He almost got me... almost got me."

Suddenly, without warning, a small twig on one of the forking branches beneath her feet gave way. Gina slipped and was falling before she could react. Her last act was to reach out for the trunk as she fell, feet first between the two forking branches. She would probably have survived the fall from that height, but her hip bounced against one of the forks, knocking her backward into the y-intersection of the two branches. It was three days before they found her hanging. Gina's head was jammed in the junction of the two forking branches. Death came for Gina Grant on December 15th – as scheduled.

- the end -

5

DADDY'S HANDS

Maddie stumbled toward the narrow, sandy pathway. Twilight had begun to steal the remaining slivers of light from the canopy of trees, and the girl understood that night would soon be upon her. Maddie wasn't afraid of the dark, though. That kind of darkness had never been a thing to fear. Some children were frightened of the dark shapes and shadows that came as apparitions when nighttime overtook the day. Her friend Bobbie always talked about the scary things that she saw in the darkness of her bedroom. But that was never the case with Maddie. Somehow, the nighttime had always seemed a comfort to her.

Even though darkness was not a problem, the girl was nevertheless struggling. She couldn't quite understand what was happening to her. There was a strange buzzing in her head and behind her left eye. She'd never experienced anything like that before. The buzzing sound echoed so close that she couldn't tell if it came from within or outside her head. When it had first started – right after she had awakened on the floor – Maddie had been sure that it came from something nearby, and she'd looked around her bedroom, trying to locate the source of the sound. Now, on the pathway, she wasn't so sure. She was inclined to think that the noise came from inside her head because instead of receding, the buzzing still sounded as if it was very close by.

Such a funny noise, she thought, *chhh... chhh... chhh*. It was not funny in a laughing way but funny in a strange and bothersome way. Maddie wanted the sound to stop, but it wouldn't go away. She thought that if she could only reach inside her head, push the noise out, and make it disappear, she might begin to feel better.

The girl began to hum, "You Are My Sunshine." The song was one of many she and her grandmother had sung together many times. It was an unsuccessful attempt to drive the noise from her head.

Maddie hadn't been feeling very well all afternoon. Ever since her daddy left for work at two o'clock, she'd been a little out of sorts. She had fallen asleep for a while after he'd gone. When she awakened, she was on the floor in her bedroom, not on the bed. She couldn't remember lying down on the floor and didn't remember falling asleep, either. Maddie just remembered waking up. Everything seemed odd to her. She'd never slept on the floor before and didn't know why she had done it on this day. At first, she thought she'd only been sleeping for a few minutes, but then she saw that the late afternoon light had cast long shadows through the worn lace of her ragged curtains. Maddie had stared at the looming shadows and struggled to comprehend the meaning. It took her full concentration to realize she'd been asleep for a very long time. That confused her. She tried to remember what had happened earlier in the day, but everything seemed sort of fragmented inside her head.

"Jigsaw puzzle," she'd whispered with a thick tongue.

She thought about her Grandma's jigsaw puzzles spread out on the kitchen table. There were so many pieces. That was just how it felt inside her head – like scattered puzzle pieces – but Maddie's puzzle wouldn't fit together properly. Thoughts seemed to come and go rather rapidly. She instinctively patted her forehead to feel for fever like her grandmother would have. She tried hard to concentrate until she finally grabbed onto one splinter of thought that reminded her of the book. It was due back at the library. Maddie tried to stay focused on the book so she wouldn't be so confused. She'd picked up *The Lion's Paw* from her bedside table, and though she was stumbling and unsteady on her feet, she had made it downstairs and was on her way to the library.

Maddie's progress was slow. She felt sluggish. The constant, rushing sounds inside her head seemed to affect her balance. The noise made her wobble more than a little bit, forcing her to move more slowly. She somehow understood that – pulled that thought from her jumbled-up brainwaves. She was being clumsy, too. That wasn't like Maddie at all. The problem was that awful, distracting sound. That noise made it very difficult to concentrate on walking.

When she had finally made it across the road in front of her house, Maddie took several steps past the wooded entrance to the worn pathway but found herself too dizzy to continue. She tottered so much that she dropped her book and grabbed onto a spindly, scrub oak to keep from falling. The tree was stunted, surrounded as it was by larger oaks, Brazilian Peppers, and strangler vines, all competing for every inch of space. It was an ongoing life struggle for the flimsy tree. It had to fight for every drop of rain, every ray of sunshine, and every bit of nourishment it could absorb from the ground to feed its heart. Weak as it was, the scrub oak swayed dramatically, fighting under the weight of the slightly built nine-year-old girl.

The give of the tree sent a searing shot of pain from Maddie's shoulder down into her oddly twisted right arm. Only then did she notice how that arm wasn't working. Without thought and induced by the pain, she sucked in a very deep breath, which immediately caused more pain in her ribs. Little bits of bright white light danced wildly before her eyes and left behind more and more darkness as they receded. She clung even tighter to the slender tree trunk as it straightened to its upright position again. She stood there for long moments, and finally, the intermingled, sparkling lights and darkness gave way to her normal vision again.

Maddie held her sucked-in breath momentarily before she eased the breath back out to protect her aching ribs. Even in the cool October breeze, sweat covered her face and glued her short chestnut hair flat against her head. She took soft, shallow breaths, and slowly, very slowly, the pain began to subside to a more tolerable level. Maddie recognized how odd it was that she had not noticed how badly her body hurt. The noise had been too much of a distraction.

The girl kept a stranglehold on the tree, trying to grasp onto some other important thing. She was disturbed by that nagging half-thought she couldn't quite sort out. Gingerly, she turned to stare back down the pathway. Everything was enveloped in darkness across the dirt and gravel roadway back toward the house. Maddie thought her vision had gone black until suddenly, a breeze lifted and spread the leaves on the foliage that nearly surrounded her. The breeze-animated branches intermittently revealed a light through her bedroom window on the second floor.

Daddy will be mad again.

94

Chhh… chhh… chhh…

Maddie's mind gnawed at the problem, fighting to make connections and make a good decision. Coherent thoughts were as erratic as the breeze around her, but after a moment, she decided.

No. Can't go back. No time.

She reminded herself to breathe gently as she bent down slowly and carefully. It was not easy, but she was able to grasp onto the book she'd dropped in the dirt beside her feet. Her whole body was wracked with pain, but there was no time to allow it. She couldn't let the pain overtake her.

Don't feel… don't feel… don't feel…

With the book in hand again, Maddie stepped back onto the pathway. At first, she moved with great caution and at a snail's pace. Each step seemed to take minutes, but she couldn't really comprehend the time thing. That part of her brain seemed to be tricking her.

Maddie had begun to regain a semblance of stability on her feet for fifty yards or so. All the while, however, the chhh…chhh… chhh continued inside her head. She continued along the path, moving slowly but with less consciously placed, shuffling steps and a little more confidence until the breeze turned into a wind that nearly took her down again.

The girl stopped and leaned against a pine. Her breaths were shallow, favoring her ribs.

I can do it, she thought. *Let me think… let me think… have to get through the woods. Not so far. Through Mr. Baskin's field… and… and… yes. Then, cross that road. I'm there. Daddy said… Daddy said… What? What? I can't remember. I smell lemon pie. Where is the lemon pie?*

Ever since she'd awakened after Daddy had left for work, Maddie kept having moments of great clarity alternately with moments of complete confusion. Now, she had lost her focus on the library. Her thoughts were again of that jigsaw puzzle until a strong thought pushed through and overtook the others. Her focus became the ever-waning light. She looked up as if the stars or moon might confirm the time. She knew that time was important but didn't remember why.

The night sky was obscured into blinking, on-again, off-again sparkles by the wind-twisted overhead canopy. She stayed in place against the pine tree and watched the intermittently visible stars for a few minutes. The blinking brightness took her back to when she had just turned seven. In a clear and orderly vision, she remembered – she saw – a happier time in her life as if watching a film reel rush through a scene. It was summer. Maddie was watching the waves that obscured the shrimper's lights in Apalachicola Bay. Her cousin Corrie showed her a game. They would watch waves play hide-n-seek with the lighted boats as they tossed about in the bay. She and Corrie would try to guess which boat would next become visible at the top of the swells. They giggled and clapped when they were right. They played on the beach every day and into the evenings. Afterward, she and Corrie ate their supper, and then Aunt Vera showed them all the pictures of Grandma and her family in her big hatbox full of photographs. So many pictures of Grandma were taken when she was much younger. Maddie had picked up each photo taken when Grandma was pretty and young and wore stylish hats and dresses. It was back in a time when her heart wasn't sick yet.

As she rested there, Maddie relived those visits. There were picnics, swimming, and sandcastle building. Like a film, she watched it and saw herself crying on the last night with Aunt Vera and Corrie. Her Aunt had said, "Things will get better, Maddie."

Maddie always hated leavings. That last visit was the most fun she'd ever had. Now, Maddie had relived it in a moment under the twinkling starlights above. Then she had felt that exact, leaving feeling in her heart again until suddenly, that sound overwhelmed her brain and brought her back to reality – *chhh... chhh... chhh.*

It took Maddie a moment to realize she was on the path going somewhere. She glanced at the book, pushed away from the tree, and resumed her journey. She did this without conscious thought. Apalachicola had seemed too real – like like she was actually there. At that moment, it seemed that the pathway could not be real.

Maddie's thoughts turned to her grandmother. Even though jigsaw-jumbled again, the pieces still brought tears to her eyes, making the pathway more treacherous. She couldn't hold back the tears, though. One of the best things in Maddie's life was remembering the good days and good times – even if the memories tangled up and made her cry.

Maddie continued to stumble along slowly. When she could pull thoughts together, she thought about the stories her grandmother would tell about the old times. Remembering was a comforting routine the girl had learned to revert to in bad times. Now, she used that routine to keep the awful noise in the background and reduce the muddled thoughts for a moment.

The girl could remember just the way her grandmother's voice sounded. Once, Maddie had written down all of the Grandma stories she could remember. She had made a booklet of the stories and drew pictures of flowers on the front. She'd tried to draw a picture of her grandma, but Maddie was better at writing stories than drawing. She thought her flowers turned out nicely, though, and kept the book under her pillow for a while. The words she'd written on paper existed only inside her head now, for her daddy had torn the booklet to pieces in a fit of anger last spring. At first, Maddie was sad about the storybook, but soon, she decided that it didn't really matter. She knew all the words, and once the booklet was gone, she'd begun adding more details in her head as she remembered Grandma's stories. There were so many tales told from the old rocking chairs on the front porch. They sat there many afternoons and sipped sweet iced tea while Grandma fanned herself with the paper fan Maddie had made for her.

Maddie knew she'd never run out of memories. She began to whisper aloud what she would say to a grandmother long gone as she staggered along the dirt path.

"Oh, Grandma, I love you. I miss you. You held me so tight when the storms came. I miss all the stories about my beautiful mama with golden hair. I wish I could remember her too. I miss your voice. All your railroad stories. Grandma... I just want..."

The girl stopped to wipe away the perspiration that was stinging her eyes. She pressed her hand against her left ear to ease the troublesome noise. It was a moment longer before Maddie could get her feet to move again, and she took breaths just deep enough so that her ribs would not ache so much.

Once she was moving again, Maddie could *hear* her grandmother's voice. It sounded far away at first – sort of hollow, and it surprised Maddie very much. She gasped with happiness and ignored the rib pain that came with that breath. Then, suddenly, she could *sense* her grandmother walking by her side. She looked there, confused. She stopped again and reached out to touch but could not see nor feel anyone. Still, Maddie knew and whispered, "Grandma..."

The voice was getting stronger every second, and Maddie

easily recognized the sing-song way her grandmother always spoke to her.

"Now, Honey... you got to get on. Keep on walkin while we talk, hear?"

Maddie obeyed and hobbled on.

"Why, child, I surely do wish you could'a seen this place way back when. It was hectic, but I did enjoy that kind'a hectic. Why... everthing was in motion. The whole house was purely animated with talk n' laughter n' movement. Folks would stay over or just come to the table to eat, but folks was just everwhere. This place was a pure beehive'a folks a'coming an a'going! Just buzzing with activity. My... my... my! Ladies dressed up so fine. Fancy frocks. So many fine folks with places to go.

"My stars! The railroad was still big business then, you see. Course, the Atlantic Seaboard had way more business than we ever saw, but you'd be surprised how many passengers we had way out here west'a the coast. See them tracks running right yonder by the house? Why them tracks is what kept this house full. Station was right over yonder where that stone platform still stands. Can't hardly see it now. The weeds has just took over the place. It was a wooden platform 'til that hurricane come in, I believe, around Cocoa Beach in nineteen and twenty-six. Storm hit us too n' took out that wooden platform. They built that stone one after that. Your Daddy weren't but 'bout two years old when that happened. I think what took it out was that ol' hurricane launched a tornado. Took part'a the station roof too, n' that had to be fixed.

"My, how I used to love to hear the trundle of the baggage cart across that wooden platform when Mr. Hughes rolled it out. The cart was a sight to behold, Child. Why, I wish you could'a seen that thing. Had big old steel, spoke wheels painted the shiniest red you ever seen! The flatbed of the cart was a bright and splendid green, and Mr. Hughes kept it shining 'til it near 'bout sparkled. After ever train, you could see him right out yonder, Johnny-on-the-spot,

taking a rag to the finish. Polishing that thing to a shine. Maddie... I was just a young-un myself then. Keep on walkin', child. Keep walkin'. I'd watch Mr. Hughes load trunks n' suitcases n' satchels of all sizes n' descriptions onto that cart. Some'a them bags looked to be made of finest leather, n' some was tattered to beat the band. There was times, mind you, if the station was a little shy'a passengers, or they was just hauling oranges, he'd give me a ride on the cart from one end of the wooden platform to the other, n' that was quite a thrill. I would sit up on that cart in royal fashion for my ride, like the absolute Queen Sheba herself. Oh my... I was a caution! Oh, I was! Now I must say... I kindly suspected that man felt obligated to give the cart something to do, too! But oh, my! I was thrilled.

Maddie's steps were slow and cautious as she stumbled along the pathway, listening to every word.

Now, Mr. Hughes was right particular about careful loading. He didn't want to scratch that green n' red cart as much as he didn't want to damage any luggage. Even some mighty ragged suitcases held together by string... he handled them bags like they belonged to a king. I'd try to imagine all the places that luggage was fixing to go to... or the places they been. Child... just imagine all the places they could go. Close your eyes, n' you can just see 'em. Maybe Cincinnati, Knoxville, or maybe Paducah. Maybe Galveston, or San Francisco, or all the way to Seattle! Some had stickers on 'em telling where they been.

"*It was some years later that Mr. Hughes went on to his maker. Had to be on past eighty, I reckon. Mr. Rand took over the job after that. I was married near 'bout a year by then, n' just had my baby boy, n' me n' your grandpa was running the house by that time. Now, Mr. Rand was a bit of an impatient man and not prone to be very careful with the luggage or the cart. I don't believe I ever did see him wipe down the cart, n' once, I even saw it left out in the rain! Oh my goodness, Mr. Hughes surely would not ever have done that nice cart that-a-way. Well... as you might imagine, after so much baggage traveling in and out of that station n' not much extra care taken... well, that cart began to lose its shine n' start collecting rust. Not a bit of elbow grease applied by Mr. Rand... ah, well... that was all so long ago."*

Maddie clutched her book and continued her slow, stumbly walk accompanied by the grandmother she couldn't see. The noises still filled her head, but she could hear the voice clearly, and somehow, in her mind, was a vision. She saw the crinkled skin around her grandmother's eyes when she talked about Mr. Hughes and the cart. Maddie watched a tear fall from her eye as it often did when she told of those old days.

"All them things occurred a while before another hurricane carried off the station - building and all. The stone platform got left behind. Poor ol' thing. Left behind, n' now it's just about took over with weeds n' scrubs. Just a haven for rattlesnakes now. Pure breeding ground over yonder.

"But, oh my, I surely do remember them days when the station was lively n' the house was just as lively too. Child! It was a busy place back then. It was a sight! Once upon a time, it certainly was! We had all we could do to keep up with the comings n' goings. Why, you never saw the likes of it. I reckon I washed a many a sheet. And feeding folks? Wonderful smells of coffee and bacon. Roast pork and rice with tomatoes. Lordy, but that big ol' table was full'a food and full'a people, near 'bout day and night. Talking of lives lived. Love n' losses. Travels and hard times n' bountiful blessings. Child, if I close my eyes, I can still hear the racket of forks n' spoons 'round that table with folks grabbing pork chops n' pawing biscuits, n'passing fried chicken right along with passing stories n' constant conversation across the table n' back n forth. There was a mess of laughter n' it was a musical kind'a sound around that

table. *Weren't hardly never a quarrel nor hard word said. Walk, Child.*

"It was a good place. See... this house was a good stop-over point while folks waited for a train heading in a different direction. Tracks switched on to Tampa way on down, and some went east, too. All gone now. Folks didn't need to stay no more after while. It started just dwindling away with the depression. Came to be a sight worse than we ever calculated. Just dwindled away. Turned your Grandpa to the drink. Turned him right mean when it all died down. I reckon his meanness made your daddy mean, too... somehow. I just don't understand how it could turn a man so. Can't even see the tracks for the weeds no more and..."

Maddie stumbled on an exposed root. Pain struck hard, and her grandmother's voice just floated away as if carried off on a breeze.

Chhh... chhh... chhh... The noise in her head became louder. Her head throbbed.

"Don't feel. Don't feel. Stop feeling."

The increasing sound and the pain brought Maddie quickly back into the moment and a need to tell her grandmother something important. She called out to the float-away voice, trying to make her return.

"Thank you, Grandma! For the books. When I couldn't talk anymore. You read to me. To make me talk again, but Grandma... I talked because I could *see* everything you read, and I needed... something... something *different* to see and to think about. But you left me. Why?"

Speaking made the girl breathless. Her chest heaved despite the pain.

"Why... does everything good... go away. Grandma? Like you? Like... the station? Like the people... around the table? Why does everybody leave? I love you. I wish I wish... I wish you didn't go."

The child went silent then. She stopped to look around. The increasing winds played through the trees, foretelling of rain. Maddie waited for her Grandmother's voice, but all was silent except for the *chhh... chhh... chhh...* and she began to move down the path again.

Even with the wind, her body was damp with sweat. A mix of salty perspiration and tears obscured her vision, and Maddie stepped into a shallow wash-out. Her body twisted and nearly went down before she quickly grabbed onto a Strangler Fig-enclosed oak with her good left hand. She managed to hang onto the book this time but paid the price as the pain shot through her body.

"Just breathe, Child... don't let the pain take you... breathe." Grandma's voice again, but through Maddie's lips. "You can get through it if you just don't feel."

Maddie let go of the coiled vine and leaned slightly to her right for balance. Then, still unable to lift the injured arm, she used her left to pull the worn cotton T-shirt up from her belly. She carefully wiped the stinging sweat from her face and eyes while struggling to hang onto the book.

Slowly, the girl turned her head to survey the area around her. She was far from the house now. The bedroom light was no longer visible, as the woods surrounded her, and the full blanket of the night filled the air. Though Maddie knew the path and woods by heart, they had confused her on this night.

"Almost at the clearing now?" she whispered. "I think. Almost to the end."

She still had to cross Baskin's tomato field and get to the library before nine. Maddie knew that afterward, she could relax a little. She could go more slowly on the way home. There would be no hurry then. Daddy wouldn't get home until a little after eleven when his shift was over if he didn't stop at the bar. She could lie in bed and listen for his tires on the road kicking up a wild tornado of dirt and rocks behind the old, dust-grayed, green pick-up truck. Then she would pretend to be asleep, like always, and hope and pray that nothing would set him off again. Maddie suddenly remembered his fury of so many hours before.

"Grandma... I try... to be good. I do. Tried not to make any noise. He works hard. Needs his sleep. I know that. No good. 'Yer always running your mouth.' He kept screaming at me. 'Yer just like yer damn mama.'"

Like your mama. Like your mama. The very words spoken by the child at that moment struck her with another memory like a flash of lightning. Maddie saw a vision that stopped her dead still. It was a vision she'd pushed away for a long time. She didn't *want* to remember it, but now Maddie had no control. The images wouldn't go away. She suddenly saw herself standing in the doorway, paralyzed with fear. Four years old... almost five? Grandma was in the hospital again with a sick heart. Maddie's memory was vivid, and she saw it all. She watched the whole thing happen again at that moment...

She saw the bare back muscles knotted. The knots were as big as the fists that pounded and pounded her mama against the wall. First, there were screams, but they didn't last long. Then her mama made no more noise, no sounds. She slumped, but he held her up to strike her again and again. Then, as he held her by the neck, Mama slid, ever so slowly, down to the floor. Her long, golden, bloodied hair made a glistening red ribbon on the wall behind her. Then Mama fell sideways. Mama? Yes, it was her. It *was* Mama. Maddie winced when she heard her mother's head crack against the wooden floor. Her soft golden hair – the hair that always smelled so nice when she held Maddie close – wasn't so golden anymore. It had quickly become a mass of red wetness. Her pretty blue eyes stared at Maddie in the doorway.

Maddie watched. She saw Daddy – quiet then – his chest heaving. He was looking at his hands. He stared at his hands – opening and closing his bloody fingers into fists. He stared at them as if they belonged to a stranger. Maddie tried to be quiet – quiet as Mama – but a small whimpering noise escaped from her lips, and he turned. Moving in a slow motion – with a face of stone – he turned and saw her crouching in the bedroom doorway. And then he took her and Mama into those woods, and he put Mama into the hole. He quickly threw the dirt onto her face because he said her eyes were watching. Mama's eyes saw. Maddie's eyes saw, too. And Daddy said, "I ort to put you in there with her and be done with the whole thing." His words all slurred together, and he poked at Maddie's chest with the shovel. "You tell anybody 'bout this, and I'll put you right in there with her. You hear?" He looked at Maddie and repeated his words. His eyes were filled with hate.

That night, the girl had learned all about hate. And Maddie never said anything about that night to anyone – ever. Even when Grandma came back from the hospital, Maddie never spoke of that night. For a long time, Maddie never talked at all, and people said she was traumatized because her mother ran off with some man and abandoned her child.

Chhh… chhh… chhh…

Maddie crossed a small clearing. She'd begun cradling the aching, swollen right arm with her left – still dutifully clutching the book. She entered Mr. Baskin's field. Her right leg was having difficulty keeping up with the left one. She was trying to make the leg work and trying to stay upright between two rows of ripe, aromatic tomato plants. She talked to keep her mind on something else.

"Grandma… you'd like this book… *The Lion's Paw*. Got to take it back. Can't let Daddy get it…. No… can't let Daddy throw away another book. Got to take it back."

Maddie looked down at her feet. They seemed disconnected from her. They went in and out of focus, but she could see they weren't moving fast enough.

Chhh… chhh… chhh…

She tried to ignore the derelict feet.

"They were orphans. Like Tom Sawyer. But they escaped Grandma… they got away. Good father… looking for their good father. No mamas for them either. Never any mamas.

"Look, Grandma! I kept walking. I see the end of the field now. I made it! See the library lights there? Cross Third Avenue… the playground. Why is it so cold? Where's my sweater? It's too hard to think.

Chhh… chhh… chhh…

What *is* that noise? My head feels too big. I can't think. What's wrong with me? I can't think."

Maddie stumbled badly and fell over a sandy embankment. She barely held on to the book. Panicked, she tried to move backward off the mound. She lifted her shoulders up off the ground and balanced on her left elbow. The dirt was piled up just like that dirt where her mother went into the ground. A groan escaped her lips. Her head told her to go, but her body wasn't moving. Maddie's body refused to move anymore.

Thoughts came slowly then. "Shut up that squalling. Throw that dirt in there. More! Cover it! Push that dirt in. Don't you tell… gonna be in big trouble if you tell.'

Secret. Never, never, never tell. Daddy! I'll be good… I promise… I'll be… good.

Very slowly, Maddie gave in and crumpled fully to the ground. She pulled *The Lion's Paw* to her chest. Maddie closed her eyes. Her breathing ended, and red liquid flowed from her ear and into the sand.

- the end -

6

A WARRIOR NO MORE

Captain Worth – a tall, commanding figure with gray hair and a full gray beard stood at the edge of a hilly rise. He caressed a small oval locket inside his coat pocket. His wife had insisted he carry it. He was glad, for it comforted him whenever he thought of her and home.

A biting wind invaded Worth's very bones. The cold winds had always bothered him more than snow, and he was sure snow would come sometime this night. It would make their situation in the morning much more daunting and deadly. The captain calculated. Heavy snow would affect their ability to see and greatly impact the movement of men and equipment. Their clothing would also give them away more readily against the white-covered ground, though perhaps not so much as the enemy's blue. Light snow would make ground conditions slippery – a wet and penetrating cold. Already, three men were sick, including the young farrier who'd become their doctor by necessity.

Captain Worth had a strong sense of foreboding. The feeling was much more intense than in previous battles. He worried for his men. He pulled his hat down tighter against the relentless wind and squinted to focus on the nearest ridge across the valley. At least fourteen small campfires were visible, but just flickers of light. He knew it had to be a pretty large encampment. The Yankees had arrived sooner than his scouts had reckoned and would likely bring his remaining infantry unit into the fight of their lives by daybreak. He didn't have nearly enough men left to survive the onslaught, and Dinsmore's unit couldn't possibly arrive in time to alter the outcome. Worth wondered, as he so often did, *how on earth did we undertake this God-forsaken war?*

Lieutenant Swilley approached at that moment and interrupted the captain's thoughts.

"Made sure Perkins got Atalanta taken care of. She's proper hobbled. Fed n' watered, Sir. Doubled her blanket, too. And night watch is done lined up."

"Good. Thank you, Thomas. See that our fires are well concealed." The captain pointed toward the ridge. "You see how they've revealed their location? "

"Yes, Sir. Maybe they don't know we're here?"

"Maybe. Maybe they do. Maybe they want us to see just how *there'* they are. Then again, maybe they have reasons we cannot conceive."

"Yeah? I reckon they could be meanin' to strike fear. Well, Sir, I'll see to our fires right away. Anything else, Sir?"

"No. Thank you. I'll be turning in soon, and you should as well. Temperature's dropping fast. Snow coming soon. Nevertheless, we can expect what tomorrow will bring. I suspect it will be a long and brutal day, Thomas. You... all our men need rest. Though we lost almost a quarter of our men last week... even with that... overall, we've been fairly in the luck. We surely could do with Dinsmore's unit, though I'm feeling more and more certain they'll not make it in time.

And tomorrow... tomorrow, I fear, will test our mettle as never before."

"We got some of the best trained men, Sir. And I tell you true... that's in no small part, thanks to you, Sir. We'll fight to the last breath."

"Indeed we will, Thomas. Indeed, we will, but no matter... I'll continue to pray our reinforcements arrive in time so it doesn't come to 'last breath.' Whatever the case... I thank you for serving by my side. And... and you, Lt. Swilley... you will make a fine captain. You have the instincts and the will. You know the men and have their respect."

The lieutenant was momentarily startled by his captain's words and stood silent. But then, quickly, he brushed any concern aside.

"It's my honor to be at your side throughout this hellish war, Sir, and God willin', I'll be by your side until the end of this thing. Tomorrow we fight again, so I'll say good night. And pray to God Almighty that we will all survive."

The lieutenant saluted and then pulled his coat tightly against the whipping wind.

"Sleep well," Worth saluted in return. "Sleep well, Thomas."

The captain continued to stare at the far campfires. Perhaps they were right on the mark, indicating an enormous force. He thought *Maybe they actually are extra fires purposely exposed and meant to strike fear. That would certainly be the best situation, but perhaps too much to hope for.* Worth gnawed at the meaning as the wind whipped around him, but the latter possibility did not decrease his dread.

The captain's thoughts turned again to Amelia and the children. Ethan was eleven, and he'd soon be able to manage the crops. Old Claudie would guide the boy even though he could no longer work the fields. Bird – Claudie's twenty-year-old boy could handle the heavy work. Though his mind was like a ten-year-old since he fell from the barn roof four summers prior, his body had healed, and he was still a strong and able man. He worked well with guidance. Claudie would keep him focused. They were both good men – sharecroppers who'd never failed Worth or his father before him. Both he and his father believed it morally reprehensible to take on enslaved people, yet the captain found himself immersed in this war. He was a reluctant warrior. Conscripted initially, he came to fight for the lives of the men under his command. Repeated bravery under intense fire had quickly moved him up in the command chain, but like most men, he wished to be home.

"Amelia… Amelia," Worth whispered as he caressed the locket. "You must be strong."

He wondered how she would manage without him. News from home had been slow, though he was sure his loving wife was writing weekly letters as they'd both determined to do. She claimed they were managing, but would she burden him with information to the contrary? He wondered. He could read between the lines enough to know that she still greatly suffered the loss of little Charlotte. Their three-year-old had died of the fever the previous spring. He'd not been there to comfort and aid his grieving wife and children and felt both guilt and grief that he'd had to subdue for the sake of men depending on him. The captain could see that Amelia tried to shield him from her anguish. However, letters before Charlotte's death lacked the tinge of sadness she could not hide in her words afterward. He felt helpless to comfort her broken heart.

The captain remained standing on the rise, separating him from the certain death he believed awaited him on the opposite side of the valley. The relentless wind whipped up the hem of his coat where the last button had come undone, yet he stood as stone. Some men moved around behind him. Some were preparing for bed, some for the night watch. He sensed their movements. He heard their whispering, and one who softly hummed, "Southern Soldier."

With none of the previous approaching battles had Captain Worth thought in terms of his own death. He never conceived of it. Even in the last fight, as some of his men lay dying around him, he rode up and down the line of men shouting commands without regard to personal safety. He'd always gone into each fight with some sense of foreboding about what his men would face, but still, he had confidence and absolute inner knowledge that he would not die. He simply knew. But on this night, watching that ridge, he somehow knew just as well that he would never return to his home. He understood this would be his last night on earth, yet he prayed not for himself but for the men and the family he would leave behind.

Captain Silas Worth looked upward as snow began to drift softly, silently, onto the world around him. He breathed in deeply and quietly thanked God for the world of beauty and love that had surrounded his life. Then, he looked back and watched the last of his men preparing to turn in for the night. He knew them well. He'd heard the stories of their families and home lives and knew that most had not asked for or wanted a war. He wished to understand how the hearts of men could lead to such destruction, but he knew that kind of understanding was beyond his ability to perceive.

Worth nodded to the night watchmen as they saluted and moved on to their assigned posts.

The Captain ducked into his tent and lit a candle. He brushed snow from his hat and laid it aside before putting his pen to ink. After writing a short letter to his wife and children, he placed it inside his breast pocket near his heart. Then, with his coat still on, the captain lay down on his cot and closed his eyes.

"Amelia," he whispered. "My kind and lovely Amelia, I will come to you in dreams." He clutched Amelia's locket as he drifted off to sleep.

It would have made no difference that Dinsmore's men were still ten miles out when the sun rose that morning. The Union men had not waited until daybreak to cross the valley. They came upon their enemy in the stealthy, earliest morning hours before the sun could show its light. The Confederate men first detected their enemy at two hundred yards, and they put up a fierce fight.

The warrior, Captain Silas Worth, led his men with the courage of ten until he no longer could. He took a rifle ball to the heart during the first hour of battle on that cold and fateful morning.

- the end -

7

THE PANDEMONIUM INCIDENT

When Detective Tullis turned onto Flora Drive, he could see what appeared to be the abandoned white mail jeep and police blues flashing. He'd been investigating a missing adult since late morning, and he figured it was taking him away from the unrelenting missing teen cases he'd been unsuccessfully working on for months. There seemed to be no rhyme or reason for the missing teens, and it was looking more and more likely that they were runaways. The adult was Trey Barnes. He was a mail carrier and a bit of a drinker, so this investigation looked at first to be pretty simple and quickly concluded.

Tullis was on a straight, flat road nearly a quarter mile long that ended right in front of a white house. The rather long driveway was wooded on both sides. The detective took it slowly over the rutted dirt road, but as he got closer, he could see both vehicles distinctly. Parked closely behind the mail jeep, he saw City of Pandemonium patrol car number twelve. The flashing blues shone brighter in the waning sunlight. Tullis continued maneuvering his unmarked, gray

Chevy over the increasingly rutted road toward the vehicles and the old house beyond.

The house was a large, sprawling two-story structure, almost obscured by trees, bushes, flowers, and vines. Though Tullis rarely got out to this sparsely populated end of town, he knew that this was the only occupied home remaining on Lake Catywumpus. The scattered half dozen others had been bought out, and most of them torn down during the previous two years. An elderly woman occupied this last house – Mrs. Genevieve Woodley – better known around Pandemonium as the Plant Woman because of the healing herb and medicinal plant mixtures she prepared. Though Tullis certainly knew of her, he'd never actually met her face to face. She was a recluse by habit and nature. Most people who knew her were older or had lived in and around Pandemonium their whole lives. The woman's reputation, however, preceded her, thanks in no small part to the concentrated efforts of Miss Ella Goodbread.

While Miss Ella – like most of the townfolk – claimed to be a good, upstanding, God-fearing person, she was, in reality, one of the busiest town gossips and not altogether upstanding either. Even though it was whispered among lesser gossips that Miss Emmaline Sweet or Mr. Humphrey Tinker could certainly give her a run for her money regarding the passage of stories, most everyone in town – including Det. Tullis – knew it would be hard to beat Miss Ella in that malicious department. She'd often raise her left eyebrow when passing something she thought particularly juicy and preface the story with "Now I hate to be tellin' this, but..."

Now, because Miss Ella was both an avid teller of tales *and* employed as the sanctimonious secretary of the First Pandemonium Church, she often claimed to have heard things from a reliable source. Many people assumed that source must have been Reverend Braverman, though he would deny it if asked. He was perhaps telling the truth, for it was also unfortunate for some who confided in the reverend that Miss Ella was – by way of too-thin walls and a carefully placed glass – privy to the reverend's counseling sessions with the sinners and troubled households of Pandemonium. These three specific elements made her somewhat of a 'perfect storm' in terms of knowledge of town secrets and burdened souls.

For years, Miss Ella and her mother Mona ("Little Mo" Goodbread, to her friends), had lived in a tiny shotgun house just about a mile from the Plant Woman – considerably less distance as the crow flies, or following the wooded, lakeside route. The aging mother, Little Mo, had suffered for years with chronic rheumatism and numerous other real and imagined illnesses. When they'd lived on the lake, she had often sent her daughter on a winding trek through the woods to the Plant Woman's place to obtain cures for her ailments.

Nearly a year and a half after Little Mo died, Miss Ella sold the house and all her twenty acres to the Great Lan-Tica Holding Company. Lan-Tica was buying up all the property around the spring-fed Lake Catywumpus. They'd built a plant just north of the lake at the creek springhead and wanted to use the lake as a cooling pond. Various representatives from Lan-Tica had tried relentlessly to purchase the Plant Woman's property, too, but she wouldn't budge. She claimed they were fouling the lake and ruining what she called "the biological system" of the whole area.

It generated a bit of chatter when old fishing buddies Henry Whiteschine and Lucas Foil complained that the fish were disappearing too, but after both men drowned in the lake and only a few parts of their decomposing bodies were recovered, no one except the Plant Woman saw the company as a problem. She thought something in the lake had dragged them under, but most folks thought the police theory was more likely. The police report stated that Henry probably jumped in to save Lucas, who could not swim. People couldn't see how Lan-Tica could have caused that. After all, the company was bringing many new jobs into the community, and Mrs. Woodley was the only person complaining or adversely affected – if she really was affected at all.

The Plant Woman eventually gave up trying to convince the town and became even more reclusive. Det. Tullis knew that she had refused all further discussions regarding the sale of her property and had finally threatened – in quite colorful terms – to use her twelve gauge to blow the head off one rather tenacious Lan-Tica representative. Two officers had been sent out to calm frayed nerves, and the representative had been convinced that it was probably best to stay off Mrs. Woodley's property. Finally, the company left her alone, and she remained the one and only resident remaining along the lake.

Miss Ella Goodbread thought the Plant Woman crazy for refusing the Lan-Tica offers and said so all over town. The people of Pandemonium were unaware that she had her reasons for wanting the Plant Woman gone from the lake. 'Crazy' became a keyword in her discussions about the old woman, and Miss Ella added little anecdotes to support her psychological analysis. Threatening people was one thing she pointed out. "Was that sane?" She'd ask. "Would you call talking to plants sane?" She'd seen this firsthand, she said. Was turning down large sums of money from Lan-Tica and threatening people with shotguns not crazy? Miss Ella herself – as she liked to point out repeatedly – had moved into downtown Pandemonium, bought a Chrysler, and had moved quite up in the world with the tidy little sum she'd received from the sale of her own home. She'd even taken a correspondence course to learn shorthand to enhance her skills as the secretary for the church. It was all she could hope for and more, and anyone who couldn't see the value in this *had* to be crazy.

The plant woman was cut from quite different cloth, though. She was odd, that was true, and unpredictable too, and many thought, likely a heathen. She was certainly never seen in any of the three churches in town. Miss Ella never missed a Sunday at First Pandemonium, so she could testify to the fact that Mrs. Woodley didn't attend there. She had "other" information that she'd been holding back as well, she said, because, of course, she didn't like to "gossip."

"… and pry if you will, but my lips are sealed on some of the more lurid details I know about the woman!" Miss Ella told people.

During the years she'd lived at the lake, Miss Ella had found little to do but take care of her ailing mother, so she spent many hours prying into the Plant Woman's business. Living in such close proximity, she discovered much more about the very private Mrs. Woodley than anyone else ever did. That gave her tales about her neighbor a certain credibility. Unfortunately, her stories were often distorted. Sometimes, this was due to her sincere but biased assumptions. More often, however, she meant to intentionally lead her listener in a certain direction for shock value. Because the woman was reclusive, what Det. Tullis and most everyone else in town knew of the Plant Woman was heard through Miss Ella's second and third-hand grapevine. Understanding human nature in small towns, most of the gossip, Tullis took with many grains of salt, but at least it gave a bit of insight into her history.

The main story Miss Ella told was this: In the late 1930s, Genevieve Woodley had graduated with a degree in Botany from some hotshot college up north. Afterward, she'd spent nearly five years living in the Okefenokee Swamp, studying plant life. She'd never been married but called herself "Mrs." because, she said, "It keeps things simpler." She received little, if any, pay for the work she did with the plants. She wouldn't reveal why she chose to settle in Pandemonium, and Miss Ella never ceased to speculate upon why she chose a place nearly eighty miles south of her precious swamp. Some of the scenarios Miss Ella's mind devised to explain this were rather sordid, and she would have been quite surprised and disappointed to learn the truth. Mrs. Woodley's place was property passed on to the Plant Woman by a distant family member on her mother's side because she was the last living heir. It became a near-perfect location for Mrs. Woodley to continue with the work that was her passion and still be close enough to the swamp to acquire new fungi samples and plants. Not knowing the truth only fueled Miss Ella's imagination, leading to further speculation and shared fiction. It was unclear to the town folk whether or not Mrs. Woodley was aware of Miss Ella's gossip because the woman rarely went to town.

Over the years, the Plant Woman led her quiet, secluded life with little distraction regarding her work. She filled her home with plants and laboratory apparatus, and when she needed more space, she had an additional room built onto the existing, modest, two-story house. These add-ons became rather haphazard over time, taking on Picasso-ish angles. The woman went into town for supplies once each month and was cordial to everyone, but was never what you'd call talkative and certainly not outgoing. She stayed thoroughly obsessed with her work. She studied and worked with her plants, grafting, altering, and making cures and concoctions. She always seemed glad to help people with treatments, but they had to seek her out. She never volunteered her services to anyone and never stated or implied that she had any medical expertise. Mrs. Woodley corresponded with and exchanged parcels with other botanists at several universities and was well respected in her field.

As a teen, Miss Ella occasionally helped her neighbor and saw several articles the plant woman had written in scientific journals. She never shared that information with any of the people in town. She told herself they were not educated enough to understand such writing and research, but she likely understood it would have diminished her other stories of the woman. Likewise, when some people in town had discussed the possibility that she was working on a cure for cancer, Miss Ella poo-pooed that line of thinking. Indeed, positive comments regarding the Plant Woman often prompted an exaggerated eye roll from Miss Ella. However, she conceded that the old woman never failed to travel back to the swamp at least once yearly – even at her advanced age – to further her studies.

The Plant Woman reproduced a swamp-like, humid environment for some special plants within her home. Some plants had many temperature and humidity variables, and she accommodated their needs. She still went to discover and collect new samples of the plants she couldn't easily propagate outside the swamp environs. In her younger years, she stayed in the Okeefenokee anywhere from one to six months at a time.

Miss Ella still told the tale about how, back in 1954, the

Plant Woman took off for the swamp and didn't return for over a year. Ella was fifteen at that time. Because she lived so close, she was hired and entrusted to care for all the plants when the Plant Woman was on one of her trips. There were specific and very detailed instructions the teen girl had to follow. Ella complained that she received "small remuneration for this service. Way too small." Actually, the plant woman had allowed Ella to set her own price for the service, but she was known to complain frequently about the situation. She said to anyone who would listen, "… and of course, it was a full-time job, and combined with high school and caring for Mother, well… it wore me to a frazzle. It was a great sacrifice of my time, of course… but like Mother always said, I just have too generous a nature. Mother said I seemed to always be giving to others." Miss Ella had confessed to her charitable deeds in great, sighing whispers.

Before her trip in 1954, though, The Plant Woman had never stayed away so long. She sent Ella a letter asking her to continue at double the fee for a few more months, and the teen happily agreed. When Mrs. Woodley finally did return, she brought with her a four-month-old baby girl. Ella and numerous others in town were properly scandalized. Many people averted their eyes when she came into town with the little girl. For a while, some people refused to take her cures, while others just hid the fact that they did. The Plant Woman never offered any explanation for the baby other than to say it was her child. People could accept it or not, by their own choosing. It didn't matter to Genevieve Woodley either way. In time, people forgot, just didn't care anymore, or needed her herbal cures more than they enjoyed ostracizing the woman.

Mrs. Woodley schooled her child, Peggy, at home, and the girl graduated three years earlier than students her age. She went off to the University of Florida, where she studied medicine. Peggy eventually opened a clinic in Puesta Del Sol Bay. It kept her so busy that she could only visit her mother a few times each year.

Miss Ella never forgot a scandal, though, and certainly not one of such magnitude. It was "just sinfully wrong and improper for unmarried women like Mrs. Woodley to carry on and indulge in illicit liaisons with men." Even so, many years later, she would tell anyone who would listen. What Miss Ella didn't say – and neither did Det. Tullis nor anyone else suspect – was that it was quite a different matter for herself and the good Reverend Braverman. She and the preacher had discussed it many times. He was a reverend, a man of God, and God guided him and sanctioned certain things in his situation. Mrs. Braverman suffered terrible headaches, which sent her into her darkened bedroom for days on end. The poor, afflicted woman was simply unable to offer him enough in the way of wifely duties to keep the evilness of the flesh out of his mind. Miss Ella, with deepest empathy, thought it her duty – nay, her mission – to take on Mrs. Braverman's place in this matter, and an ongoing affair ensued.

Only once were the lovers nearly discovered when the distraught mother of a runaway teenager burst into the church for help. Luckily, the lovers had become stimulated in the close quarters of the storage closet, and they eluded detection. Afterward, however, they decided that as difficult as it was to contain themselves, this kind of activity was best kept off the church property. Thankfully, Miss Ella discovered that Great Lan-Tica never bothered to tear down the rundown boathouse on the west side of Lake Catywumpus on the old Goodbread property. The boathouse became the rendezvous spot where Miss Ella

Goodbread could provide for the reverend what his sickly wife could not. The derelict boathouse became the routine scene of their rather frequent trysts – frequency being a key to keeping the evilness out of mind, as the good reverend had told her. Miss Ella was only too happy to accommodate Reverend Braverman.

Ella was sure her loving gift and sacrifice brought the reverend closer to God. In fact, after their sessions, he often told her that he felt as if he'd died and gone to heaven. Even though they both got a little chuckle out of the comment, if his Sunday sermons were any indication, well... it suffices to say they were always more powerful and thundering when the lovers could manage a Saturday together. So, it was for the good of all, really, even though it was necessary that they keep this fact to themselves.

This secret relationship was also the real reason Miss Ella thought it best for the Plant Woman to sell out. Under normal circumstances, the church secretary tended to be quite a loud woman, but trysting with Braverman brought out reverberations above and beyond ordinary decibels. With the other houses gone from the lake shores, sounds carried much further in those woods and over the lake. Miss Ella knew that the Plant Woman's proximity to the old boathouse could present a potential problem to the lovers. She'd learned that fact the hard way when the old woman had once happened upon them. It was quite unfortunate that Miss Ella's screams as the Reverend Braverman brought her to the heights of ecstasy also brought the plant woman running. Mrs. Woodley had actually believed that a murder was taking place and had brought her trusty twelve gauge to save the supposed victim and as protection against the possible killer.

Once again, luck was with the lovers. The Plant Woman

drove around to the boathouse to investigate. When they heard her car approaching, both were already dressed again and ready to leave. The reverend was forced to hide while Miss Ella spontaneously established a story to explain the screams that Mrs. Woodley said she'd heard. Ella said that she'd been gripped in a fit of nostalgia for the old place, and it had gotten the best of her. The Plant Woman had looked a bit skeptical, but Miss Ella thought she had eventually bought the story along with the fake tears that she'd been able to produce just as spontaneously to give more credibility to the tale. It was another stroke of luck for the couple that they'd left the reverend's car at the Walmart, so they'd escaped detection. They were more careful after that, but it put a damper of sorts on their lovemaking, as the reverend took to stuffing a handkerchief in Miss Ella's mouth at the crucial moment of their rapture. Miss Ella Goodbread fervently wished her neighbor would just go ahead and sell to Great Lan-Tica so that she and the reverend could let loose without the aid of the handkerchief.

The indiscrete Plant Woman bringing home that baby in 1954 was a different matter entirely. In Miss Ella's book, it was strictly a sin and sanctioned by no one. She never failed to share this favorite bit of information with any new members of the community or church. The majority of the other town folk, however, just weren't interested. It had happened over thirty-five years ago, and it wasn't important. The cures were the important thing. Most of the old-timers in town swore by the Plant Woman's home remedies and said you couldn't get a better cure anywhere for what ailed you. Carl Beamer swore that the Plant Woman had cured his tuberculosis, and Roxanne Sutton, always a fidgety and nervous sort, said her chamomile mixture had changed her life. People tried to pay for the cures, but the Plant Woman would not accept their money. After a while, laws and strict regulations would have prevented that anyway. When people came for a cure, though, they'd leave a ham, some fresh eggs, canned butterbeans, peas, or tomatoes. One fellow routinely brought earthworms in exchange for a concoction of lavender and oil for his wife's irritability problems. The Plant Woman understood their need to compensate in some way, and she accepted their gifts graciously, though financially, she seemed to be in no need of this or any other method of payment.

As the years passed, things changed, and people came less frequently for cures. The composition of the quiet little city – so inaptly named – was what had changed so dramatically over the years. It was a phenomenon that happened in a lot of small towns. Some of the old, established businesses couldn't make it in the late 1970s and early '80s; President Jimmy Carter had ruined things, they said. Det. Tullis thought there were just some very smart people without a lick of common sense, and when those people ran the country, the country was run into the ground or taken over by the crazies. Without a doubt, outsiders like Great Lan-Tica and its subsidiaries of chemical companies and plastic manufacturers could take advantage of people caught up in or distracted by other life crises. The company experimented with amalgams, which generated by-products never before introduced into the surrounding soil and water. Instead of operating in areas safer for such manufacturing, they moved to where they found it cheaper to operate and easier to overcome regulations or manipulate politicians.

Most residents were grateful to have a new company start up in such bad general economic times, and they said that Pandemonium would be a ghost town without Great Lan-Tica. All that was probably true to some degree, but they nevertheless did change Pandemonium. Perhaps it was inevitable. The old-timers – mostly farmers – seemed to be a dying breed because their children no longer followed in their fathers' footsteps. Many young adults transitioned to the larger cities and those who remained usually relied on conventional medications and remedies. As a result, the Plant Woman rarely had visitors and, therefore, became even more reclusive. When she did have visitors, they were of the unwelcome sort. The plant woman became a rather frequent caller to the Pandemonium Police Department because of that undesirable sort of visitor – the teenage rowdy.

Det. Tullis knew that local teens, and some from as far away as Puesta Del Sol Bay, partied at the lake. Some inevitably ended up in the Pandemonium jail. The kids most often used the southeast side of the lake for parking and partying. Those who used the area as a lover's lane were usually no trouble, though two of the couples were some of his missing teens. Generally, though, those there for romance tended to stay on the little white sand beach opposite the plant woman's property with their skinny-dipping and lovemaking, but the beer parties always seemed to turn rowdy. The boozers often went thoroughly wild, tearing through the lakeside in their souped-up automobiles. They raced around, whooping and hollering and sometimes even shooting off guns. They passed stories about Mrs. Woodley. Sometimes, they thought her a witch and sometimes a voodoo priestess. The teens took special delight in invading her property. Her home was on the north side of the lakefront, surrounded by about twenty acres of her plants. Several acres of her prizes plants and herbs had been destroyed. It happened more than once, but unfortunately, the kids were always gone by the time an officer could respond. The house was right at the edge of the city limits and easily two miles from the nearest paved road.

Tullis went to Flora Drive on this day, however, not because of teenagers ripping up the landscape – patrol handled that – but rather to investigate why Trey Barnes' mail vehicle was there. A missing adult case was a rare situation in their small town. It all began just before lunchtime. Supervisor Hollingsworth at the Pandemonium Post Office had called the police to report mail carrier Trey Barnes missing. His mail jeep was also gone, and there was no indication that he had returned from his route the previous day because his car was still in the employee parking lot. His edge-of-town rural route made him the last one to return to the post office each afternoon, and since he lived alone, no one had been alert to the fact that he'd not returned from his deliveries the day before. Trey was known to imbibe a good bit, so his supervisor thought he might be sleeping one off when he didn't show up for work or answer phone calls to his house. If that was the case, Hollingsworth had full intentions of writing him up because he'd done that once before, and taking the post office jeep to go drink or even to drive it home sober was not acceptable. When Trey didn't answer his phone after five tries, his supervisor waited for his other mail carriers to get underway before driving out to the man's house. Just as he suspected, the jeep wasn't there. Hollingsworth began the rounds of checking all the local watering holes, looking for Barnes – hence, his several-hour delay before calling the police.

When he was assigned the case, Det. Tullis considered several possible angles regarding the missing man. First, he placed a call to Hollingsworth to get the full details known about the time frame, mail route, and Trey's habits. The detective narrowed the search area to a reasonable grid based on the information he gathered. He put out a BOLO – Be On The Lookout – to patrol. Tullis then contacted various patrolmen through dispatch and sent them to check certain grids within the city limits as well as fanning out to the fringes of town. He had officers check with a sampling of residents to see if they had received mail the previous day. He wanted to determine Trey's last delivery. Det. Tullis heard back from all but one officer when finally, at about four-thirty in the afternoon, Corporal O'Neill and his partner had stumbled upon the mail jeep at Mrs. Woodley's place.

Tullis had already begun to head in that direction after the officers in town had responded. O'Neill had taken his sweet time, and Tullis knew it. Corporal O'Neill was a constant thorn in the detective's side. He had requested that O'Neill search all roads within his assigned grid early on, starting with Mrs. Woodley's place and working back toward town. The annoying officer, however, had decided it was a waste of time to go all the way out to Lake Catywumpus.

Mrs. Woodley's mailbox was three-quarters of a mile back off the main road where Hog Waller Wash met Isolene Road. That wasn't up near the Plant Woman's house, so it just hadn't made sense to O'Neill to check where a mail truck wasn't even supposed to be – plus, that would have cut into his lunch plans. He'd been trying to make headway with Pearlie Mae Waverly for weeks, and if he didn't get to the Bobcat Diner by twelve sharp, Hubert Swark would steal his regular seat at the counter section where Pearlie Mae served. The other seats would quickly fill, and O'Neill would be relegated to sitting in Dollie Throgmorten's section. He considered Dollie homely beyond redemption and thought she was always after a man in a uniform like himself.

Now, as Tullis pulled up behind the patrol car of the

recalcitrant cop, the burly, six-foot-two Cpl. O'Neill struggled to extricate himself from the tight space between the steering wheel and the seat of his vehicle. At the same time, the corporal's large partner-in-training, Larry Munt, heaved his own two-hundred-plus pounds out through the passenger side. Tullis heard a whooshing sigh from the overburdened vehicle when both men finally emerged.

Adjusting his gun belt as he went, O'Neill slowly sauntered toward the detective's car while Munt faced an unforeseen and challenging problem. He found himself quite trapped and struggling to decide how to get around three tightly parked vehicles so close to a thorny hedge that he was completely pinned in. Munt started toward the jeep, then, stymied, turned back. He took several steps and stopped – clearly ambiguous regarding his dilemma. The officer-in-training was considering the feasibility of squeezing between the bumpers of the patrol car and the unmarked detective unit when he noticed O'Neill, red-faced, swinging his arms overhead emphatically, indicating toward Tullis's vehicle. Munt took off as quickly as he could in the direction the older cop motioned while trying to avoid the thorns that tugged at his sweaty uniform.

O'Neill smoothly regained his composure, hoping the detective had not noticed the inept rookie. He removed his hat and smoothed back the few sweaty hairs still clinging in vain to the top of his head. He deliberately posed by the front bumper of Tullis' vehicle. He stood with legs apart and hands on hips, trying to appear as aggravated as he actually was. O'Neill waited as Tullis, still seated in his vehicle, ignored him and made notations on a small yellow notepad.

Tullis always dreaded working with O'Neill and had hoped that Barnes and his jeep would be found in Officer Culbertson's zone. Ever since Chief Houser promoted him to the detective position, passing over the bungling O'Neill for a third time, the corporal had continued trying to make Tullis's life miserable. Under the best of circumstances, O'Neill was a pompous, arrogant, lazy cop. Tullis was grateful that most of the officers he knew in Pandemonium and other departments were hardworking, conscientious people. Those like O'Neill were few and far between. As a three-time loser, he was a sullen and disruptive force within the department. Tullis knew that there were people like O'Neill in every walk of life, and that's just how it was, but he avoided contact with the man whenever possible.

Tullis finished his notes and stepped out of the Chevy. He removed his jacket and draped it over the back of the seat, then adjusted the 9mm Sig in his shoulder holster. He clipped his radio to his belt. Just in case, he grabbed his flashlight and a pair of latex gloves, which he shoved into his pocket. The detective finally stepped face to face with the profusely sweating O'Neill. Not a breeze stirred, and the heat descended upon them like a heavy woolen blanket.

"Corporal?" Tullis finally acknowledged him without looking up. "Besides the obvious mail vehicle, what've we got so far?"

O'Neill hitched his gun belt higher on his bulging stomach, shoved his hat back off his brow, and flipped open his metal notebook with great exaggeration. He stared at the tall, slim detective to make sure Tullis understood that he was taking his time. O'Neill licked his fat thumb and used it to push aside several pages before locating the one he wanted. With great deliberation, he pulled a pen out of his pocket, shifted his eyes to the notebook, and began to check off points.

"Patrolled zone seven. Located missing mail truck. No Trey Barnes. No sign 'a struggle. Miz Woodley don't answer the door, 'n that's far as we got. Oh yeah... radioed Vernice to put a call in to Miz Woodley's daughter over in Puesta Del Sol Bay to see does she know where her mama is."

Tullis continued to make notes as O'Neill spoke. "And did you check around the house or back by the lake?"

"No, sir-ee! Nuh-uh. No! Figured that was D-tective work," O'Neill smiled and elbowed the slow-witted Munt, who had maneuvered himself to stand close by his partner's side. O'Neill wanted to make sure Munt had picked up on this inflicted dig.

Plus," he smirked, elbowing Munt again, "figured in this jungle, liable to end up with Poison Ivy, snake bit, or something a whole lot worse Some people say this old woman's crazy... grows all kinda weird stuff out here... ain't no tellin' what all. No sir-ee. Waited for you. Wouldn't want to YOU surp no authority nor nothin' you know."

"Postmaster notified?" Tullis ignored his performance.

"Postmaster's still on vacation. Hollingsworth's on his way w' somebody to pick up the jeep." O'Neill toned it down a bit when he realized he'd not get a rise out of the detective and that Munt, overly excited by his first big case, wasn't being a very attentive audience.

"Alright. Let's try the door again. Maybe the woman's hard of hearing."

Tullis took a quick look inside the jeep. Everything seemed in order, but there were two boxes of undelivered mail, and the keys were still in the ignition.

He started toward the door, scanning the massively overgrown yard as he went.

O'Neill and Munt leaned against the side of the patrol car and waited for a direct order while Tullis alternately knocked, rang the bell, and called out to Mrs. Woodley. She didn't answer, though he thought he heard a slight rustling and creaking within the house as if someone were moving around inside. He stopped and listened for a moment – nothing. Then, Tullis tried the door, but the knob didn't give. The drapes were pulled tightly closed on the window next to the front door, and it was either locked or possibly frozen shut from disuse. By the looks of it – with vines and weeds growing over the steps and threshold – he guessed that this door had been out of use for some time.

Observing each step, Tullis worked his way through the twisted mixture of grass and shrubs on his left up to the next window. This small glass square, more like an afterthought than a window at all, was quite high, and tall as he was, the detective struggled, stretching on his toes to see through a lacy curtain.

From his vantage point, Det. Tullis could see part of both the dining room and the living room. He caught a fleeting glimpse of some movement, but whatever it was, it was gone too quickly for him to identify. Maybe a cat, he thought. Struggling to stay on his toes, he saw that the dining room table was skewed, with one corner shoved up against the wall. A white tablecloth was mostly off the table, and an overturned vase of dead flowers lay on top. One chair was inverted, and another leaned against the table on two legs.

"Come have a look at this," he called to O'Neill.

The cop swaggered slowly toward the house with Munt stuck like a remora to his heels. At the window, O'Neill stretched his heavy frame upward and peered inside.

"Looks like a ruckus been goin' on. I can kick the door in and..."

"One step at a time," Tullis cautioned. "Could be she's gone off, and some of those kids she complains about have gotten in here and had a time. Maybe Trey Barnes saw them up to no good and came here to check on the woman. We need to find Trey. Listen, my radio's on the blink and won't reach the station out of the converter. Get your radio and check with Vernice to see if she's heard from the daughter yet. Also, have her call Mrs. Woodley's number... see if there's any response now. And... switch to channel three to communicate with me after you talk with Vernice. We'll keep the regular channels free for dispatch. I'll check out the back of the house... see if there's forced entry or what's up. For now, you guys wait for Hollingsworth so he can take the Jeep.

O'Neill headed back to his car to grab his radio. Officer Munt traveled so closely on his heels again that twice he stepped on the older cop's shoe, nearly pulling it off his foot. The already irritated O'Neill finally let loose with a string of curses and shoved his partner ahead of himself.

Tullis scanned the area but could see no easy way to get to the back of the house. He began working his way to each window through the tangled foliage against the house. As he rounded one corner of the house, he stepped on a huge black snake. The startled snake jerked forward in terror, and Tullis, equally startled, jumped and then fell backward. The snake slithered further into the underbrush, and the detective gingerly picked himself loose from the thorny clutches of the rambling rose into which he'd fallen. He pulled thorns from his scratched and bleeding face and arms and then noticed the torn sleeve of his pinstripe shirt as he wiped his arms with a handkerchief.

"Damn!" he whispered." Brand new shirt."

Disgusted, sweating, and feeling the oppressive heat in the jungle around him, he gave up trying to wipe away each new trickle of blood that welled up and continued to work his way around the house. There were many outcroppings of rooms to work around, as the house had been haphazardly enlarged at different points in time for space requirements only, with no particular attention to any aesthetic or architectural detail.

He could hear the phone ringing from somewhere deep within the house, but no one was picking up. It seemed clear that either the woman was not home or was unable to answer. He figured it was possible that she'd fallen or stroked out or something, but that didn't quite connect with the disturbed furniture in the dining room or Trey Barnes missing for twenty-four hours, for that matter.

Det. Tullis checked each window that he passed. Each was locked tight, and all he could see inside through the dust-laden glass panes were test tubes, beakers, low-hanging lights, and plants of every description. He passed three more rooms and several windows past the dining room. Then, Tullis rounded a corner and reached a brick wall extending away from the house and into the yard. From there, the wall made a ninety-degree turn. The detective followed the wall and once more had to pick his way through a tangled jungle of plants and thorny vines. He was sweaty and disheveled before he reached the end.

The brick structure turned out to be the back and side of a carport. Tullis looked into the opening and was surprised to see a metallic brown Volkswagen with antennae-like extensions protruding from the hood and painted with markings to make the car resemble a cockroach. Large yellow letters on the side proclaimed 'BERNIE'S BEST PEST CONTROL AND EXTERMINATORS.' In smaller letters, underneath was 'Call BERNIE'S BEST in Puesta Del Sol Bay to kill your pests,' 555 PES-TERD. The roach car was parked behind an old, wood-paneled station wagon. Det. Tullis recalled seeing the station wagon in town a few times. He thought it likely that it belonged to Mrs. Woodley.

Tullis stepped out of the extraordinary jungle and into the clearing of the carport. The little hairs at the back of his neck stood up. His hand automatically went to confirm the shoulder holster. It was quiet. Too quiet. *Something's definitely not right here,* he thought. He stopped in his tracks for a long moment, eyes scanning all within his vision. He smoothed the standing hair, but deep down, that cop instinct gnawed at his gut.

His mind raced through several possibilities, none of them pleasant. The little hairs on his neck stood again, begging for attention, and his hand stayed on the leather holster under his arm. Still, everything was quiet – not even the sound of birds or crickets. Tullis wanted to believe it was just the overwhelming heat, but – that gut instinct.

The detective stepped slowly and quietly past the two vehicles and looked inside. Again, everything was orderly. Nothing was amiss. His hand never strayed from the holster, though, and the sound of his leather-soled shoes on the sandy cement floor seemed to reverberate in the hollow of the carport. As he moved forward, Tullis touched his left hand to the hood of each car. Both felt semi-cool to the touch – consistent with a temperature he would expect, if not recently driven and parked as they were under the carport canopy. Beyond the carport was a long dirt driveway. It went around the dense jungle of plants toward the lake, and then, as far as he could tell, it turned back toward the front of the house at some point that was not visible to Tullis. He'd send O'Neill and Munt to come up from that direction. They could walk the area to look for anything amiss.

The detective cautiously stepped toward the front of the station wagon. He saw three cement steps leading up to a door with a window inset. A light was on, and from his vantage point, all Tullis could see was a three-tiered basket filled with onions and sweet potatoes hanging just inside the door.

Tullis pulled his radio from his belt, clicked the mike open, and spoke softly. "Delta One to Baker Four."

The radio hissed and crackled before O'Neill finally responded with exaggerated, singsong sarcasm.

"Baker Four...Vernice is still trying to get through. Ain't heard nothing yet, or I *would'a* let you know."

"Ok. Get back to her and have her call Best Pest Control in Puesta Del Sol Bay. One of their cars is parked back here. See what the deal is with that. Then, after Hollingsworth shows up, take Munt, and you two work your way around the other side of the house. Use that dirt driveway or road or whatever it is. Walk it so you don't miss any evidence if kids have been in here. Looks like it circles down by the lake and winds up at her carport. I'm gonna see if I can get in through the back door. Tell Hollingsworth to stay put out front till we know what we got."

"Oh yeah... forgot to tell you... Hollingsworth's got delayed... won't be out till this evening to get the jeep."

Tullis cursed under his breath. He started to open the mike and then hesitated. He stared at the radio in frustration as if it was O'Neill himself.

"Just no accounting for that kind of stupidity," Tullis whispered. He sighed deeply and clicked the mike open.

"Look, O'Neill," he said in a controlled voice. "We have a possible serious situation here. Got an abandoned vehicle out front and apparently one back here, too. Not a soul in sight, and nobody answers our calls. I want to know immediately whatever information is coming in. Immediately. Anything you hear from anybody. Anything. You got that? You copy?"

"I copy, De... tective." O'Neill's irritation was on full display.

"Great..." Tullis hesitated but kept the mike keyed so that O'Neill could not interrupt. "We may need to get another unit out here. I hope we'll know exactly what the situation is in just a few minutes, but I got a bad feeling here. So you guys go check out the area by the lake... then... since we're no longer waiting for Hollingsworth... then work your way back up and meet me in the carport. Behind the house."

He waited for a response while O'Neill made silent, obscene, copulating gestures toward his own radio as if to abuse a substitute Tullis. Munt erupted in loud laughter until his partner signaled for silence with an index finger. The rookie quickly covered his mouth to contain any audible laughter.

"Well..." O'Neill finally drawled into the radio. "What *exactly* are we looking *for*... SIR? Trey?" He grinned at Munt, who still had hands-over-mouth to control his laughter.

"Trey... any of them, for God's sake. You can't be that... Look. Be a cop. Look for anything out of the ordinary. Maybe those kids have been here. Look for beer cans, destroyed vegetation... anything that looks like evidence, Man. Keep your eyes open and get back with me ASAP if you see or hear anything... and that includes anything from dispatch."

"Alrighty, then, Ten-four." O'Neill switched his radio back to channel one. He pulled his hat off and, once more, smoothed back his sweaty, thinning hair.

"Want me to take the lake?" Munt begged. "I can do it!" He snapped and unsnapped his holster strap, dancing around like a six-year-old with urinary urgency.

"No." O'Neill snapped. He was deep in thought now and ignored his partner's nervous dance, which would ordinarily have caused him to slap the younger man about the head with his own hat.

"A-hole giving me orders. I'm gonna check with Vernice. I'll do that much," he said finally. "But be damned if I'm gonna be at his beck'n call. Know what? *I think* we'll just stay on channel one... after all," he winked at Munt, "we gotta listen for Vernice. Right? And... he's the detective... so let him just frickin' detect and..."

"But, can't we go looking for something like he said?" Munt interrupted. "It's gonna be gettin dark! We'll miss everything."

"Just calm down! We'll walk down by the lake. Got nothing else to do. But we ain't gonna find nothing."

O'Neill reached into his vehicle and grabbed a flashlight. "We'll just take our own sweet time, is all. Long ways back there... gotta look for stuff, right? Might take us... oh... half hour to make it to the back of that house."

"But maybe there's some psycho killer holed up in there. Could be holdin 'em all hostage or something." Munt, this time pulled his gun from the holster, thoroughly excited by his suspenseful, evolving theory and his first big crime.

"Put that gun away, damn fool! Ain't no psycho killer. Like as not, that crazy old woman's in there having herself a orgy with old Trey, and who knows who. She's a loon. Always has been. All this other mess is just hogwash. Detective, my ass."

O'Neill pushed Munt toward the path they would take to the lake and began calling Vernice on the radio as they walked.

———

The back door was locked, and Tullis had just used his knife blade to jimmie it when he heard a hissing noise coming from somewhere up above him. When the door opened, he tried to turn the release button on the lock, but it was stuck. He pushed the door back to a nearly closed position again, careful not to let it close all the way. Tullis stepped back and drew his gun. The snake was still fresh in his mind, though the hissing noise didn't sound like a snake, and he'd never actually heard one hiss. He looked all around him, but nothing moved. The only sound was that of his shoes crushing the gritty bits of sand on the concrete floor of the carport.

Then he heard it again.

"Sssst. Pssst!"

He stepped cautiously to the end of the carport from where the sound seemed to be coming. He looked around, then upward, following the sound that had begun again. That's when he saw the fingers. They were hooked around the sill of a second-story window partially opened to about ten inches.

"Mrs. Woodley? That you?" he called.

"Shhhh!" The old woman's face suddenly appeared behind the wavy glass of the window. Her white hair was loose and wild around her face as if she'd been caught in a heavy wind. One lens in the glasses she wore was broken and smeared with a red substance. She kept blinking as if she struggled to see. She looked stricken – haggard and fearful. "My God," she whispered hoarsely. "Don't make any noise. I think they can hear. I don't know where they're at."

"Who Mrs. Woodley? Trey Barnes? What's wrong here?" He spoke in a normal voice level as he looked up.

Her face disappeared from the window, though her fingers still clung, white-knuckled, to the sill. Tullis could see a shower head and part of an open shower curtain. When she looked back again, anger had spread over her face. She seemed on the verge of hyperventilating, and it took her a moment before she could speak again.

"Please..." she gasped. "Be quiet. You'll get us killed. They'll hear you!" Then, her face was gone again.

Tullis subconsciously rubbed his fingers over the small pouch attached to his belt; it contained an extra clip.

"Baker four," he whispered into the radio.

Tullis hesitated. He received no response. He moved a few feet away from the window and spoke a bit louder. "Baker four, respond, please..."

Again, there was no response. Det. Tullis then tried to reach Vernice in the dispatch office on the off-chance that his transmission would be heard back at the station. He knew the chances were slim. He'd been experiencing radio problems for a week, and with radio repair swamped, as usual, he'd been making do like everybody else. He tried O'Neill once more before he finally gave up on it and moved back to his position underneath the window.

"Mrs. Woodley," he whispered.

"Mrs. Woodley," a little louder now, straining to see her face again as the sun began descending behind a curtain of Pines.

She looked down at him. Her face was almost serene now as if her thoughts were somewhere far away. Her lips moved, but she was silent as in prayer.

"Mrs. Woodley, is it Trey? The other guy? What kind of weapons do they have?"

"Weapons? They don't have weapons. Cover you. Surround you." She spoke calmly, monotone. "Came up out of the water, down by the limestone cave, I think. Damn, Lan-Tica. May be a... fungus? No, think, think. No. Got to be

Physarum. But smart. I think… How can that be? That can't be, can it? And… they move so fast."

Her rambling made no sense to Tullis. He just stared at her, waiting for some kind of clarification. She seemed to lose her train of thought, though, and stared out toward the pines. She was silent for a moment, then began to speak quietly and so rapidly that Tullis could barely understand what she was saying.

"Trey may be dead. I saw… I know the Best man is dead. Pesticide… I thought maybe pesticides would work. Got him in the seed room… day before yesterday… tore him apart… just awful to see. And… no one came looking for him? We needed help. We needed help. I left him there… just left him. Had to. How could I help him? Then Trey came with a package. He tried, but no use… no use a'tall. It happened too fast."

Her voice trailed off, and her face faded from view again. "Mrs. Woodley… stay with me here. Mrs. Woodley!" Tullis called. "Who's tore somebody apart… who's in the house?"

Instantly, she was back again, her voice nearly venomous. "If you don't hold it down," she warned, "they're going to be on you like piranhas on a … You've *got* to be quiet!"

"Look, Mrs. Woodley," he whispered to appease her. "I've got your carport door open, and I'm just going to come up…"

"My God, No!" She seemed to be disconnected from all reality. Her voice, still quiet – almost too low to hear – took on a sing-song quality. "Shouldn't have opened that door! Shouldn't a done it! Shouldn't a done it! I tried to tell you… Quick! Get up! Get yourself up on the carport roof… get out of their way… don't go in… Don't go!"

"Mrs. Woodley, I've got to get in there to you. You need help. I'll use your phone. Call an ambulance. You're in shock…"

"No!"

Her other hand suddenly pressed against the window. Tullis could barely make out her bloody, mangled fingers, tightly gripping a pair of hedge-trimming shears in the last remaining rays of worn-out sunlight. Tullis thought her hysteria was total now as she began to babble in a whisper he struggled to hear.

"No... No... Don't go in there. Get off the ground... they spread all over. They got Trey... Got Trey. Lake's probably full of 'em. Got someone over at the boathouse this morning. Screams. Oh, God, the screams. Terrible. You hear the screams? I keep hearing the screams..."

She ranted on and on, nonstop now, almost convincing Tullis that he heard screams down by the lake, too. Her statements became more and more convoluted until, finally, she was completely incoherent.

He had to get to her, help her – with or without backup. She was probably in shock. She needed help. There was no other way.

But who the hell is in there, and how many of them, he wondered. *And what's keeping O'Neill and Munt?*

Det. Tullis tried the radio twice more but still got no response. In most other situations, he would have been fuming and ready to rake O'Neill over the coals, but the prickly hairs on his neck kept him on high alert.

He wouldn't figure out until two days later, when Munt's body was found at the edge of the woods on Isolene Road, that it probably was actual screams he'd heard coming from near the lake. That information, however, was to come after the fact and no help to Tullis at that moment.

No matter how many perps were in the house, Tullis knew he couldn't wait for backup. He could wait no longer. The detective left the Plant Woman mumbling incoherently at the window. In the fast-waning sunlight, with his weapon still drawn, he cautiously approached the door again. Tullis found the door standing wide open. He froze in place for a moment. He'd not seen nor heard anyone leave. His heart beat faster. He looked around and checked between the vehicles. He looked behind and underneath the cars. He decided that the door must have slipped from where he'd left it just barely inside the frame, or maybe a breeze had released it. Tullis had been careful not to close the door completely because of the faulty lock – but no – there was no breeze interwoven into the still stifling heat.

Peering cautiously into the kitchen, Tullis whispered into his radio once more, attempting to raise O'Neill. He received nothing but dead silence. He stood in place, trying to take in everything at once, and then stepped onto the first step. Immediately, his foot flew sideways, and he grabbed the doorknob just in time to avoid falling onto his rear into a sticky, orangish, slightly phosphorescent substance that partially covered the steps.

"What the...!"

Tullis felt sure that goo was not there when he jimmied the lock. His attention had been focused on looking beyond the lit but empty kitchen into the dining room when he'd first taken the step. He saw this oozing substance clearly now. From the kitchen light, he could see a trail of the stuff going out the carport and into the brush. It looked somewhat like a larger, stickier version of the slimy trails left by snails and slugs but with a yellow-orange color and horrid smell. Det. Tullis turned back toward the kitchen door, struggling to comprehend what he was seeing and how it got there. He deliberately tested the substance again, tapping into it with one shoe. When he lifted his foot, long strings of the sticky stuff clung to his shoe. He recoiled as it released more of the pungent odor. The smell was vaguely familiar. He couldn't place the smell that was somewhat like strong vinegar mixed with... *What?* Tullis wondered as the stink wafted upward to assault his nose. *Formaldehyde?* It was so strong after the intrusion of his shoes that it brought burning tears to his eyes.

Tullis wiped his eyes on his sleeve and smeared the gooey stuff attached to his shoe onto a dry portion of the cement floor. Some of the leather from the sole of his shoe came off as well.

"Damn! Just what the hell is she doing out here? We gotta get the state lab out here to examine this," He whispered.

Det. Tullis wondered if kids were coming out to this area because this was some sort of new drug to abuse, but he dismissed the idea quickly. With the overpowering odor, burning eyes, and melting shoe leather, he doubted anyone could stand much contact with the stuff. He knew he had to avoid walking in the sticky goo, which was inside the house, too.

Avoiding the slime, Tullis stepped cautiously through the kitchen and into the dining room. He turned on every light switch he could locate, even though the phosphorescent goo emitted that slight glowing trail just about everywhere along the way. Twice more, the detective tried to raise O'Neill by radio. He switched channels and called out to anyone else who might hear – all to no avail.

Tullis knew he needed to get upstairs to Mrs. Woodley as soon as possible. She was in rough shape, but he also needed to search first for Trey and the Best man, who were probably injured more severely than she was if her rambling was to be believed. Had she gone crazy and attacked them with the shears? That was the thing that kept running through his mind, the thing he kept trying to dismiss as he crept through the house. He never believed the church secretary's gossip about the woman. Miss Goodbread called her crazy, but she was as well known for her exaggerated gossip as The Plant Woman was for her eccentricities. Tullis didn't put much stock in rumors. Mrs. Woodley was currently crazed, that was for sure. That, however, didn't seem exactly unnatural in this circumstance. Her hands were bleeding and looked mangled. Something happened here. She was most likely in shock and maybe suffering some after-effect from the odorous slime.

What is that stinking stuff she had in her house? He wondered. Scenarios ran through Tullis' mind. *What was she experimenting with? Did that slimy stuff alter her perception somehow? She seems to drift in and out of reality. Maybe someone else has actually attacked them. Her wounds could be defensive, for sure. Who would attack people this way, and where the hell is O'Neill?* All these recurring and competing thoughts rushed through his mind as he moved slowly.

Silently swearing at the bumbling officer, the detective gave one last try at raising O'Neill on his radio. He also tried calling Vernice back at the station and then switched channels to seek out any officer listening. He still received no response, and then the light grew dim in his flashlight. He banged his hand against the battery tube and instantly got a better connection and light.

Tullis kept an eye out for a phone as, one by one and methodically, he checked out each of the irregular, first-floor rooms that contained mostly plants and lab equipment. His search for a telephone seemed to be in vain. He'd expected to find it in the living room, but if it was there, it was well hidden by the abundant plants. It seemed that there was no room in the house devoid of plants. He found plant stands, plants, and apparatus in disarray or overturned in two rooms.

The area Mrs. Woodley must have been referring to as the seed room was obvious to the detective, for seeds were strewn everywhere. He could see that much from the hallway, but the wall light switch didn't work. The detective turned on his flashlight. He saw containers marked with seed names lying broken on the floor. The room reeked of pesticide – he recognized that odor, and there were definite signs of a struggle. Tullis splayed his light across the room and first saw a large pesticide tank with a hose and sprayer nozzle still attached. It appeared that it had been smashed against one wall. The liquid bug solution pooled on the floor and discolored the wall. Then, he saw a red-stained, white baseball-style cap near the tank. Emblazoned on the hat was "Best."

Tullis' skin began to crawl even before he approached a huge, dark pool of what appeared to be partially dried and smeared blood behind a plant stand. He knew that it was too much blood loss for human survival. The Best man was likely dead somewhere in the house. While visible in several areas, the goo had dried up, and barely any odor lingered. Underneath another overturned plant stand, Det. Tullis brushed aside some spilled seeds for a better look. He saw four reddish-brown marks streaked across the wooden floor. He placed his flashlight on a table, pulled a latex glove from his pocket, and slipped it on his left hand. He bent down to pick up a curious-looking curved object. His brow furrowed as he rolled it back and forth between his fingers. With his light set aside, it took him a moment to realize what he held. Suddenly, Tullis jumped up and dropped the thing abruptly. He saw that he held the remains of a human fingernail, now dried out and curled up with a chunk of desiccated flesh still attached. Det. Tullis cringed, thinking about how this man may have met his end, and still, he continued his search.

Further examination of the room revealed no body. With his gun and flashlight still in hand and heart beating wildly, Tullis cautiously stepped back into the hallway and focused his light up some stairs. He stepped into the next ground-floor room. It appeared to be an office. On full adrenalin alert, he tried to calm his breathing. He saw a phone on the desk and picked up the receiver. The phone made no sound. Detective Tullis clicked the disconnect button several times, but still, no sound came from the phone. He tracked the cord to a melted-looking end where it lay in a dried puddle of goo. He figured the slime had eaten through it.

Tullis moved on, ever cautiously. Books, magazines, and papers – stacks and stacks – filled the room. Several piles had been knocked over, and the stinking slime was still in liquid form and everywhere. With hands holding a flashlight and gun, he continued to wipe away burning tears using his sleeves and carefully chose each step to avoid the stuff.

Det. Tullis knew he'd found Trey – or what remained of him – when he saw the closet. It was open only a few inches, but with the last stream of daylight coming through a dusty window and the meager help of his now-faltering flashlight, he could determine that it was most likely Trey. He could see enough to grasp the situation. The mailman had probably tried to reach the relative safety of the closet.

The detective's stomach churned. "What kind of madness could make this old woman... or whoever... do this?" Tullis whispered.

The sound of his own voice – his trained policeman's voice – seemed to steady his resolve in the face of this gruesome discovery. Slowly, with the toe of his shoe, Tullis opened the closet door wider. Just inside was a large pool of congealed blood, a ragged piece of the man's postal uniform shirt, and further inside the closet, a black shoe with most of a black sock clinging to the foot still inside it.

Later, they all agreed that the detective had no recourse but to use deadly force.

After finding convincing evidence that both men were undoubtedly dead, Det. Tullis rushed to finish the downstairs search and returned to the bottom of the stairs. They were the open type, with the first floor visible beneath each step. He hadn't noticed it before, but now he saw that the slimy substance pooled in front of and underneath the first step, with only a little on the step itself. If the whole scene had not confused him enough, this small detail thoroughly did so. He hesitated going on to the second floor and tried to clarify in his mind why this felt significant. *Slime on the floor that ran under the first step but not on the stairs. The killer or killers possibly had second thoughts and declined to go after the woman with their poisonous substance. However, Mrs. Woodley might be the perpetrator.* Tullis had considered that earlier but kept his theories fluid. Possibilities.

The detective tried again to raise O'Neill and the dispatcher to request backup. He waited a moment but received no response. Tullis took a deep breath, ignoring the obnoxious smell around him. He slowly mounted the stairs with his now flickering flashlight and gun still drawn.

At the top of the stairs, Tullis could see into one large bedroom. He stepped inside and searched the room. Everything appeared neat and in place, and no humans or remains were found. He stepped into the hallway again. Only one closed door remained to be searched. It was opposite the bedroom and above the carport area where he'd seen Mrs. Woodley. He knew it had to be the bathroom.

Det. Tullis stepped into the bathroom to try to subdue the

crazed woman. She was leaning against a counter by the window and seemed to have drowsed off. She still clung to the window and held onto the shears. One leg was bleeding through what appeared to be a hastily wrapped bandage.

Tullis spoke in soft, low tones of reassurance. She didn't respond.

"Everything's going to be alright," he said. "You don't need to be afraid anymore, Mrs. Woodley."

The plant woman's eyes fluttered open, and she stared blankly at him as if she didn't know where she was. Then her lips moved, though no sound issued forth.

The detective was halfway across the bathroom and continued to speak in soothing tones as he took small steps toward her.

At that moment, Tullis picked up the sound of sirens in the distance. He figured that O'Neill must have gotten a call through to dispatch, or someone picked up his call for backup. Distracted, he turned momentarily toward the siren sounds, and at that same moment, Mrs. Woodley lunged at him. He caught her movement just as the sharp pruning shears struck him in the back of the neck, and he instinctively wheeled around and fired. The Plant Woman fell dead at his feet.

The woman had gone insane, they said, and he was lucky that her aim had been off and his wound, though deep, was not life-threatening. Det. Tullis was cleared of any misconduct during the subsequent investigation. The killing of Mrs. Woodley haunted him for the remainder of his life. He knew if he'd hesitated, he could have been fatally wounded, but the man always regretted allowing himself to become distracted. Another thing bothered him as well. Simply stated, and though others disagreed, all the "facts" of the case just didn't add up.

He found out after the incident that O'Neill had desperately called out for backup. There was never enough evidence to determine precisely what had transpired between O'Neill and Munt. Something violent had indeed occurred, and O'Neill's frantic screams for help on his police radio had at least brought more police units racing to the scene.

Some speculated that Munt had taken all he could stand from the abusive O'Neill. They declared that he'd finally flipped out and gone savage on the corporal and thrown him into the lake. O'Neill was never a strong swimmer, and he must have quickly floundered. Some of the corporal's shredded clothing was found washed up the following day. Evidently, before O'Neill's body could be located, he'd quickly become gator chow. Munt was found with his weapon in hand. It had never been fired. Most people believed he had simply run through the woods until his heart gave out. The terror frozen on his face showed his horror at what he'd done.

The people at Best Pest Control in Puesta del Sol Bay had been trying to track down their man, Timmy Buford, for two days. After much investigation on their own, they began to understand why the bug vehicle was found at Mrs. Woodley's home, which wasn't on his route. It turned out that Timmy had been trying to make some bucks extra. He'd been taking a few jobs on the side without the knowledge of the company. They'd had no idea he was even in Pandemonium.

Miss Ella Goodbread ran off with the Reverend Braverman – or so it was told all around town by Emmaline Sweet. Emmaline said she had suspected something was going on between the reverend and his secretary for quite some time. Mrs. Braverman suspected something as well, for she had found her husband's car at the church when he didn't come home. Miss Goodbread's Chrysler was found abandoned at the old Goodbread boathouse. Some said that was a tactic to throw people off their trail, and neither she nor the reverend was heard from ever again. That was enough proof for Emmaline Sweet. Mrs. Braverman moved back to Birmingham, where all her people were from, and the last word was that her migraine problems had improved dramatically.

By the time the state lab people arrived at the scene, the sticky substance had mostly dried up, disintegrated, and blown away. Officers had opened all the doors and windows in the dwelling to rid the scene of the lingering stench. There was so little of the substance left that the lab technicians believed officers had vastly overstated their claims about the stuff. Analysis of the small remaining bits of dried-up slime indicated similar characteristics to the mucus secretions of snails. Lab biologists said it was completely harmless.

Investigators from the state could only speculate on how Mrs. Woodley had killed the pest control man and Trey. So few remains were found that the cause of death couldn't be determined. The medical examiner thought she had possibly used some chemicals to dissolve the men, but he could identify no chemical present in what little remains remained.

Great Lan-Tica bought the Woodley place at an excellent bargain, for no one wanted any part of it. They burned the property to the ground, and after several high-level internal meetings initiated by their staff biologists, they secretly undertook a massive clean-up of the lake. Memos were sent throughout the company, explaining that the actions were taken preemptively – in case Mrs. Woodley had released anything dangerous into the lake.

It proved to be an altogether calamitous few days for the

City of Pandemonium. Many of the town folk said that for a short time – and quite unfortunately – the ill-conceived name of their little city actually fit. After the initial uproar that accompanied the whole chaotic situation of the Plant Woman murders, the town gradually returned to its regular routine of runaway kids, shoplifters, and drunks. Pandemonium resumed its quiet, small-town, slow pace – for a time....

- the end -

8

THE DEATH OF A BABY

When they got to the crumbling, clapboard house, the baby was dead.

Rebecca sat in the rocking chair, holding the tiny body. The only sign of life between mother and child was the monotonous rocking back and forth of the chair against the rough-hewn wooden floor. Rebecca, stony face, drained of all color, seemed as dead as the child in her arms.

She could hear the drunken men coming down the path. She'd known they were coming long before she heard their horses. Now they were here. The wild laughter and evil words echoing up from the path would have struck fear in her heart before – but no more.

Lucius, riding in ahead of the pack, was first to stagger through the ragged screen door. Tall, wiry, and unshaven, he smelled as if moonshine seeped from the pores of his skin. He pushed his sweat-stained, wide-brim hat back off his forehead and reached out, intending to pull Rebecca from the chair. Suddenly comprehending the scene before him, Lucius snatched his hand back as if he'd touched hot coals.

He staggered backward and fell more than sat on the sagging bed opposite Rebecca. The man said not a word, though his mouth opened and closed like a fish gasping for air.

Tipton, Zeke, and J.T. tied up the horses and stomped up the steps. They stopped and tussled on the porch for several seconds before finally stumbling into the room. The screen door slammed behind them. Zeke and Tipton continued the half-hearted fight for possession of a jar of moonshine until J.T.'s angry voice broke into their consciousness. They instantly fell silent.

"What in hell's goin on here? His voice boomed as he stood spread-legged before Rebecca's chair.

"She ain't workin' is what she ain't doin'," Zeke accused, slurring his words.

J.T. turned and stared at his son with a look that withered the man-boy instantly. Zeke spat tobacco on the floor, wiped spittle from his mouth with his shirt sleeve, and hung his head.

Her father turned back to Rebecca, but she made no attempt to answer. She seemed to hear nothing but the crickety sound of the wooden chair rockers squeaking against the pine floor. The girl remained stone-faced and continued rocking at the same, even pace.

No one spoke a word.

Finally, J.T. stepped on the front edge of one rocker with his huge, mud-crusted, black boot, effectively stopping the chair in its forward motion.

"Gal… you show me some respect and answer when I talk to you. What's a matter with that young un?"

Rebecca slowly lifted her gaze to meet J.T.'s hard brown eyes. The other men, still as tree trunks, watched in silent shock that their sister would stare so at their father.

"She's dead." Rebecca's voice was without inflection and barely audible.

J.T. stared into the baby's staring-back, brown eyes. Unconvinced, even by the bluish hue of her lips, he poked a long, dirt-encrusted finger against the baby's already stiffening arm.

"What you done?" His voice was both threatening and filled with contempt.

Tipton and Zeke stepped a little closer, only just beginning to grasp what was happening.

"She couldn't breathe. She died," Rebecca said. "Just died."

"You done this, gal!" Lucius's voice was shaking. "She done it, Pa. Weren't a thing wrong with that young un. You know damn well she done it. Try and keep us from it is what she done. Seed we was comin' for it."

J.T. removed his foot from the chair and stepped aside. Rebecca stared straight ahead and fell back into rocking as if she'd never been interrupted.

"Tip… git out yonder behind them pines and dig a burying hole. Zeke, you git out there and help." J.T. ordered.

Zeke started to protest but thought better of it and followed his younger brother out the door. He knew it was dangerous to question his pa when he used that tone of voice.

"We'd a'found somebody to take her. Weren't no reason to do this," said J.T. "You done shamed yer brothers here." He used the back of his hand to wipe brown spittle from the corner of his mouth and onto his filthy overalls. "And shamed yer ol' pa, too."

Rebecca looked down into the baby's dead eyes.

"You tried to sell her to Wanda's, J.T. You done tried for Godsake to sell a baby to a whorehouse." Rebecca's voice quavered slightly before she got it under control.

Abruptly, the girl stopped rocking, slowly lifted her head again, and stared up into J.T.'s eyes. He suddenly became uncomfortable – uncharacteristically so – but there was something different about how the girl looked at him. There was something different in her eyes. It was some fierce and fiery thing he'd never seen in his daughter before, and his alcohol-saturated brain could not comprehend the meaning. It was worrisome, though. J.T. staggered and took a hard step backward. He struggled to understand what he saw in Rebecca but quickly began to take control again.

"Gal... I done..." He stammered, but only for a moment. "I done told you... quit callin' me by J.T. I'm yer pa. Show respect. You... you don't talk to yer pa that a'way. I reckon you know... you know we was only trying to help you out. Doin' fer you! How you expectin' to get yerself a husband? You with a young un on yer hip and all? Sight more apt to git one if yer shy of a kid. Wanda refused her anyway, so you ain't lost nothin' on that score. And today... today, we done found it a place. Ol' man Parsons was fixin t' take it. We fixed us a deal for you an'..."

J.T. placed his hands on his hips in an effort to regain some unnamed, lost ground. "You... with a young un." He wiped his mouth of the foam accumulated there and shook his head. J.T. opened his mouth to speak again, but the girl spoke first.

"Me? You saying me with a young un? Me?" Rebecca let out a disgusted sigh. "Something wrong with ya'll. *Me* with a young un. You don't take no responsibility. You 'n them boys... ya'll really don't."

"We was only... it was you!" Lucius jumped up from the bed and pointed a tobacco-yellowed finger just inches from Rebecca's face. "You know better'n to stay around when we been drinkin'. Should'a lit out. Took off down the road yonder and hid in them woods. It was you… got us all… all… gal, you ort to'a knowed to git gone! 'Sides that… we don't know but what you been trifling around on yer own. "

Lucius backed away from Rebecca's chair. "She killed it, Pa. You know she done killed it. She's a damn killer."

Tipton and Zeke returned to the porch carrying their shovels. They stomped dirt from their boots and arrived just in time to hear their brother's accusation and witness as J.T. backhanded Lucius so suddenly and savagely that his eldest son was caught off guard and landed hard on the floor.

Tipton held onto the screen door handle like a statue. He made no move to enter.

"Ya'll don't never be sayin' that, you hear?"

He turned to point to the men outside. "Nary a one a ya'll."

J.T. stood towering over his son. Lucius lay still on the floor, not daring to move as J.T. pointed to the men outside the screen door. "Ya'll hear me now? Ain't gone be no asking twice. Ain't gone have my rep-atation sullied about in town nor nowhere's else."

"Yessir," Zeke called out from behind his brother. He shook his head and wiped his grimy neck with a dirty handkerchief.

"Yessir," Tipton responded but still did not open the door.

"Ya'll done heard what the gal said." J.T. looked directly – pointedly – at each of his sons. "That youngun got sick and died. Now. I ain't gone hear no more of it."

J.T. snatched a faded red shawl from the back of the rocking chair. He clumsily spread it out on the bed, then turned and lifted the staring baby from Rebecca's arms. He half expected his daughter to resist, but she made no move. J.T. held the fully stiffened baby out and away from his own body as if it might somehow contaminate him. He laid the brown-eyed little child onto the center of the shawl and folded each side around it before enclosing it with the top and bottom of the cloth.Lucius finally struggled to his feet again and limped to the screen door. Tipton and Zeke moved to the porch steps, then into the dirt yard and safety. They held onto their shovels and watched as Lucius held the door open so his father could pass through with the wrapped body. Lucius looked back toward Rebecca. She stared down into her empty hands and continued rocking. Lucius let the door slam behind him and stood staring at Rebecca through the ragged screen. Disgusted, he turned away, spat into the yard, and descended the steps. He followed his father and brothers into the pines."I didn't kill her," Rebecca whispered to no one. "I saved her a life."

- the end -

9

MCALLISTER'S LAST DEAL

When he asked me, I said, "What? It's like selling your soul, right?"

And he said – so calm – but half-amused, I guess, "Well… there are many other things for sale besides your soul. Perhaps you watch too many movies."

And I thought then, *perhaps I do*. But I knew for sure this guy didn't look like no DeNiro in that flick with Mickey Rourke. He wasn't slick, or polished, or evil-looking with the long, egg-peeling fingernails like DeNiro. Yeah… he was a bit creepy, and his fingers were long and bony but with square nails, and he was… he was…

Ok. It's hard to describe Tolbertz even now. After all this time. Ordinary. Ordinary but in some indefinable creepy way. I guess that's the best I can do. He was just so freakin' ordinary. Early fifties, maybe. Lips a little too fleshy, maybe, but just any guy off the street. Million guys similar looking. Nondescript… that's a good word. And words don't come so easy no more.

I was down on my luck, see? That's the thing. Yeah. That's

the thing. And drinking way too much... but... no... I won't use that as an excuse. Can't. I was cold sober at the time. Leastways, when we first started talking, I was sober. By the time the deal was struck... well... who knows? The details fade somehow.

Point is... I thought it was just your come lately, half-cocked philosophical conversation. One of those oddball discussions that get started once in a while when you're straddle a barstool in some dingy little dive just like this one. One's get started when you're a middle-aged guy down on your luck.

And that's what I was, alright? Down on my luck. Me. Who two years before – and after years of struggling, I might add – who two years before that had been at the pinnacle of my career, as they say. Nothing less than an Oscar, if you can believe it. Best original screenplay. Freakin' *King's Desire* it was. You remember it? Hell, everybody remembers it. Made Haywood a bundle, I can tell you.

John. Holcomb. Haywood. What a guy he was. Producer *and* director extraordinaire. Procurer of scripts from the downtrodden of Hollywood and Vine... the struggling unknowns. A true Hollywood machine in living Technicolor. Pimp, any which way you look at it. Bought it outright – bought up all my rights to *King's Desire*. Hey... so it goes, right? So I shouldn'ta sold it, right? Not like I was some hick from the farm. Not me. I had some savvy in this area and had a gut feeling about it on top of all that. But I needed the dough... you just don't know what it's like out there... Hollywood, I mean.

You gotta fight to make it in Tinseltown. And then, of course, fight to stay on top or just stay somewhere in the middle. I fought Haywood pretty hard over the deal, though. After the fact, you know? Had to. It's just that... I don't know, pride or ego thing happens inside a man. When you've reached your limit, and you gotta do *something* to still call yourself a man. Had to take that fight all the way, you know? Course, he won. Course he did. That's just the way it is. Whatcha gonna do? Money is power. Freakin' money always wins. I never really had a chance. Jeez... I look back on that now and think... well, what a dumbass, you know? Didn't listen to the people who tried to tell me. Warn me, you know? It was the principle of the thing. You know what I mean? Sometimes it's just the damn principle of the thing. Accomplished nothing. Zero. Just ticked him off good and proper is all it did, and I swear, he blackballed me after that. They say there's no such thing in Hollywood anymore, but don't you believe it. That's a whole different story, though, and I digress... water under the bridge, as they say.

Point is, for a full, long two years after losing to him in court, I barely sold a word. Cleaning up a scene or two on this or that script. Fixing other writers' messes. And that under the table if you just want to be real accurate about it. Nobody daring to use my skills or my name in plain view. Got just enough work to scrape by, and that was scraping the bottom, let me tell you. Still, I read the trades, you know? Kept up with the business. Expecting people would eventually forget, or Haywood would lose his clout. You figure... just how long can this blackball thing go on, right? I thought not long. With the right material... I mean, I had at least two Oscar-level scripts. Well, whatever. I thought wrong. Still, kept looking for opportunities... Mr. Optimistic, that was me, always looking for opportunities.

And actually, I was still quite prolific with the writing, even if I couldn't sell it. Hell, at that point, I was halfway through another screenplay that I thought could beat *King's*

Desire. So I was writing. That's the important thing for a writer, ya know. Just keep writing. Creating.

Trouble is… I started drinking. That's what really started taking me down. So yeah… I *was* drinking at the time. But when I met Tolbertz in Cravey's Bar, I wasn't drunk. Not by any true measure.

I remember the day I met him like I remember my last shot of Comfort. See… I was in Cravey's Bar. It stunk like stale beer and old vomit, but it was my watering hole. No Hollywood types likely ever set a foot inside. It was a little after ten in the morning, and far as I could see, the bar was empty 'cept for Cravey and me. Not that I was checking. Be honest… at that point, I didn't care anymore who saw me starting out at ten-thirty in the morning. Don't know if I was trying to build up my nerve for another round of rejections that day or just…

Well, I threw one back and slapped the glass hard against the bar top for old Cravey to lay another smooth Southern Comfort on me. Southern Comfort… my new best friend in those days… hell, my only friend back then, now that I think about it.

Well… old Cravey – leathered, and white-haired, and looking for all the world like a preserved mummy, unwrapped and on display – he gives me this long look that there's no way to interpret, and slowly he pours that cool liquid heat that lights the fire and eases the soul. Then… without taking his rheumy old eyes off me for a second, he sets that bottle down on the bar so quiet you'd think the freakin' thing was padded. Kept it on *his* side of the bar, though. Wasn't relinquishing that bottle to me.

That's when Tolbertz slides onto the next stool. I give him a hard look. Must'a been sitting in one of the dark booths at the back. But I scanned the place pretty good when

I walked in – damndest thing. I never saw where he came from. Didn't come in through the front door. I know that for sure. Just seemed to materialize like a vapor becoming solid. I turn back to my business.

He looks at me and says, "Rough night, eh?" Then he slowly sips from his glass. Sips smooth and easy. Hooded eyes. Half-closed. I see some kind of weird-ass smile creep up on Cravy's stone face.

I shoot him this sarcastic, side-wise look, like, it don't take no freakin' one-fifty IQ to see it's been a rough night and a rough year. I'm well aware. I look the part. Then I cut my eyes back to the glass in my hand and toss back the one Cravey's just poured.

Guy's still staring at me. I see this out of the corner of my eye. Got this half-smile twisting his blubbery lips like he's privy to some inside joke.

Pisses me off a bit. Shithead is what I'm thinking. Who's he to give me a look like that? Who's he to crowd me in that empty bar? So I turn to face him, straight on. I stare directly back at his staring eyeballs. I pointedly wipe my mouth on the back of my hand and pop the glass down hard in front of me again. Then I turn away without a word and watch Cravey on automatic pilot, fill 'er up again.

"Lighten up," says Tolbertz. "Relax… We all got bad days."

I swallow down this next shot and wipe my mouth again. I see this guy's for conversation… not gonna freakin' give up. So I figure, what the hell?

"Yeah," I says. "Bad days, we all got." I'm dripping sarcasm, but still, I don't give him the courtesy of another glance. I see his reflection in the cracked-design mirror behind Cravey, though, and he has this sly-looking kind'a smile. That design in the mirror twists that smile beyond the sly. The whole image sort'a gives you the creeps in some enigmatic way.

"And these things too shall pass," he says.

"Sure," I say. "These things pass, and so do we... trouble is... sometimes, the latter precedes the former." I'm staring full-on at his twisted face now... reflected in the mirror behind the bar, and he's staring right back at me.

He smiles, points upward for emphasis, and says, "Ah, but not if we empower ourselves and become the seekers of our own destiny rather than allow destiny to drag us down some loathsome road not of our own choosing."

As he's saying this, he gets this look on his face – recognition. "Say," he says, wrinkling up his brow now and snapping his fingers. "You're that writer... don't tell me," he says, "I know it... I know it. Yeah, you're that McAllister guy... Brian McAllister! The writer, right? Oscar... yeah, Oscar... am I right? Best Screenplay, for... let me see..."

"*King's Desire*," I say, and now I turn to look at him straight on. "Yeah, that's me." And I don't let him see it at first, but I'm softening up on this guy a bit, thinking maybe he's in the business, and contacts, you know, connections are everything. Never let a possible opportunity slip away. I'm entirely on board with it now cause I'm thinking he's in the business, see? Cause who else remembers the writers? Who else is gonna remember me from Oscar night four years ago? Nobody, that's who. Unless... unless they're in the business. And hey... one contact. That's all it takes. And I've got stories. I got stories ready to freakin' sell. I just need someone... the right someone to hear my pitch... read my scripts... get 'em into the right hands.

"'Elias Tolbertz," he says, offering a hand which I reach around and take firm hold of as I nod my head slightly. I'll never forget the cold, clammy feel of that hand long as I live. Gut feeling ignored.

"Oh man," he says. "I'm a fan." He snaps his bony fingers

at the bartender, who's fiddling with something behind the bar. "Cravey... come pour this man a double, Cravey. This one's on me... in fact, just keep 'em coming and put it all on my tab."

And Cravey obeys. He smiles that freaky smile again and pours, and I throw this one back, too. To give him a chance to fill it again in case the offer fizzles out too soon.

Tolbertz just watches me. He's smiling again, that crooked smile. Then he shakes his head, and the smile widens out, breaking all over his face. It's like he's not believing that he's got this good luck to meet this Oscar-winning writer.

"Man," he says. "When Gloria takes everything from King, and he's down to the final hour... totally unexpected! It's great! Great stuff! How you guys come up with these stories... It's unreal.

"Imagination," he continues without giving me a chance to answer. "That's what it all boils down to. Talent and imagination. What I wouldn't give for that. You guys are just born with it."

He taps a finger on the bar top, and Cravey tilts the bottle my way once more. Before I can even say thanks, he's filling my head again with the BS.

"It's a gift, you know. You look around and... Hey... you've seen it. Plenty of guys toss the words around and come up with nothing. They re-hash the same old stuff over and over... little curve here... little detour there, but the same old hash in the end. You, though... and writers like you... the really great ones, I'm talking about... the ones with the true, creative talent, the imagination... man, I tell you, it's a gift you're given."

Finally, he stops with the talk and sips nice and slow on the drink he's been nursing.

I nod my thanks for the praise, but frankly, he's taken it so far that now I'm a little embarrassed. I want to get off this creative crap and move on to what he's got to offer... who his contacts are in the business. I swallow Cravey's last pour and feel it burn down deep in my belly.

"Unfortunately," I say. "What I need a talent for is negotiating and selling the stuff. So far, I'm batting zero on that score. Don't trust agents," I advise him. "You need 'em. You do need 'em, but you can't trust 'em, and in the end, I wonder if they don't cause you more damn problems. Compromise? They want you to compromise everything and shut your mouth. On the other hand, though, I sure haven't developed the knack for selling myself yet, so it's the perpetual Catch-22. And you find yourself riding that tornado in the toilet as you're sucked down, down, down after your agent presses the handle to flush." I suddenly realize I've been running off at the mouth and making little sense while severely downgrading agents... which he might be

Tolbertz sits up a little straighter when I finally shut up and says, kind of hesitantly, "Well, you know... perhaps I could actually help you out a bit there."

And finally, I get in the line I've been holding back. Busting a gut to say ever since the guy started all this.

"So, you're in the business," I say this casually but with finality, cause I know for sure now that I pegged him right. "Man! I hope I didn't offend you if you're an agent! Not all agents are bad. Just mine." I give a little laugh. Only half-assed apology I can summon. Me and my big mouth, I'm thinking, and I silently curse myself, but then I open my arms wide in supplication and say. "I figured maybe... agent? Way you was talking and all. Who you with?"

"Ah... No. Alas," Tolbertz says, throwing his hands out

sideways. Sort of mirroring my movement. Like as if to say, Whatcha gonna do?

And I'm thinking... well, first I'm thinking, who the hell says "Alas?" But I'm thinking, just my freakin' luck... foregone conclusion. And I'm already disgusted inside and feeling the double burn – burn from the liquor and burn from the sudden loss – and somehow... somehow, deception. I'm feeling like a chump. I feel like giving him a *real* mouthful of the words – a gift of words – he's been so hopped up on. Nevertheless, one little part of me figures he still might be good for another drink or two. I hold my tongue.

He sips his drink again, still eyeing me.

"I'm not in *the* business," he says finally. "But I do quite a little bit of work for Harold Blasintime over at Closter Film Studios. You know... books, accounts, a little procurement here and there... that sort of thing."

O.K. I was quick to dismiss. Now, he's got my undivided attention again. I got no beef with Blasintime. I think to myself... ok. Blasintime's good. Sure, he's no Haywood, but it's a start, and maybe he's not in the blackball loop.

He taps the bar top next to my glass again, and Cravey automatically pours the Comfort. This time, I sip, however. Even though it took me three-quarters of the bottle to really start feeling it in those days, I wanted to stay clear.

"Haven't seen any of your stuff in the last couple of years. You must be working on a big one, huh?"

"Not exactly," I say... not thinking it through. I quickly recover, though, and fix that blunder. I say, "Course, a writer's always working on something. But I've got several projects... uh, several screenplays ready to go... you think Blasintime's looking?"

"Oh... well... I couldn't say about that," he says. "But as I told you... I do a little procurement here and there... and you know producers... they're always looking for good stories. With an Oscar in your pocket, you should have no problem selling your stories, right?"

"Well, Oscar... freakin' awards... don't mean squat if nobody'll let you in the door. Happens all the time. Not just to me, but see... thing is, I had this little tiff with Haywood. He cut me out of the massive profits on *King's Desire*. Hidden little loophole there... well, hell, I didn't read it thoroughly. I was too green, ya know? They count on that. They should have to reveal that kind of stuff. Anyway, seems no one has time now to say hello to me, much less listen to a story pitch. And that movie's *still* raking in the dough. Still going."

I shut up quick after that spiel. Now I'm feeling downright foolish. Flapped my trap to a stranger like I knew the guy. With this sudden realization... hell... I don't wanna drink more, but I can't stop myself. I toss back the hot, freakin' Comfort, wipe my mouth, shut it, and wait.

"Ah, yes." He drums the counter with those long fingers, can't seem to hide that crooked smile, and rattles on. "Seems I do remember reading some little tidbit about some litigation involving you and Haywood."

He goes straight face now. "But... maybe," he says. "Maybe I could convince Blasintime to look at your stuff. He's not fond of Haywood himself, so perhaps. Although... you know the politics of Hollywood. You saw it firsthand. However, funny coincidence – I just love coincidences, by the way. Don't you?'

I just stare at him. I'm stone-faced now and controlling my mouth, but Tolbertz didn't wait for an answer to his question anyway. He just rattled on.

"Coincidence is... I'm seeing Blasintime tonight. Yes. Quite a coincidence. He and Laurette are having a little party for Fiona Demone, and I've got to run a couple of things past him... anyway... maybe I could..."

"I got some stuff in the car," I jump up and cut right in to stop him. Didn't try to hold my tongue or my feet. I'm moving for the door before he can give it more rational thought.

"Two... three, perhaps," Tolbertz calls out as I exit the door without waiting to hear him finish.

Out in the street, I'm momentarily blinded by the sunlight. I'm dizzy. Breathless and my heart is doing this funny, racing kind of thing. I lean against the building, trying to get this stuff under control. Never had anything like that happen to me before. I tell myself it's the drink or the sudden shimmering heat outside. Later, in retrospect, of course, I decided maybe it was a red flag trying to get me to jump in my car and get the hell out of there. Whatever. I didn't leave.

After I catch my breath, I'm able to move again. I start digging through the fast-food containers and trash piled up in the back seat of my '75 Camaro that leaks, wheezes, whines, and threatens to lie down and die every time I turn the key in the ignition.

Finally, after much rummaging, I find *Paraffin Soldiers*, which has a huge, freakin' coffee stain splattered across the front cover, and several pages stuck together. Then, I pull out *The Harridan Years, Magdalene's Maze,* and *White Shutters,* which, by the way, Haywood would have creamed for if he'd read it. These, too, are either stained or crumpled, but *Soldiers* is in the worst shape. It's a great screenplay, and I riffle through it but decide it's just too messed up. So I throw it back on the floor with several others that aren't my best. I mentally kick myself in the ass for not being more careful with my life's work. Anyway, I return to the bar with the other three.

Back inside the dark of the bar, I'm suddenly woozy and sweating like crazy. I stop just beyond the door and grab onto the back of a Naugahyde booth, sticky with God knows what and smelling like sweat on top of sweat. In a minute or two, I begin to get myself straight again, but I'm still hanging onto that nasty booth. Must be the sun, I tell myself. It's cause I'm coming back into this dark hole from the heat and bright white outside, that's all. I convince myself that's why I'm woozing. *Had* to believe what I was telling myself. Not that hard to do in my condition. Another red-flag? I pay no attention. But, hindsight. Ah, yes… good ol' hindsight.

So, okay. Finally, I pull it together and release my tenuous hold on the nasty booth. I slowly make my way over to Tolbertz, and all the while, my gut is telling me something, but my head's not listening. I slap the scripts down onto the bar in front of him and shakily slide back onto my barstool. Cravey's refilled my glass, and, of course, I down it. I needed it bad at that point.

Tolbertz sips his drink and stares down at the smeared and battered papers but doesn't touch them. I see the look on his face. It's like he's suddenly seen a disgusting cockroach crawling across the bar. And I *know*. Of course, I know. The scripts are in bad shape – really sorry shape. He doesn't move to touch them. But then I see his face relax ever so slightly, and I think he sees something in me through those disheveled scripts that makes him *know* that I'm in sorry shape, too. I think he's gonna tell me forget it. Pound sand. And my heart is racing again, but different than when I was outside. Panicky. I can't look him in the face now. I disappear another whiskey, stare at my glass, and wait in silence. He doesn't say anything, but bonus prize… Cravey refills my empty glass for what I figure is the last freebie. I look at the liquid. I tilt the glass and make the whiskey swirl inside, but I don't drink. Savoring.

Tolbertz stares at the manuscripts in front of him for several eternal moments before he reaches inside his jacket, pulls out a business card, and offers it to me between two skeletal fingers. He holds it out to me for the whole five seconds or so that I hesitate before pulling it from his fingers. His demeanor suddenly changes then. He stares. At first glance, he seems kind'a bored-like... or, I don't know... unreadable. Then, I can see a subtle change in his eyes, even though his face is suddenly contorted with that twisted grin again.

I'm getting uncomfortable with his silent stare when he finally speaks.

"I make no promise," he says. "I'll show them to Blasintime, and we'll go from there. You available tomorrow? About the same time? Same place?"

"Well..." I hesitate just a bit – like I had a mental schedule to consult, and his crooked smile goes wide. Then I realize the freakin' futility of this – like, who am I fooling? This guy has looked too deep into me in this short time span, and I don't know how he did that, and I can't hide... and even though that discomforts me, I ignore my gut again -- flag, flag, flags everywhere. But ya know how that sliver of hope can creep in? Hope edged out the flags.

"Yes," I say – real firm and determined sounding. "I'll be here."

He nods, then eases off his barstool and tips forward slightly like a real gentleman might have done in the early 1900s. He pays up and then slides a crisp, fifty-dollar bill onto the bar as a tip. Cravey snaps the green up before I can give a good howdy-do to Ulysses S. Grant. When I look up again, Tolbertz is gone. Just gone.

I had a fitful sleep that night, I can tell you. I tossed. I turned. I felt sick to my stomach. If this thing didn't go with Blasintime, I knew I might just as well pack it up, dreams and all, and go back to Tampa. Try for a job over at the Tribune. Whatever was gonna happen, I figured this was my last chance to make it in Hollywood.

The hours seemed to drag by like a bad play in slow motion. I started for the new bottle of Southern Comfort sitting on the bureau 'bout a dozen times, but I didn't succumb that night. Maybe it helped that the seal wasn't broken yet. I don't know. I remember I was determined not to put another drink in my gullet. I could stare at the bottle and hold out till ten-thirty in the morning. That's what I told myself. I could freakin' wait that long. I really struggled through that night, though. You can imagine how I questioned my sanity for allowing this guy – who I didn't know from Adam – to take my original manuscripts with nothing but a nearly blank business card in return. That damn card had the name Elias J. Tolbertz and a phone number. That's it. No business information or address. How could I give up my work like that? What's worse... I had no copies of my manuscripts. But I wasn't thinking clearly then, see? Mostly the drink, but hope and the possibilities had taken over my decision-making by then. But, no... No. I said I wouldn't blame it on the booze. I made the decision to hand over my work. I take responsibility for that. But back then, I *did* blame it on the alcohol, and I suffered greatly that night, thinking maybe those scripts were gone for good, I can tell you.

When Tolbertz finally showed the next morning, I'd already killed two. I was swirling the third and sweatin' bullets – as they say – like I never had in my life before or since. When I saw him walk in, my sigh was audible, and my pure relief must have been abundantly clear, for he smiled that freakin twisted smile again as he pulled up on the stool beside me. I could just detect the slightest bit of tooth showing between those too-fleshy lips.

I immediately saw the pitifully stained manuscripts rolled up in his left hand. I felt momentary anger at his mishandling my already mistreated work that way. My heart sank as my mind acknowledged what this meant to me. He was returning them. There was no cause for doubt. No deal. No sale. I was finished in Hollywood. I could literally feel my body sag into the barstool.

"My friend," he said, again offering me his hand. I barely touched the outstretched, leathery fingers to acknowledge. I hadn't noticed that leathered look on those fingers that were just so bony, and – not meaning to – I instinctively jerked my hand away. I quickly turned back to swirling my drink. I didn't want to think about this guy and his weird fingers. What more could there be to discuss anyway?

But what I didn't know then was… he wasn't finished with me at all. Not by a long shot. Cause if I could have known… *if* I could have just grabbed my scripts and walked out right that minute… But I didn't. And there's no way to back-space and white out what's written in my life. I can't get it all back. It's gone. Done deal.

"My friend," he said it again – cause I guess he could see I really wasn't hearing. "You have great talent."

Now, frankly, I don't need to hear this. I swallow my drink and stare at him. I don't need that fawning praise he spit out the day before. That and a quarter still won't get you a cup of coffee. It don't mean nothing. At that moment, it's freakin' worthless cause I know what's coming. I've seen rejection a thousand times. So I give him this dirty look. I mean, for real. My face is telling him forget it. I don't wanna hear it.

He takes my cue, shuts his hole, and nods to Cravey, who quickly fills my glass. Then he waits till I toss that one off before he continues.

"Blasintime is… well, he can't use anything right now…"

"Or ever," I say without looking at him. "Just like the rest of 'em. Guess I could'a told you that and saved you the trouble of asking. Doesn't matter," I say. "I was planning on heading back to Florida anyway."

Suddenly, I don't have the energy to lift the new glass that Cravey's pouring, so I just stare at it. Ya know that sinking feeling you get when plans fail? Well, I was sunk.

"This is a vicious business," Tolbertz says. "Seems Haywood has not only a long memory but a long arm as well. He's been around too long. Holds a large stack of chips. You understand Blasintime's position, I'm sure."

"All too well," I say, not wanting to hear more and anxious to turn the conversation off for good. "But hey, you tried… Thanks a bunch. You get me… thanks for trying, thanks for the drinks, et cetera, et cetera, et cetera."

I lift my glass in a proffered toast to this weirdo's generosity and quickly toss back the last Comfort as I slide off the barstool. I throw ten bucks down on the bar and reach for the rolled-up manuscripts that Tolbertz's still holding, but he's not letting loose of his grip.

I let go. I'm startled for a second, not expecting this.

"Take your money back." Tolbertz grins wide now, stretching his rubbery lips.

"I have a proposition," he says. "Sit back down… relax." He drags out 'relax' like a hypnotist trying to put a guy to sleep. "Hear me out… fill the man's glass, Cravey…" he nods toward my glass again. With one finger, he slides my ten-dollar bill away from the silent bartender and back toward me.

For one moment... for one split second, that little nag-ass voice in my head said, *'DON'T'*... but did I listen? No, I did not. I told that internal voice to kiss off – or something – and then it was gone. That moment for 'don't' was gone, and I was sitting on the barstool again with another drink in my hand.

"As I said, you have a great creative talent..."

I started to stop him, but he held up an insistent finger, motioning me to hear him out.

"'Imagination," he continued. "You perhaps don't realize the true value of this. Many artists do not. Some people would give... well... some would give a great deal to have... Well, they'd give *many* things... great sums of money... to have such talents."

"Okay. I get the compliments and thanks, but like I told you, that info and two bits... well... won't get you a cup of coffee these days," I say this cause this guy's not offering me nothing. Nothing I can take to the bank. "So what's the proposition?"

"What would you take for it?" Tolbertz asks me. He's dead serious. The smile is long gone.

"Take for what? For these screenplays?" I ask. I'm getting angry now cause either this freakin' guy's intentionally confusing the hell out of me, or I'm just plain drunk, and I *know* that's not so.

Quiet now, almost whispering. Conspiratorially. He says, "Not just these." He holds up the roll of stories. "For your talent, Mr. McAllister. For. Your. Talent. Your imagination. For your cre-a-tivity." Now, he lays out the manuscripts on the bar between us. He smooths them out so that they lay almost flat. We both stare at the stack silently.

"Pure bull shit," I say – and I say this out loud right to his face. "What looney bin did you just escape from? You want stories? I got stories. You said neither Blasintime nor anyone else is interested, so what are you asking? You wanting to buy my stuff? These manuscripts? Is that what we're talking about?"

"What are they worth to you, Mr. McAllister? How much? For your talent. Your imagination. Your creativity? And… of course, whatever you have written to this point."

He calls these points out firmly, counting each one off with his boney damn fingers like creativity and such are tangible items on a shopping list.

I'm thinking this guy is gone. I mean, like fully gone in the head… for real. I tell myself that I know this for sure, but if he hands me money, I'm not gonna kick, right? This is so far gone that I figure, what the hell… let's just see how far he goes with this bull. I'm gonna just freakin' go for it. It's not like I'm scamming him. He made the offer, not me.

"What are you willing to pay?" I'm smiling real big now.

"I'm willing to pay the full value. What you think it's all worth."

"Well, as you know, right now… right this minute… they're worthless," I say as I riff through the pages of the stacked manuscripts.

I'm still thinking somehow in terms of scripts. Even though Tolbertz enumerated certain intangible qualities, I let that part whiz right on past my head. Who would have taken that seriously?

"Appears nobody wants the scripts but you." I look him straight in the eye, and I'm smirking like hell cause this guy's gone, and I know it, even though he remains cool. Face unreadable. Yeah. Cool cat, this guy. Staring and silent. That's when I make reference to his intangibles, and I say,

"But sell talent? What? It's like selling your soul, right?" And inside, I'm stifling to keep from laughing in this jerk's face.

And he says, calmly... really calm, but suddenly smiling like a damn Cheshire cat, "Well, there are many other things for sale besides your soul, Mr. McAllister."

So that's when it happened. I just blurted it out like it was a legit business deal, but not in any way believing the words I was saying. No. Not at all believing, but ripe to take his BS to the fullest extent just to see.

"Two hundred and fifty thou," I said to him. "Cash," I said. "No. No, man... three hundred thousand."

I knew full well how stupid the whole conversation was. But I figured, hey, I'll play this out and use it in a scene someday.

"It's done then. For the scripts and the other things discussed." He grabbed my hand and shook it so fast it was almost comical. As he pulled back, I held on, and bad as I didn't want to be touching that hand, I wouldn't let go yet.

"One other thing," I said. "You asked my price... I also want Haywood to come down with some dread disease and suffer. Really suffer... and die," I said. See, I'm showing him that I'm fully involved in his game at this point. I'm figuring, hey... I can play... he's got his fantasy... I've got mine. Definitely, something I can use for some scene in some bar... someday.

"'Any particular disease?" Tolbertz asks. He's dead serious. Straight as Crosby to Hope in all those road pictures I grew up watching on T.V. His face is serious. No twisted smile. He's making like all this is real. A business deal.

I wrinkle my brow and squinch my eyes like I'm trying real hard to decide, and then I say, "Naw... Mr. Tolbertz, you feel free to choose just whichever disease you like."

"Consider it done," says Tolbertz. He taps a long, skeletal

finger on my manuscripts lying on the bar. "Pleasure doing business with you, McAllister."

He seems genuinely happy, like he's concluded this great deal, cause he tosses a hundred dollar bill on the bar for Cravey and tells him to keep the change. Then he's off the barstool and heading for the door. No plans for see-ya-tomorrow... same-time-same-place.

A few months later, after I'd sobered up a bit, ya know, I thought about that man's fingers again. I was a bit surprised that I hadn't noticed how skeletal those fingers were right at the beginning. Yeah. I had noticed they were a bit bony, and then, at some point later, I saw the leatheriness. Then, finally, I saw how skeletal they were and, worse, felt them. It struck me as odd... like the man was deteriorating in front of me. Why didn't I see that right away? I still don't know. Maybe, at the time, I was too distracted by the whole implausible scene. I wasn't thinking about the fingers at the time, though.

"Damn," I say to Cravey. "Can you believe that guy?"

Cravey ignores me and heads to the cash register with his C-note.

Well... I can tell you, any further thoughts I gave this Tolbertz were of pity for someone gone round the bend, as they say. There was no deal... just as I thought. I figured I was damned lucky to get my manuscripts back from him.

When I returned to my dingy, overpriced, dumpy efficiency that evening, I threw my unwashed clothes into a broken-down suitcase and tossed all of my manuscripts into a cardboard box. I piled them onto the back seat of the Camaro, along with my Oscar and my trusty Royal typewriter with the Q key missing. I left the remaining stained manuscripts on the floor of the back seat where they'd resided for months. I figured I could probably pawn the Oscar, but I could do that along the way when the bucks ran out. I grabbed the rest of my meager belongings and added them to the back seat.

When the car was packed, I went back inside and counted out my money on the sagging, broken-down excuse for a bed. My full net worth at that moment appeared to be two hundred and forty-eight dollars and seventeen cents. I figured it was enough to get me back to Tampa if I was careful. The biggest problem, I expected, was going to be the Camaro. I blew big bucks on a brand new, shiny red stingray after my payoff for *King's Desire*, but after attorney's fees on the Haywood thing and too much high living... well, it wasn't long before I was selling off everything and living on nothing. I bought the old Camaro, and it served me pretty well, but it was going downhill fast, and I wasn't sure it would take me all the way to Tampa. I figured to cross that bridge when I had to.

With everything loaded up, I hit the sack early, planning to head out of town whenever I woke up the next morning.

That's when the surprise came – that next morning. I decided on one last drink at Cravey's. Sort'a for old time's sake, you might say – one for the road.

Over the past few months, Cravey had learned to pour a Southern Comfort as soon as he saw me at the door. This time, he didn't do it, though. He just stared and waited until I sat down. I stretched my arms out as if to say, 'What?' But Cravey, he's still silent – dead-faced and staring.

"Cravey?" I say.

Without a word, he pulls a beautiful leather briefcase from below the bar and puts it in front of me.

I thought, *What the F?* I was confused, but before I gathered my wits enough to say anything more, he'd already turned and walked away.

My heart was pounding, that I can tell you. Slew of things

running through my mind all at once, to where I couldn't think straight. All the time, though, I guess I was denying the possibility – the implications.

I opened the briefcase right there on the bartop, and it was full of money. I was stunned but quickly shut the case. Of course, I got the hell out of that bar tout suite. I didn't count it till later, but it was three hundred thousand dollars. I counted every dollar. When I could gather my thoughts, all I could think of was, just take the money and run! Not my fault some crazy guy's out there giving away free money.

So I did. I did run. Didn't even take that planned last drink at Cravey's Bar. I took the briefcase full of money, threw it onto the front seat of the Camaro, and hit the road.

My mind whirled. Tingled. Ya know that electric feeling you get in your body when you're incredibly sleep-deprived or shocked senseless by some unexpected event? I felt out of control, sort'a. And it wasn't till Vegas that I thought to check on my stuff in the backseat. Oscar, typewriter, clothes, and my other stuff all there. Then I opened the cardboard box with my manuscripts. It was empty. I checked the floor and saw that those stained and ripped stories were gone, too. Manuscripts all gone. Just gone. I panicked at first. Those stories... the characters... it's like they're part of you... they belong to you. I gotta say... it freakin' shook me. I kept thinking... what did I just do? But then I soon came to my senses and said, what the hell... so he got a few stories. Couldn't sell 'em to anyone else, and I got the three hundred G's. Hell, I can write more stories. So we were square. In my book, we were square. That's how I looked at it then.

I partied in Vegas for a week. Sure, I went through some dough and went through some women. Who wouldn't? Hell, it was Vegas, man! I had money, and I felt like burning some green. I guess when the reality hit me – really hit square in the face – was when I saw the freakin' newspaper.

I think it was Cherry... or maybe it was Leeann. Damn, I can't remember which it was now. Anyway, the girls always ordered room service for breakfast, and the hotel always sent a newspaper up with the meal. One morning, the girls were giggling at the table, and I was still half asleep when I heard one of 'em discussing Haywood. They said he was real sick and how sad it was because he was so great and was up for an Oscar again. That got me awake real quick. I jumped up and grabbed the newspaper out of Leeann's hands, and there it was. Middle of page one:

'HAYWOOD CRITICAL-STRICKEN WITH CHOLERA-OYSTERS LIKELY CULPRIT'

The story went on to say that he failed to seek immediate help, and his prospects for survival were not very good. I was shocked even though the reality of what I'd done was beginning to seep into my alcohol-soaked brain. I never meant the guy that kind of harm. Course, I thought I meant it at the time. How could I have known it would all be real? I thought about how the doctors said his survival probability wasn't very good. Guess I was the only guy at that point in time who knew his chances were nil. Guess I was the only one, too, who knew that Brian McAllister would never be able to sit down and bring characters to life on the Royal typewriter again and... no, come to think of it... I guess Tolbertz knew it, too.

- the end -

10

THE SUN BEARING DOWN

S eemed like we'd been travelin' a good long while, and I
was right thrilled when we got to Independence,
Missouri. It was an excitin' town. Papa went to fetch our
wagon and oxen. Him and my brother Jesse was fixin' to put
a cover on it to save us some money cause Mama was fussin'
right smart about how much everything was costin'. When
they got that done, we was fixin' to load up our supplies and
head to California. I reckon we was all itchin' to start a new
life. Well, not Mama, but I sure was happy. To me, it was
excitin' new adventures ahead of us.

Oh, my! Independence! I liked that word, and just to be in
the city made my heart flutter. The street was mighty
crowded. Wagons and horses and people'a all kinds just filled
the streets. Goin hither and yon, wrapped up in all kinds a
business. They had right nice wooden walkin' boards in
front of the stores, and I stomped my brogans hard on the
wood to say, *"Here I am!"* Mama gave me a look, but I
stomped one more time anyway.

Oh... and the ladies in such nice-lookin' frocks and

bonnets. They was right colorful, and I wondered why Mama didn't wear prettier colors. I looked down at my own skirt. It weren't ragged, but I hoped nobody would notice that the blue flowers was so faded they looked downright gray.

Independence was a noisy place. Wagons and people everwhere. Oh... it was like a bee hive with people runnin' 'round doin' things. Back home, Preacher Courtoy always said that folks make a mighty big noise livin life. It made me wonder if California folks would be so loud like that, too.

Mama and me went into the general store. Lizzie, being the oldest, had to stay with the wagon and take care of May Belle, Camilla, and our new baby brother, Ferney C. – who we been callin' Brother. My older brother, Jesse, went off with Papa. I had just turned nine and was glad I was old enough to go to the store and young enough not to have to watch a newborn baby like poor ol' Lizzie did. Lizzie's twelve, and Mama lost two baby boys in between me and her. Mama always says nine is plenty old enough to be looking after Brother, but she says I'm too scatterbrained. Says she can't trust me, but I just get excited about things and tend to lose track'a time and what I'm supposed to be doin'. I don't know why I'm like that. I just am.

About a month before we left Knoxville, Mama sent me to the garden to pick a mess of turnip greens, but the sun was bearin' down on me, so I stopped by the creek to cool off first, and there was a heap of minnows. The water was so soothin' on my feet, and I watched the minnows and lil' ol' tadpoles play around my toes too long. Them turnips was wiltin' in the heat, time I got out there and got 'em picked. I remember Mama got real, extra mad that day and said I wasn't worth my salt. Fussed at me a extra long time and finally told me I weren't fit to feed. I guess it scraped my feelins a mite. But I reckon maybe I'm not fit.

I don't know why, but when I go down yonder to the creek, I get too excited. I see wondrous things there in the cool shade. Papa says there's a heap of nice things to see if you just get quiet and take a look. I lie down in the soft grass by the creek and look at the world. I see the clouds and the blue sky and the trees swayin' around me. I smell flowers bloomin' if it's warm outside. Sometimes, I sing, but mostly, I'm quiet and just seein'. Ever now and then, a dragonfly will light on my fingers, and I can bring him close for a good look.

I found a nice little green snake one time. I played with him for the longest time, 'fore I turned him loose to go on his way. I love to watch them brown lizards that change colors and stretch out their throats, too. Looks like they got a little sunset right there under their necks. I'm just inclined to see where they're goin' or what they're up to. I reckon they might be using their throats to send signals to each other. They move their bodies up and down, too. Might be signaling to some gal lizard nearby or something. Maybe that's how they talk to each other. Papa says that's so.

I sometimes wonder if Mama ever saw the prettiness in the world when she was little. Maybe not. She come from Georgia and had to pick a heap a cotton. She said them cotton boles tore up her hands. I reckon there weren't no creek and grass and trees nearby for her to watch critters. She don't understand how I get so taken when I get to watchin' creatures and such and forget about my chores. But I don't rightly think that means my brains are scattered. I think it's plain ol' forgettin'and gettin' tangled up in time. I sure hope they have some creeks and little critters to watch when we get to California.

Well… after we got inside the general store, Mama made me stick right by her with my hands in my pockets. Told me not to touch nothin'. She weren't just aggravated with me, though. She was already a mite peeved. That man at the stables like to'a give us a half lame ox. Whoo-wee. She made Papa go right back over there and fix that sitcheration. Said we'd a'been in a fix sure enough with a ol' ox that quit on us halfway to California. I think she was likely right about that.

Oh, but how I itched to take my hands outta my pockets. The Independence store had so many more things than our store back in Knoxville, so I'm sure I would'a had to touch somethin' if my hands was set loose. I was purely struck dumb by the things they had there. I saw a mighty fine lookin' silver harmonica I wished I could get for my brother, Jesse. Uncle Augustus showed him how to play, and he learned to make some good music, but he don't have his own harmonica. I saw some right nice marbles me and May Belle could'a rolled and played with. It was fun to look, but we didn't get any of the good things.

Mama warned me not to ask for nothin. Said we could only get what we just couldn't do without, like sacks of flour, bacon, lard, sugar, and coffee. She paid for the seed corn Papa wanted, too, but we had to go back and pick that up from the feed store when Papa got back. Mama didn't like that one bit. When we was in that store, I could hear her grumblin' about it, real low-like. Her teeth stayed tight together when she was sayin'… 'that seed was one of them things that could'a waited, Fern.' And sayin'… 'leavin' too late in the season, Fern.' Ferney – that was Papa – had took Jesse, and they went after other things I reckon we needed for the journey. No matter. I didn't have to have them play-purtys. I was just excited to see whatever I could see in Independence and the lands ahead of us. To me, the world seemed such a big and wondrous thing to be in then. I learnt that word from Pastor Courtoy. He read to us from the Psalms n' said, "...tell of all His wondrous works." That's what I'm tellin' I saw – a bright, shiny, wondrous world.

I did enjoy the lookin' around, but I was right anxious to get goin' on the rest of our adventure, and when we got all the things we needed, and money was 'bout runnin' out, Papa pulled our wagon behind some others waitin' at the end of town. Him and Jesse finished working on the top covering our wagon. It didn't look as nice as some of the other wagons, but Mama said it was passable. It would do.

We was the fourth in a line, soon to be twelve wagons. Papa said fourth was a good spot cause if it was rough going up ahead, we would know it in time to take it slower or dodge some extra problem.

We would shortly be crossin' the plains, and Uncle Augustus told us it was mostly flat land far as the eye could see with a few scattered hills and mountains far off. He'd already crossed and tried his luck at gold minin'. Told us that backbreakin' work weren't worth the piddlin' nuggets he found. He come back two years before we left and sold his stake to Papa. It took what Papa had saved up, plus two years' crops and helpin' other folks harvest theirs, to get the money to go. Papa didn't care, though. Simon Cooper come back a sight richer, and Papa heard where a passel of other fellers was gettin' rich too. He told Mama he reckoned Uncle Augustus didn't work it hard enough. Said him and Jesse was fixin to dig day and night, and we was fixin' to get rich minin' for gold.

I heard the wagon master, Mr. Purcell, tell Papa he heard about a better trail to get to California. Said he was gonna cut due west at Fort Bent and get us there quicker. I hoped it wouldn't be too quick. I wanted all the adventures that ever day might be fixin to bring.

Mama got things all settled in the wagon how she wanted, and it was right quick after that when the other wagons joined up, and we headed out. It was early in the morning and just broke daylight. Oh, how excitin' it was. I picked a spot up where I could look out the front. I could see Ursula wavin' at me from the back of her Papa's wagon. Her two little sisters sat beside her. They all had the prettiest, white-lookin' hair, and I wished my red hair looked like theirs cause Mama said my hair was a rat's nest.

Me and Ursula had played with little stones we found while we waited for the rest of the wagons to line up. We lined up our bigger rocks to be wagons and put little pebbles around to be people. Ursula always sang or hummed little songs that I didn't know. Papa said their family came from some faraway place across the ocean that was called Norway. None of them could speak English very good, but they was friendly, and Ursula's mama had given me a sweet biscuit before we loaded up. I hid it in my pocket til me and May Belle moved to the back of the wagon, where we nibbled on it real slow to make it last. Camilla was asleep, but she was too little to eat biscuits anyway. She couldn't even walk yet, and the way her foot twisted in, Mama said she might never.

We rode near 'bout all day. Ever now and then, some young folks would get out of their wagons and walk for a spell. Mama let me get out once to walk with Ursula, but we tired out directly, and Mama got right vexed trying to help me back into the wagon.

Mama had cooked up some meat and bread before we left Independence, so she gave us all some pan bread with bacon for our dinner cause Mr. Purcell said we wasn't stoppin' till he found a good spot and decided to stop us. He said that would be right close to suppertime. It was gettin' on to sundown when he finally quit us for the night. The wagons circled 'round, and the families started sortin' things and gettin' their meals ready and their animals fed. The children played close by, but me and Ursula slipped out underneath our wagon. We went and picked some flowers and laid down in the high grass where no one could spot us. I was teachin' Ursula how to say things in our language, usin' finger people to show "walk," "run," "jump." We would start laughin' when she tried to say the words. I could tell she was learnin', though. I was, too, cause we traded her words and mine. Like one, two, three… en, to, tre. It made me happy to have a friend and learn words, too.

Come nightfall, we went to our wagons. I was right bored and, I reckon, fidgety, but I steered clear of Mama. Campfires was burnin', and grown folks seemed to be mighty busy. Mama kept movin' things inside the wagon while Lizzie helped cook. Seemed like Mama weren't able to make up her mind on how to keep things sorted in the wagon. I wanted to ask her something, but I saw her jaw set tight, so I crawled under the wagon and sat alone outside the circle. The night was so black, but I was never afeard of the dark like Lizzie. I could hear folks talkin' with the words all runnin' together, so it sounded somethin' like a long hummin'. It was kind'a soothin'.

I could smell the stew Lizzie, or somebody was cookin', and I was hungry, but earlier, Papa and Mama had got purely aggravated with me talkin' too much again, so I stayed sittin' in my little sliver of darkness. I felt like I was seein' the whole world before me. My world. It seemed right magical, and I felt like them stars was callin' out to me. I wished I could be a star right up there with 'em in the night sky lookin' down on the world. I slipped off to sleep there against the wagon wheel and woke to Papa yankin' me up off the ground, smackin' my bottom, and shovin' me into the wagon. I reckon I scared 'em, but I didn't mean to do it. I didn't get to eat. Still, gettin' sent to bed was better than gettin' sent to the outhouse back home.

Seemed to me like it was quick gettin' to Fort Bent, and nobody had too many problems along the way. At the fort, some folks repaired things or, traded animals, or re-supplied, but Mama just got some more flour, and Papa refilled our water barrels. We was at the fort for a day, and a man there told some of the folks it weren't a good idea to go that trail Mr Purcell spoke of. In the end, the wagon train stayed together goin' the wagon master's way.

After a short time at the fort, we was traveling again. I don't know how many days passed, but it was a good many. We bounced along with the wagon, sometimes jerkin' real bad, for we had done run outta good trail long ago. When the wagon jerked like that, Brother would wake up hollerin'. He never seemed to get used to it. Poor Lizzie.

We was travelin' a heap slower on that new trail, but I didn't mind cause when we quit for the day, I had time to play with Ursula and May Belle. One night, I heard Papa and some other men complainin' about not usin' the other trail. Mr. Forrester in the lead wagon was right put out for having to clear some rattlesnakes for the oxen to get through a tight spot at one place. Some of the other men run up there to help, but Mr. Forrester was vexed all the same. Papa said he fussed about it half the night, but the next day, we went right on the way the wagon master wanted to go. I reckon it was too late to turn back.

Sometimes folks would get out of the wagons and walk for a spell cause it was rough ridin', but Mama never did that. She worried about the snakes and said she was stayin' inside.

A day or two later, she got a mite sick, and Papa had to pull aside and let the others pass. Mrs. Taggert and her family was behind us, and she offered to stay and help, but Papa told her to go on. Finally, Mama felt better, and we caught up and fell back in line just before dark, but stoppin' made us last. I couldn't wave to Ursula no more, but we could still sit and play a little when we circled. I wished we could go back to being behind her wagon, but Papa said no because Mama was havin' her headache spells, and we was mighty likely to stop for her again.

We traveled on, and some days went smooth, and some days was hard. We just had to get through them hard ones. It was hot in the daytime and cold at night. We come real close to runnin' outta water. Mr. Purcell had told everbody that there was a waterin' hole close, but we hadn't found it the day he said we would. Papa was gettin' terrible mad about that and said he was fixin' to get fired up like they ain't never seen in all creation. It was plain lucky we hit a big stream the next afternoon cause Papa could get real fierce when he was put out with folks.

The men folks had a big talk the night we camped by that stream. Children weren't allowed to listen in, but me and Ursula snuck up right close by. I told her how that wagon master was tellin' 'em they was not as likely to run into Indians on his trail. Said he went the side trail three times, and it was just as good and faster, and Indians was lookin' for folks on that other path.

Mama was gettin' weary of the trip. She cried a heap a'times and had terrible headaches. Lizzie was mostly cookin' and takin' care of Brother. I felt right sorry for her and tried to help when she'd let me. I fetched water a good bit.

The days rolled on, and I reckon you could say our

wheels rolled on, too. One hot day after another. Seemed like there weren't no breezes like in Knoxville, just hot wind. I could see the little children was gettin' a mite weary like Mama, and I would sit in back and hold Camilla and put my arm around May Belle and sing little songs to them, and we'd rattle on. After while, the day would begin to be gone, and we would circle for the night and do all the same things again the next day.

It always got hot shortly after daylight. When we come across water, it always felt special. Sometimes, we had to ford a shallow stream or a sliver of a river. That gave us time to get out and dawdle so we could cool off and wash down a little. Every now and then, somebody's wagon would need work, or a wheel would break. One time, when we was still fourth in line, Ursula's Papa's water barrel broke loose and tangled up between our oxen. Everyone had to stop when somethin' went wrong. But the children got a chance to stretch their legs or play a little if they didn't have to fetch things.

The days began to bore down on everbody – even me. I was gettin' tired of the trip, but I was still excited about gettin' to Papa's gold mine in California. One night, just me and Papa was sittin' by our fire. Papa was combing the dust out of my hair. He leaned down by my ear and whispered to me that when he struck gold, Mama would be happier about leavin' her Ma and sister in Knoxville. He squeezed my hand and told me to be patient and help Lizzie. I promised him I would.

The weather had got blazin' hot and terrible dry. Worse than I ever knew before. The wagons rollin' before us whipped up dust everywhere. Papa and Jesse sitting up front drivin' the oxen had to wear kerchiefs over their faces, and Mama closed the front of our wagon with a blanket.

After Fort Bent, Mama stayed mad at Papa near 'bout all the time, and seem like the weather made it worse. Brother was cryin' a mighty lot, too, and Lizzie still had to take care of him. Came a time I couldn't seem to stay off Mama's nerves, then she'd fuss at Papa, and he would fuss at me or punish me. I think it was hard because there weren't much room to move in the wagon. I couldn't understand how Ursula's mama was always singin' or hummin' songs, but Ursula said she did. Papa used to say that Mama was havin' a bad day, but I told him it seemed like every day was a bad day for Mama. He scolded me right smart for that.

I don't rightly know what I did, but finally, somehow, I got on Mama's last remainin' nerve, and she screamed at Papa. It all happened mighty fast, and Papa yelled back and told me to walk by the wagon for a spell. I had to climb out the back in a hurry. Papa slowed down, but we couldn't stop, or the oxen would try to quit on him. Real quick, I grabbed my bonnet but couldn't find my brogans.

The ground was stickery with dried-up little plants here and yonder and hot as fire. It hurt my feet bad, and even the tears on my face was burnin', but I stayed quiet. I stayed patient. The sun beat down on my bonnet and on my back, and the dust just kept on comin' at me. After about an hour, as the sun told, I could feel dust fillin' my insides. I started to fall behind. I couldn't catch up. I couldn't call out. My mouth was too dry and full of dirt, and words wouldn't come out. It hurt to breathe. I looked down at my dress. It was all dusted brown – the color of the sand. I couldn't see the faded flowers anymore. Then I fell behind. I told myself to hurry, but my feet failed to move faster. They finally quit on me. The last thing I remember before I fell out that day is seein' Papa's hands holdin' the reins as the wagon turned just a mite toward the west. Then I sat down in the hot sand. I'm of a mind to think Papa forgot I was walkin'. I don't know how far they got before they come back. I just know it was too late. I watched as they buried me out here in this hot land with the sun bearin' down. I tried to tug on Papa's shirt and hollered, "Here I am," but Papa couldn't hear me. I don't know what territory this is, but... I still walk this parched ground in my faded dress and bonnet with the sun bearin' down.

- the end -

11

SHADOW OF DEATH

L eslie adjusted her seatbelt and backed the silver
Mercedes from the parking space. The sun had taken
on a slight orange hue to signal its beginning descent. The
still shining brightness reflected off the hood as she wheeled
the car around the large circular drive. She grabbed her
sunglasses from the console and, as an afterthought, tugged
at eight-year-old Pamela's seatbelt.

"Mum!" Pamela pushed her hand away. "I know how to do
it! I'm not a baby anymore, ya know." The girl, properly
annoyed, brusquely adjusted the book on her lap.

"I know, Darling. Well done. Indeed! You're quite the big
girl now." Leslie sighed. "I'm just checking. That's mum's job,
my love."

She brought the car to a stop where the driveway
intersected with County Road 423. Cautiously, Leslie turned
south to connect with the main highway that would take
them back to her sister's home in Pine Meadows. Giant oaks
quickly obscured the low-lying brick buildings of the
Palmetto Woods Convalescent Village.

"I know you're a bit impatient, Pammy. You'd rather be with your friends... but because you *are* such a big girl, Mummy expects you to understand why we must visit your grandmother. You mustn't be so grumpy about visiting."

Pamela frowned and twitched uncomfortably in her seat. "Well, I *don't* like that place, and I *don't* like Nan's doctors."

"Now, Pamela... why would you say that? Dr. Becker is quite nice. In fact... I don't think you've actually been there when he was in with your Nan... He's the only doctor she has. And David... the tall one who takes care of Nan... he's a nurse, Darling... Not a doctor."

"No, Mum." The child sighed loudly. "Nan's *other* doctor. The one who always wears a suit. The one who's different. You know who I mean. The one who went in Nan's room after."

"Pamela... there was no doctor today. Only David."

"Oh, Mum! Yes. There. Was!"

The girl sighed dramatically again and displayed her exasperation by hitting the book with her fist five times to match the beat of her words.

"He had a gray suit like Daddy's."

Leslie took a deep breath but held her tongue. She felt tired.

"And black hair. He looks like Mr. Shing... my tutor back in London, ya know? But with a scary face. Mr. Shing has a nice, smiling face. I saw that man down the hall last time and the time before. He goes to other rooms, too, and he came into Nan's room just when we were leaving. You saw him. You looked right at him. And he watches us, Mum... he always watches, and I don't like that."

"Alright. *That* man. I think I know who you mean. I don't think he was a doctor, though," Leslie said. "I'm not sure. I don't remember him working with your grandmother, but he did go into her room, didn't he? Now I'm wondering why. Well... I'm just going to have to check on that. He's certainly not Nan's doctor. Perhaps he's a priest. No. Maybe pastor. I'm not sure, *really*, who he is. So many people coming and going all the time. I'm not sure. But truly Pammy... the point is, Darling... we must visit your grandmother. And, I don't like to, but I shall remind you once again... I do not like your attitude, nor do I care for your use of language. We don't say, 'ya know.' Understand?"

The child breathed another exaggerated sigh as her mother slowed the car for a pickup truck approaching an intersection ahead. When she was clear of the truck, Leslie glanced at her watch.

"We must work on that," Leslie continued reminding her daughter. "And... you *shall* visit your grandmother. I think you understand how important it is to visit Nan, don't you, Darling? Nan may not be with us much longer. We've spoken about this. The doctor says that the angels will come for her soon."

"And then shall we go back to England, Mum? Or must we stay on? I'm tired of staying in Auntie Delia's house. She's quite cranky, ya...you know. And I don't think she likes children very much. And I miss Pru and Vanessa. I have no one in America for sleepovers. Leah's mum always says no to sleeping away. It's not fair. I don't want to be here."

"Pamela Jean... you mustn't be so selfish," Leslie scolded.

Mother and daughter were silent for a long moment, and then Leslie gently stroked Pamela's arm.

"You remember when Nan was well? Back in London? You two had such lovely tea parties with your dollies. Nan dressed you in silly hats from her big trunk, and you laughed so much. Remember? You had such great fun. It was grand.

So... So, you must think of Nan for now. You must be patient. You do love your Nan... surely?"

"Yes," Pamela sounded contrite. "I do love her... but Mum, she doesn't even speak to us anymore. And it's quite awful to see all those tubes and things sticking from her arms. And her mouth. It's not nice. I don't like that place. It smells yucky."

Leslie cringed at the slang, but it wasn't the time for more corrections.

"I know. It isn't terribly pleasant. But I think... I hope... that your grandmother knows we're there. That's important. And your auntie and I try to share visits so that Nan sees us often. So she doesn't have to be alone there. She needs us, Pamela. I don't insist you come too often, but you must visit sometimes. And someday, I think you shall be glad that you did visit her."

"Nan should have proper stayed in London, and she wouldn't be sick now. That would be brilliant." Pamela's tone was softer now.

"Well, Darling, that's not true. Nan could have just as easily had a stroke back home. She wanted to visit your auntie. No one knew this would happen."

"When are the angels going to come for her, Mum?"

"Soon, I'm afraid. Too soon."

"I don't want the angels to take me away, Mum!" The child's voice was suddenly urgent. "They can do that. I don't like those angels. I want to go back to England, and if the angels come for Nan, they may try to take me too!" She riffled the pages of her book, then snapped it shut.

"No. My Darling! No... You're just a little girl. You shall grow up and live a long, long time. Just like Nan. The angels don't want to take little girls. And we'll be going back to London before you know it. Daddy is only an adjunct professor at the university here. He's only here for the summer term. When this term is finished, we'll return home. So don't worry... you'll see."

"Even if Nan keeps sleeping?"

"I... well, I'm not sure. Perhaps I may stay on for a while. For Nan. And perhaps you and Daddy might return. Daddy must return to the university there for the fall term. She patted Pamela's knee and tapped the cover of the book.

"Let's think about something else, shall we? What sort of trouble is Ramona getting into now?"

Pamela described her heroine's latest adventure and soon became engrossed again in the book.

Leslie followed Highway 423 for a couple more miles. The road wound through the retirement community of Willow Hills and connected with State Road 62 in the center of town. She pulled the Mercedes into the right turn lane at the traffic light and waited. When the traffic had cleared, Leslie turned onto Main Street and glanced again at her watch.

"Four-fifteen," she said. "We're running a bit late, I'm afraid."

"Uh, huh," Pamela whispered and continued reading.

Mentally, Leslie began to tick off upcoming points to finish her day: Another hour back to Pine Meadows. No matter... if traffic flows smoothly, I shall have the steaks on and a nice gin and tonic waiting for Neville when he arrives. And for Delia, of course. Brilliant timing if all goes well.

Leslie crossed the tracks, turned again, west this time onto 62, and after two more traffic lights, she was out of Willow Hills.

The long drive home on this road was something Leslie dreaded. She wished her sister had chosen a facility closer to the town where she lived, but Delia had insisted on "the best." Leslie found it odd, however, that Delia had called visiting a chore but had decided to move their mother farther away to Palmetto Woods. She did that only after learning that Neville's job would bring Leslie's family nearby. Leslie suspected it was a convenient excuse to make it *inconvenient* to travel to the nursing home and, therefore, require more visits from Leslie. It was suspect, too, because Delia immediately began to work longer hours and could no longer manage even semi-regular visits to the nursing home. She deftly delivered up the "chore" to Leslie. Delia's visits dwindled to once each week. The whole thing became a rather obvious plan in Leslie's mind. Though Leslie actually wanted to spend the time with her mother, she knew Delia could have kept her in a nearby facility with the same result. Her sister's decision had cost time better spent with her mother and much more difficult travel.

Highway 62 was well known as a grueling drive to its frequent travelers. Leslie hated it. It was fifty miles of heavily traveled two-lane highway – the only direct route back to Delia's home in Pine Meadows. In addition, it was primarily a cross-state truck route with a generous sprinkling of elderly drivers from several retirement communities. The mix made it a potentially hazardous drive. During her many trips, Leslie had seen several accidents on the two-lane. It made her extra cautious, and she passed other vehicles only with the greatest care.

Leslie was always cautious. It was just her nature. Certainly, it had taken time to adjust to driving on the "wrong" side of the road in America, and she paid more attention, but still, she tried not to overthink the traffic issue. When she felt her death grip on the wheel, she eased up the tension and stretched her fingers. Leslie purposely allowed some of her focus to go toward the scenery surrounding her.

The countryside was beautiful. There were rolling hills, lakes, and trees. With a gap in traffic, she took the time to notice.

It's lovely, she thought, *to see that not everything in America has become concrete, fast food and convenience stores.*

"Can I have some chewing gum, Mummy?" Pamela interrupted Leslie's thoughts.

"May I. May I, Pamela, and no. Not in the car. You remember, Darling, what happened last time? We'll be at your auntie's very soon now. You can read or look out the window. It's really quite lovely."

The child glanced out her window for mere seconds and, with another of her deep sighs and exaggerated sarcasm, said, "It's only trees and cows, Mum. Trees and cows. I don't fancy looking at trees and cows, thank you. It's quite boring! Boring. Boring."

Leslie glanced sideways at the child to disapprove with a look rather than words. Pamela, however, had already returned to her book.

She decided to let it slide as she had done so often lately, but she worried. If children spoke this way in 1985, Leslie wondered, what on earth would it be like when Pamela had her own children in the next fifteen years or so? Awful, she was quite sure. It seemed best, however, to let it pass without comment once more. She'd been correcting the girl too much lately. Pamela had begun to close her ears to much of her mother's attempts to correct the impudent behavior. If the corrections were perceived as nagging and continued, Leslie felt it would eventually drive a wedge between her and her daughter.

Over the last two months, Leslie had become increasingly anxious to return home to London. Part of the anxiety she knew came from the issues with Pamela. It seemed as if the child was becoming more American than British. It was happening quickly. The children surrounding her were decidedly arrogant and endowed with sarcastic little mouths – and these were the eight-year-olds. It was all rather frightful. Leslie was quite aware that Pamela was catching on all too quickly. She'd have to talk to Neville about the problem again, and she dreaded that because lately, it seemed that her husband had been tuning her out as well. Leslie knew the truth. They all felt the strain of their living situation.

Her sister, Delia, was difficult even in the best of times. Now, Leslie felt that her family's invasion of Delia's home was becoming a territorial issue. The university had offered Neville an apartment for the summer, but Delia absolutely insisted they stay with her. Leslie believed that her sister had truly wanted that at first, but the living arrangement was wearing thin for all of them. Delia had many rules, some of which remained unspoken until the rule was broken. As a result, Leslie felt compelled to restrict Pamela much more than usual inside the house and allow her to be outside with her American friends more often.

Leslie experienced more anxiety due to her mother's stroke. Her mental capacity and bodily functions had deteriorated, and the doctors gave no hope for recovery. Leslie recognized that these issues frequently occupied her mind, but something else also bothered her. It was something that she couldn't name. It was a generalized anxiety that caused her heart to race and made her feel she should run – but from what Leslie did not know. She felt an ever-growing need to suppress that last thing, which was ironic since she knew not what it was.

As they continued the drive on Highway 62, Leslie turned the radio on low volume to a classic station. A soothing piece she recognized as Mozart began to push the stressful thoughts slowly into the background of her mind.

For the first few miles, the traffic on 62 flowed reasonably well. The rhythmic humming of tires against pavement combined with the music was relaxing, but the sun's constant glare kept Leslie from succumbing to the otherwise hypnotic blend of sounds.

Soon, the mix of cars and trucks on the highway became thicker. Leslie checked her watch, sighed, and accepted the fact that she probably wouldn't make it in time for Neville after all. She abandoned the music in her mind and returned to the thoughts of her sister. Delia would undoubtedly be irritated when she came home from work and found that she'd have to start the dinner.

Only a couple more months, Leslie reminded herself. *Still, we should have taken the apartment the university offered.* She'd worried from the start and resisted, but Delia had been so persistent. Leslie knew Delia would have reminded her of the "offense" for years to come if they had chosen the apartment.

Though she had never been able to stand up against the stronger will of her sister, Leslie did see some merit in sharing quarters. The more Delia spoke of it, the more the idea had begun to jell. There would be hours of sister time, she said – time to catch up after so many years apart. Delia's home was geographically superior, too. The apartment would have made the drive to the nursing home an hour longer. Delia also had three extra bedrooms in her huge house, where she lived with only her little cocker spaniel. The probability that Delia would have taken it as a slap in the face if they'd refused the offer pushed the decision over the line. In retrospect, Leslie decided it would have been better all-round if they'd taken the apartment. Her sister was too set in her ways to give way to others in her home. When Leslie thought back to their teen years, she realized that Delia was, at that time, *already* set in her ways and quite stubborn about her wants and needs.

"Just let it go, Leslie," she whispered. "It will be just a while longer now, just a short while."

The traffic slowed, and Leslie approached two cars. Directly in front of them was a large truck stacked with logs. On a slight uphill grade, the truck was trying to pass another vehicle, traveling well under the speed limit. The semi finally made it past the slow vehicle, but the effort produced violent puffs of black smoke from the exhaust pipe on top. A row of four oncoming cars whizzed past just as the truck pulled back into the safety of his westbound lane. Leslie gasped at the sight of such a close call. She backed off the gas even though the dangerous event had expired.

With the massive, oncoming traffic, it was nearly ten more minutes before Leslie was able to pass the slow car. As she passed, she saw that it was driven by an elderly woman, hunched up to the steering wheel and barely able to see over it. Once past that obstacle, Leslie increased her speed again. She hoped she could regain some of the lost time. Finally settling on 65 miles per hour, Leslie soon closed the distance between herself and the cars ahead while quickly pulling away from the elderly lady.

Leslie's thoughts turned once again to her mother. Back in London, her mother lived close enough to visit several times each week and have tea or dinner with the family. Leslie always enjoyed the visits. She also spent a month with Delia in the United States once a year. This time, the visit was short. Her mother had a stroke two days after she landed. Now, her eighty-year-old mother was dying by inches before Leslie and Delia's eyes.

Leslie knew that her mother was close to death. At first, she was conscious but couldn't speak, and then she went in and out of consciousness. Now, she couldn't even respond by squeezing Leslie's fingers. She wished that Delia had not insisted on the feeding tube. The doctors said that would only prolong the obvious, but Delia couldn't bear to think of her mother lying there hungry. Leslie, however, wasn't sure her mother could even feel hunger. She truly believed that her mother would prefer that her life not be extended in that way, but they'd never discussed it while her mother could. Now, there seemed no quality to her life and no kindness in prolonging the inevitable, but as usual, Delia won that argument. Leslie had just never considered that it could end in such a way.

Leslie drove on, and thoughts drove her. *Why mother? Why someone so outgoing and vibrant? Even now, it simply doesn't seem possible. Death should be swift and merciful.*

Leslie's eyes turned to Pamela. The girl had fallen asleep, and her head was oddly tilted. After an extra glance at the traffic ahead, she gently pushed her daughter slightly to the right so the child's head leaned against the door panel. Then, when she seemed to be at a more comfortable angle, Leslie turned her full attention back to the road. Like the glare from the sun, the oncoming vehicles were relentless. The traffic heading westbound along with her was still heavy but moving along at a good clip. She glanced into her rearview mirror and saw the lead car behind her running with headlights on. She figured it to be more than half a kilometer back. She glanced at her watch again. It was four forty-seven. *With luck, I might still make it,* she thought.

Rather than soothing, the music suddenly became much more of the frenetic and somehow threatening type. Leslie turned the radio off. She glanced out the window and tried not to think of her mother for a few minutes. Instead, she focused on the beautiful countryside. In this area, it was marred only by the occasional convenience store, upon which Americans seemed so utterly dependent – so many more than in England. *Do they think convenience is everything?* She pondered that point and, ultimately, decided it was true. Americans seemed to hurry, hurry, hurry.

Off to her right, Leslie saw a chestnut pony prance and jump behind its majestic mother in a rolling pasture. It presented such an ideal image of a carefree life. She supposed only animals led such lives, free from worry and hardship – and mostly pain-free. She rechecked her rearview mirror just in time to see a small car pass the headlight-bearing vehicle. They were still, easily, a half-kilometer behind her. She reached out and brushed stray hairs away from Pamela's face, and as she brought her hand back to the wheel, a sudden red movement in the rearview mirror caught her eye. The same car that only seconds before had been far behind had closed in on her so quickly and so closely that its front end was entirely obscured by the back of her own car.

Leslie was startled.

"My God!" she said to the unhearing driver. "Back away! Can't you see it's impossible to pass? Why drive right up to the boot of my car that way?"

Leslie accelerated another four miles per hour.

The car, a Porsche, duplicated her increased speed.

So close was the bright red Porsche that the passengers almost appeared to be in her back seat. Leslie could clearly see the two men in the car. The driver appeared to be late middle-aged and had a pasty, white face with small eyes encased in puffy flesh. He wore a flashy, Hawaiian-style shirt. His companion was a dark fellow with narrow, slanted eyes. He appeared to be in a suit and tie. She managed only quick backward glimpses, but their close proximity made them easy to see. The dark one, she realized, was the same man who had entered her mother's room just as they were leaving. The one Pamela thought was a doctor – the one she didn't like. Leslie's glance continued to alternate rapidly from the congested road ahead to the passengers in the Porsche behind her. The man from the nursing home sat mute and seemed unconcerned with the driver's recklessness.

The Porsche driver pulled his vehicle out several times, crossing into the opposite lane and attempting a pass, but opposing traffic forced him to return to his position behind Leslie. She began to back off the gas, and finally, the man managed to get around the Mercedes in between a barrage of oncoming cars. She slowed even more and watched in amazement as he pulled up quite close behind the next vehicle in the same foolhardy fashion.

"He's mad," she whispered. "Absolutely gone 'round the bend."

The driver of the Porsche continued haphazardly. He passed the next car and the next, as they also backed off to allow the crazed driver to pass. That process continued as far as Leslie could see. Then, a large box truck pulled out from a side road. That put her fourth behind it, with three cars ahead of her. The truck caused every car behind it to slow down, and it blocked her view of the erratic Porsche. Two of the vehicles in front of her managed to pass the slower truck, so being closer to the boxy vehicle obstructed her view of the traffic ahead even more.

Leslie checked her watch and sighed. "Positively no chance we're going to be able to make up time."

Her thoughts turned to her mother and Delia's feeding

tube decision. Leslie suddenly felt so physically tired. It was as if she had the wind knocked out of her. In a snap, it drained her, and it made no sense. "Persevere, Leslie," she whispered. "Persevere." She wiggled in her seat and stretched her fingers against the wheel, tying to fight the weariness.

Within a few minutes, the traffic began to slow down and quickly stack up, moving by a few feet at a time. From behind the box truck, Leslie saw huge gulfs of black smoke billowing up just before the next hilly rise.

That's strange, she thought. *It looks like the smoke is coming from the middle of the road. That can't be... must be a brush fire on a curve ahead.*

"I can't see from where... Optical illusion?" Leslie whispered. "Quite odd."

The traffic continued to move at a snail's pace, and finally, all the cars ahead came to a standstill. The oncoming traffic had also stopped, and Leslie realized the fire *must be* in the middle of the road.

All around her, people began getting out of their cars and walking toward the inferno. Pamela was still sleeping, so Leslie pulled her car a few feet closer to the truck for shade against the sinking sun. She opened the windows a few inches and stepped out of the car and into the eastbound lane for a better look. Her eyes watered, and she shielded them with her hands against the relentless sun. It was directly in her line of sight on the western horizon. Even with her dark sunglasses, it was still difficult to see what lay ahead. Leslie looked back at her sleeping daughter. She locked the car and joined several people approaching from behind and heading toward the fire.

"Was it that Porsche?" a young woman asked.

"Fool flew by me like a bat outta hell," said a young bearded man with a thick southern drawl. "Bet he's D.O.A."

"Musta been doin' ninety… ninety-five, easy."

"More'n that when he passed me." Said another. "Hunnert… hunnert five more like it."

"One helluva fire," said an older gentleman.

"Was it the Porsche, then?" asked Leslie. "I hope they were able to get out of the car."

The group of strangers began walking more quickly toward the burning mass about a dozen vehicles ahead. Leslie looked back to her car. There was no movement from Pamela, so she walked with the group.

"Likely dead. I ain't sure… can't tell," said the man. "Dang, sun… sittin just right to blind ya. Whoever it was, must'a hit that truck."

He pointed toward an area thirty feet off to the side of the eastbound lane where a large furniture delivery truck had come to rest leaning against a tree. Leslie hadn't noticed that truck because many vehicles had pulled off the eastbound roadway to avoid the crash and fire. The scene resembled a slightly jumbled parking lot with a half dozen people milling around the damaged truck and a dazed-looking young man sitting on the ground. An older woman knelt beside him and appeared to be checking his condition. Leslie figured she likely had some medical expertise.

"Man! It knocked him for a loop! Yeah. Oh, man! Look at that! Damn! Impact knocked the wheels right out from under that truck!" He pointed again to the shoulder of the road but closer to the burning car. Leslie saw the two huge truck wheels still attached to the axle.

Other walkers commented as they walked on, but Leslie listened mostly to the observant man pointing out details.

As they got closer to the fire, the man continued. "Yep… it's that Porsche, awright. Reckon that guy ain't gonna be in no flat-out hurry no more. Sure was a purty car, though. Oh!

Look," he said. Looks like that's him lying next to his car there. Must'a tried to get out or else fell out the door. He ain't goin' nowhere fast no more. He done got wherever he was goin'."

Leslie sucked in a breath as she recognized the now-darkened Hawaiian shirt on the form lying beside the inferno.

She was amid an ever-enlarging crowd, and something nagged at Leslie's mind as she listened to the comments of those around her.

"Ain't anybody gonna try to pull him outta that fire?"

"Too hot. Those guys over there tried at first. Couldn't do it. See that one guy? Right over there. Looks like he got him a burned arm for his efforts. Already dead anyways. Weren't no use."

"Some guy went to call for help."

"Did you see him when he almost hit the beer truck?"

"Yeah, pulled right out on the guy. Unbelievable. Truck driver was damn lucky. Swerved that truck and got it back under control. Crazy, man."

"We're gonna be here awhile. Whole dang road's blocked... both ways."

"That guy was looking to die. No two ways about it. You don't drive like that looking to live."

"Some nurse is over there with the truck driver. He's okay... maybe in shock. Shook up real bad for sure."

Leslie listened to the ongoing conversations and suddenly realized what was bothering her – the passenger. *He must still be in the burning car. Could he possibly still be alive? Probably not, but...*

"Where's the other man? The passenger," Leslie asked.

"There was only one guy," said the young woman who'd walked toward the crash site beside her.

"No," said Leslie. "No. There were two... the man in the suit... the Porsche was right up on my bumper. I saw him very clearly. He *must* still be in the car."

"If there were two, there's none now," another man said.

"I only saw one. Yeah... there was only one. For sure," an older man said.

"Can't we do something?" Leslie pleaded. "Something? I mean... surely someone should at least try to get the other man out?"

"There ain't no other man, Ma'am." someone said.

"That car could blow, Lady," another added. "Guy with a fire extinguisher, tried. Useless on that inferno. Nothing we can do but wait for the fire department."

An older woman chimed in, "And you're mistaken about a second man in that car. He was on my bumper, too. Stayed there cause he couldn't get a clear opening to get around me... so he was tight behind me for a while. There was no other person in the car."

"She's right, Ma'am. I got a good look when he passed me, too. I even gave him the finger, and he looked right at me... the other seat was empty... nobody else in that car."

"I am sure. *Very* sure. I *saw* another man," Leslie insisted. "I think he may have been a doctor at the convalescent home in Willow Hills." Leslie's voice began to trail off as she realized the people were no longer listening. "He was there today. I saw him..."

When the fire truck and two police cars passed the line of traffic, Leslie and the others watched as the firefighters extinguished the flames. The police began motioning people back out of the way. One policeman worked his way around to the people on the westbound side of the fire.

"Move back, folks," he said. "This is a dangerous situation here. Move back, NOW... go back to your vehicles."

Leslie touched his forearm as he worked to get the crowd moving.

Officer... there was a second man in that car."

"Hey... what? How do you know that? You know him?"

"No. Officer. Nothing like that. I saw him when they passed my car.

"You sure about that, ma'am?"

"Quite sure," Leslie said, though others in the crowd continued to dispute her claim.

"Hey Jake," the officer called back to the fireman, "might be another one in the car. Can you get close to the passenger side?"

The fireman edged closer to the car as water poured onto the fire, but he couldn't get a full view through the smoke and steam. "Not sure. Don't think so..."

When the flames were finally doused, the thick, black smoke continued and hovered like a cloud over the roadway while water-diluted smoke drifted into the roadside pines. The car continued to smolder.

The firefighters poured more water onto the car until they could see clearly inside the fire-shattered window.

"Nobody else," a fireman yelled. "Empty seat. Well... looks like a burnt briefcase. Just the one DOA on the ground."

As two newly arrived ambulance attendants placed a white sheet over the body, Leslie began weaving her way slowly back through the crowd.

"Empty," she whispered. "Empty."

Leslie felt lightheaded and confused. She stumbled and bumped into the grill of a pickup truck. She leaned there for a moment and wiped the perspiration from her forehead. Taking deep breaths, Leslie struggled to make sense of what was happening. She began to walk faster as the full gravity of the situation started coming together like pieces of a puzzle. Suddenly, it all became very clear to her.

It was Death. Thoughts and sudden understanding struck Leslie hard. *He took this man in the Porsche, and he'd been there to take Mother, too. We saw him enter Mother's room just as we were leaving. Why had I not paid more attention until Pamela pointed it out and insisted that he'd been there? And he's been there before, and he must have taken others.*

Leslie could come up with no other explanation – none. She was sure she'd seen him in the car, and now the Hawaiian shirt man was dead. She was in a near run. Her mind raced too as she thought... *and none of the other witnesses saw him at all. How is that possible?*

Leslie was out of breath and perspiring when she reached her car. Pamela was just beginning to wake.

"Mummy, it's hot in here... why have we stopped?"

"We've got to go back," Leslie said flatly.

"Go back? Home? Where?"

Tears rimmed Leslie's eyes but did not overflow. "Just go back to sleep, Pamela. I've got to make a phone call."

With cold air conditioning quickly filling the car again, Pamela slipped easily back to sleep, and Leslie wheeled the car around and headed back eastbound on Highway 62.

How could this be possible? What I'm thinking is quite mad... it can't be, Leslie argued in silence. *I'm simply over-stressed, and I must be imagining all this. Or it's a dream. I'll wake up any minute.*

Leslie knew it wasn't a dream as quickly as that thought had come to her. She was grasping. Her father had told her years ago that he'd seen Death come for his own mother. Other family members disputed his claim, but her father had insisted that it was true and that he'd seen it with his own eyes. He'd remained adamant about that all his life. Whatever the case, Leslie felt sure her mother must be dead.

In ten minutes or so, she pulled into the parking lot of the Minute Mart. She left the car running, grabbed her purse, and hurried inside to get some change for the pay phone outside. The clerk was nowhere in sight. As Leslie looked around the quiet store, she became impatient.

"Hello! Please! I haven't time for this! Is someone there?" Leslie called out but got no response. She became agitated as the moments that seemed more like minutes passed.

"Anyone here?" she called again. "Please... I'm quite in a rush if you don't mind. I need some change. Please!"

After another moment, exasperated, she decided to forego the phone call and drive back to Willow Hills. Leslie had just turned around to head toward the exit when a wild-eyed man with straggly, dirty blonde hair burst through the storeroom door and grabbed her.

Leslie started to scream, but the man's filthy and bloody hand covered her mouth as he shoved her through the door from which he'd come. He threw her onto the floor, and she landed next to the bloody body of an elderly man. The name tag on his shirt, nearly obscured by blood, showed her that he was Frank, the store clerk.

After that, everything seemed to happen in slow motion. Leslie looked up and saw the man with the slanted eyes in the dark gray suit. He wore an almost imperceptible sliver of a smile on his thin lips. He stood with arms folded and legs crossed casually at the ankles. The man leaned against the wall in a rather bored-looking repose. His shiny leather shoes were so close to the dead clerk's head that he need only barely move a toe to touch the man. All this, Leslie's eyes captured in that unrealistic, slow motion. She opened her mouth to scream, but no sound came forth.

The crazed man walked in circles. He mumbled incoherently. His bloody, frantic fingers pulled at his hair while he clutched a gun. Leslie left the wild man's world. He no longer existed for her. She became completely engaged with the entity in the suit.

"I'm the collector," he said. "I've been waiting."

From somewhere close by, Leslie heard an explosion. It seemed to echo in the room. She fell backward, clutched at her chest, and raised a bloody hand toward the man in the suit.

"Mother?"

"Not today." He shook his head and held out his hand to her.

- the end -

12

I'LL BE SEEING YOU

Lucas Harnage lived alone in his cabin in the backwoods of North Florida. He had chosen to live this solitary life ever since his wife Genevieve's death. It had been thirty-three years plus a few months. After her funeral, he'd left their little bungalow just off Main Street, taking his tools, meager belongings, and a picture of his beloved Ginny. Some folks in the town of High Suwannee thought it odd that Lucas – or Luke as he was more commonly called – never felt the need to leave his place in the woods.

Some folks in town thought a man of fifty-five needed to move closer to doctors and such. Plus, a man should mingle and enjoy community, they said. Most folks shared their thoughts amongst themselves, however, and though it made no difference either way, they never gave more than a hint to Luke.

Over the years, a few people had other reasons to get him back to town. Those few were the several women who'd seen him as a good potential husband. It was well known that he'd loved and taken tender care of Genevieve during their married life. They saw that he knew how to treat a woman. Many of Luke's admirers – even some married gossips – concurred that 'a good-looking man like that should not be alone.' Luke was tall, wide-shouldered, and with his thick black hair still showing no gray and deep blue eyes, no one could deny his good looks. However, most sensible women came to recognize the die-hard recluse he'd become and gave up rather quickly.

The widow, Dulcie Haven, was different. She'd begun her quest two years before and was still going strong. She dropped off salt, flour, lard, and a healthy portion of chicken & dumplings – or some other delicious stew – whenever she decided his stores had to be getting low. Her actions were, in fact, a reason to get close to him. The groceries and treats were always more than Luke needed or wanted. He kept telling her to quit it, but she continued anyway, figuring tenacity was the key to winning him over – and she fussed with him to boot.

"Lucas Harnage, I declare! You need to eat more. Big man like you. You need some good taking-care-of. And you ain't been to church in a coons age." Dulcie always called him by his true name and assumed that set her apart from other interested parties.

Luke would deny her accusations regarding his needs and remind her, as he had many times, that he had no intention of going back to church.

"God is everywhere, Miz. Haven." Luke would say. "He's in them pines right yonder and in that ol' Suwannee River running black-red with tannins back of the property. God's in that dragonfly sitting on that dandelion right there. He's in the wind, the rain, and every little thing in this world, and them stars out yonder in space. Don't try and tell me I got to go into no building to pray. Ain't no sense in you keep telling me such."

"Oh, the things you do say, Lucas Harnage! Why, our Lord God is sitting right up yonder, far past them clouds sitting on a golden throne!"

Dulcie would laugh or giggle and prattle on and on until he'd finally hold up a hand to stop her.

"Miz Haven," he refused to call her by her first name.

"Miz Haven, here's your bowl from last time. It was mighty good, but I'm telling you... you got to quit it. Here's money for the goods. I can get to town in my old truck if I need something, so don't be bringing no more food parcels out here. I done told you 'bout a hunert times. Quit bringing things out here."

Dulcie's refusal to listen to Luke's simple request had prompted him to head into the woods to avoid her if he heard her car coming in time.

Luke didn't require much. Never had. Dulcie knew this. Just about everybody in town knew it, but Dulcie had set her sights on Lucas Harnage. She started making moves from the minute she'd returned from Cedar Key to High Suwannee to take care of her dying father. Once her father had passed, she'd felt that she had to make her moves quickly because she saw that the recent widow, Lawsie Mae Slade, had the same idea. Lawsie Mae, however, didn't have the same brand of fortitude as Dulcie and had given up after a year of baking and taking sweets to Luke. Dulcie, on the other hand, simply was not the give-up type and had no way of knowing that her goal would never be achieved – and not just because of Lucas' undying love for Ginny.

High Suwannee was a small town. In towns like that, people tend to know quite a lot about their neighbors, and most people knew much of the story of Lucas and Genevieve Harnage. They understood when Luke said he could never have imagined that his life with Ginny would end so quickly. They sympathized – how could any young married couple imagine such a thing? After thirty-three years, he still suffered her loss. Even though Luke rarely came into town, people knew he was still not over her. Most of them understood that folks handle grief in all kinds of ways, and one can never predict how another might react.

The makeup of the town had changed little over the years. That's how it often goes in very small towns. People grow roots and stay even if some of the younger generations tend to move on. So most of the townfolks had lived their lives around Luke and Genevieve, and they gave the man the breathing space he wanted.

Luke and Ginny had been childhood sweethearts, although they'd claimed to be just friends for most of that time. As children, they walked into town together, hand in hand, for Saturday morning matinees at the Strand, sometimes featuring Abbott and Costello, Shirley Temple, or The Little Rascals. They also sat in the grass and listened to the little town band playing music in the gazebo over by the courthouse. Some of the older folks would chuckle and get a real kick out of watching those two youngsters singing along to "Let Me Call You Sweetheart" or "Moonlight Bay." Many predicted they would one day marry. Some said it seemed those children were destined to be together. The predictions proved correct, and the couple married just before Luke enlisted.

Before the romantic part of their relationship began, however, Genevieve's mother died. Ginny had just turned fourteen and was the only child who remained at home. Her father was a solemn, solitary man who understood little about how to comfort a girl child. Luke, whose father had passed away ten years prior, was the only one who could console her. She spent hours down by the river, and Luke stayed beside her, laying his hand over hers, quiet – only speaking when she needed conversation.

When Japan bombed Pearl Harbor in 1941, Wally Briner, the clerk from the feed store, Luke's only male confidant – and, more recently, a Navy seaman – was there. He happened to be ashore on liberty and was hit during the bombing. Wally became an immediate casualty. His death hit Luke hard. Because Luke was only fifteen and could not join the fight, it was Genevieve's turn to try to console her friend. Luke's way was to get angry. He listened to the radio every night, hoping it would not be over until he could go "Over There." Atlantic or Pacific, Luke didn't care. He just wanted to fight for Wally and America.

When Luke's mother was sent to a tuberculosis sanitarium near Miami, leaving the boy alone, he felt like a man – thought he could handle it alone. She left him a small savings account, and he had part-time work to finish his school years. Even with worries about his mother's unexpected illness, Luke's desire to do his part to win the war never waned, so when he turned eighteen on May 11th, 1944, he enlisted that very day. Ginny was only seventeen, but she understood his need to join. By then, they had long planned their future together. They were married at the courthouse the next day, Friday, the 12th of May.

Knowing he would soon depart for training at Camp Blanding, the newlyweds decided to stay in his daddy's old cabin in the woods by the Suwannee River. They wanted to be alone together. They had only four days, but they were glorious days of young married life. The area around the cabin was heavily wooded and quite secluded. Each day, they'd run naked to the river, play in the cool water and make love. As a surprise, Luke etched their names into a live oak tree where they often sat beside the water. He carved an elaborate heart adorned with curlicues around their names. They found every moment together blissful. Luke loved to hold his sweetheart tight in his arms as if something might pull her away. Ginny felt safe in his arms, and they just knew that God had put them on earth for each other.

They decided to spend their few days together like a married couple, so Luke cut wood for the fireplace and patched a small hole in the roof. Genevieve was a good cook and always added special touches to Luke's dish, like a heart with an arrow painted with butter into his fry-pan toast and forming his eggs into twin hearts. Each evening, they spread a blanket in the clearing, lay down, and watched lightning bugs display their blinking, sparkling lights until the stars outshone them. One night, a sudden thunderstorm chased them back into the cabin early, and they removed soaked clothing and loved each other by the fireplace. The two relished every moment they had together in the woods before Luke had to leave for training. It was to this cabin that Luke returned and continued living after Ginny's death.

The couple shared a beautiful time of "honeymooning." Soon, however, it was time for the inevitable departure, and Genevieve went to the train station to see Lucas off. The station master, having lost his son on D-Day, kept a Victrola in his office and played music over the loudspeaker when military men came to take what might be their last train ride from their hometowns. Though it wounded his heart and brought tears to his eyes each time, the man made it a custom to play his son's favorite song, "I'll Be Seeing You," by Dick Todd, as the men and boys started to board. The newlywed couple found it difficult to tear themselves apart as the song played, and the train began to roll slowly, wheels squealing as the conductor called a final, "All aboard." Luke jumped onto the steps of the rail car at the last minute. Ginny followed along the platform, arms outstretched to hold his hand. The song had ended, but as the train proceeded, picking up speed, Luke hollered, "I'll be seeing you, Sweetheart!" Then their fingers lost touch, and he was gone. The words of that idiom became the couple's sign-off to each other in every letter written. Luke always added, Sweetheart to his letters, and Ginny ended hers with, My Love.

Luke rode the train to New York, where he was then transported to Europe on a Liberty Ship. It was being used to carry a load of ammo and was protected by a convoy of destroyers. After a brief stopover in England, they landed in France. By then, most of the action was over in France except for a few skirmishes. They were mostly taking out strays who chose to fight and taking prisoner those who surrendered. Luke's unit quickly moved toward Germany but never saw much action beyond those few Germans left behind. He heard rumors that his unit might be sent to the Pacific, but they were returned home to guard POWs. Throughout his time overseas, Luke wrote daily letters to Ginny and received as many in return. The following year, the war was over in Europe, but work was still to be done there. He returned to the States shortly before the war ended in the Pacific.

While Luke was in Europe, Ginny's father sold their old house and moved to Clewiston to work with his son. Ginny got a job at Lula's Five & Dime and shared a one-room apartment nearby with two girls from school. She and Luke each saved as much as possible so they could buy a house in town when the war was over.

When Luke's unit was sent back to the States, he only had

a few months of enlistment left and was stationed back where he trained, at Camp Blanding. He finished his time there guarding the German and Japanese prisoners of war. He and Ginny rented a small house outside the base. When his off-duty time allowed, they spent every minute together. Ginny had purchased a small Victrola and a recording of the song they considered "our song" after the station master played it the day Luke left on the train headed to war. On his return, Ginny played the record each time Luke walked up the steps. He'd take her in his arms every time, dancing close and holding tight as if he thought something might pull them apart.

Upon Luke's discharge, they returned to High Suwannee and rented a tidy bungalow with a sleeping porch for when the weather was too hot. They discussed buying it but decided to wait until they saved a little more money to pay it off.

Luke immediately found employment with Ol' Tug Morrison, with whom he'd worked part-time during high school. Tug handcrafted furniture and sold it in a little shop on Main Street. While his mother was in the sanitarium and after her death a few months later, it was the only place Luke could find steady work. He'd been a quick study and had become quite an excellent craftsman. Ol' Tug was happy to have the boy back. Tug thought of Luke as "the boy," but in truth, he was only three years older than Luke. Unfortunately, a childhood accident left Tug with a bent back. He appeared much older, acted old, and, thus, was affectionately tagged as such by the folks around town. During Luke's time away, Ol' Tug had fallen ill twice, and he told Luke how lucky he felt to have him back again. Luke – in his mind – was the lucky one. He'd counted his blessings and thought them many. He'd made it through the war uninjured and had a beautiful wife, a bungalow, and a job he enjoyed. Luke knew that other returning servicemen weren't all as lucky as Luke felt himself to be.

All went well for the couple living in town for a few months. They talked of children and what they could do with the bungalow if they bought it. Their loving, playful lives continued, and then Ginny became ill. At first, she just lacked energy. She felt tired. Then her hands and feet and her beautiful face started to swell. Soon, other symptoms began, and the doctors seemed unable to help her in any productive way. Doctors and hospitals became their way of life for a while. What the people around them didn't know was that Genevieve tried to make it easier on Luke. She wouldn't complain even when things reached the lowest point, and she could see him breaking. She tried alleviating *his* pain and would recount their life in those days and thank him for making such a beautiful life for her. Ginny told him, "Always remember how we loved each other in those days at the cabin." Luke never forgot.

Just over two years after he had returned from Hitler's war, Genevieve, the love of his life, whispered, "I'll be seeing you, My Love." Those were the last words Genevieve ever said to the man she'd loved all her life. She never opened her eyes again and died in Luke's arms the following day. Kidney failure took her, just as it had taken her mother – Bright's disease, they called it. It had seemed unfair to him that she should be taken when they'd barely gotten started in life. But that's how it was, and he swore he'd never love another. Now, even with so many years gone by, Luke had let no other into his heart.

Dulcie's visits bothered Luke. He wanted to be left alone, and she was intrusive. She'd sometimes make awkward advances – touching his arm here, a shoulder there. She didn't seem to notice that he recoiled at her touch. Her maneuvers only served to bring painful memories of his beautiful Genevieve. If caught off guard, Luke would dismiss Dulcie as quickly as possible while trying not to appear rude.

After watching dust whirl up behind Dulcie's new 1981 Plymouth Fury and then die down as she passed the big curve, Luke would retreat to the front porch rocker and cover his face with his large tool-ravaged hands. The pain would hit him all over again, and he wondered if people ever got past the death of a loved one. It had been so many years, but Luke still wondered if his love for Ginny would fade. Sometimes, he feared it. When he worried he'd forget her face, he would stare at the fading photograph before drifting off to sleep. Despite his worry, Luke's passion and memories had never diminished, and he didn't want them to.

Luke went through the same thing every time Dulcie intruded. He'd be planning to complete an order or finish assembling a chair or table by sanding, staining, or some such chore in his workshop. The painful memories would fade into the background when he could stay focused on the work. Dulcie's intrusions caused his creative energy and focus to dissipate. He'd get her gone as quickly as possible, but memories of Genevieve in his childhood and their married days would soon flood him. He'd begin to re-run scenes through his mind like an old film reel and be lost for hours.

Most people in town knew of the couple's last years together. Many knew of their closeness in childhood and even their dating years in high school, but they only understood their connection on a surface level. True soulmates since childhood, the couple had kept a certain amount of privacy to avoid adults' playful but embarrassing teasing.

Lucas and Genevieve had been friends and neighbors since early childhood, but their friendship took a romantic turn in their teens. Ginny had long, sunbleached hair and green eyes. She was thin and could run like a gazelle, but her movements were luxurious, like a cat. Luke's heart seemed to skip a beat when she'd coyly turn to walk away, look over her shoulder, wink at him, and run so he'd have to chase her. Then, with her long hair playing in the breeze, he'd lift and swing her around before easing her down into the grass for a kiss. This playfulness became almost a ritual in their courting days.

After Ginny's death, Luke never felt like the bungalow was home again. He'd always felt excited when he walked up the steps and had that sweet, playful girl embrace him at the door. When she died, it left a hole in his life so large that he couldn't climb out of it. So Luke turned away from it all. He retreated to the cabin until Ol' Tug asked him to return to work again. Luke agreed, but only if he could build the furniture from his workshop at the cabin.

One afternoon, Luke had knocked off from work after finishing a ladder-back chair and side table for Tug. He planned to take them into the shop the following day. He was sitting on the porch carving into an intricate specimen of dead wood he'd found. He planned to put the carving as a centerpiece on the mantle. The sun was just striking the treetops when he heard the growl of a motor from the road out of his view. He could tell it wasn't Tug's ancient truck, and though it was late, it sounded an awful lot like Dulcie's Fury. Luke quickly folded and pocketed his knife, grabbed his shotgun leaning against the wall, and stepped off the porch. He stopped, listened a moment longer, saw that he had time, and returned to grab his unfinished carving. Then, with the car still not in sight, he turned and followed the trail behind his workshop into the woods.

Luke could not see Dulcie from his vantage point, but he could certainly hear her yoo-hooing. He knew she would persist for a while before she gave up and left, so he went further into the woods to the pond. Years before, an old tree had fallen in front of the live oak, and Luke sometimes sat there, eyes closed, listening to the whispering pines that nearly surrounded the pond. Ginny loved hearing the pines and claimed they weren't whispering but softly whistling.

After laying his gun aside, Luke ran his hand over the spot where he'd carved his and Ginny's names so many years before. It was higher on the oak and less visible, but he could still reach it. Afterward, he straddled the log, leaned against the oak, and started working on his wood carving again. It was finished except for small details.

Luke wasn't sure how long he'd been working on the piece, but darkness had overtaken him by the time he was finished. He listened intently for a moment and was confident that Dulcie was gone. He stood up from the log and immediately fell back to sitting. Luke tried again, feeling a bit wobbly, but picked up the carving and used his shotgun for a makeshift cane. He quickly sat down again, placed the carving in his lap, and laid the gun aside. Luke's heart was not racing. He was calm but unsure of what was happening. He looked up toward the swaying pines, and for a moment, he thought he heard Ginny's voice there. Finally, Luke put a hand to his chest, and without any pain, he felt his heartbeat slow and then stop.

When Luke failed to show up with the finished furniture, Ol' Tug Morrison drove out to check on his friend and employee the next morning. There was a mess on the front porch. He saw Dulcie's smeared and partially eaten note indicating she'd left some peach cobbler. All that remained was a broken casserole dish and lid, traces of blood, and the message. Evidently, raccoons had gotten to the cobbler first, and he hoped one had gotten cut and the blood was not Luke's. That was a big worry for Ol' Tug. He hollered for Luke but got no answer. He checked the cabin and then the shop. He saw a beautiful finished ladderback and table but quickened his pace, following the trail toward the pond.

Ol' Tug found Lucas Harnage where he died – slumped against a live oak tree with an ever-so-slight smile on his lips. Clearly, he was deceased, but Tug checked his wrist for a pulse anyway and then sat down on the log beside Luke. The wood carving had fallen to the ground, and Tug picked it up. Carved into the wood, he read…

I'll Be Seeing You Sweetheart

- the end -

13

THE LAST DANCE

Miami was extraordinarily hot that August. With her chores done at home, Linzy walked toward the school at the end of her block. A light breeze lifted tendrils of pale blonde hair off her slender shoulders. Perspiration dotted her freckled face, and she knew that by the time she reached the school, her thin T-shirt would be sticking to her body, outlining each rib and exposing the fact that her body wasn't changing yet. She'd recently begun to wonder if it ever would.

It was 1959, and though most homes in that modest, almost-middle-class neighborhood had air conditioners, very few families had the resources to run them routinely. How could they when kids were running in and out all day long? The air was rarely turned on at Linzy's house unless company was expected. With five kids to feed and clothe, her parents made it perfectly clear that using electricity to cool the house was an unaffordable luxury. In those incredibly rare, electrically-cooled times, if one dared open the front door, her father's angry voice would resound immediately and loudly, "Close that damned door! You're letting all the cold air out!"

In those Miami summers, though, the worst time was at night when the sun had long retired. It would seem logical that the heat would subside in the evening, but that would take many more hours. To Linzy, nights were when the temperature was most unbearable. She found it impossible to sleep at night unless she moved from her bed to the cool terrazzo floor. When the spot she lay on warmed up from the heat of her own body, she simply rolled over onto a new, cool place. During the day, however, she had little time to think about the scorching summer heat in northwest Miami. There was just too much to do.

While school meant hours away from home and her harsh, disciplinarian father, summer was a whole different kind of freedom. No longer trapped by a watchful father or a school desk, she saw summer days as real freedom. Though schools would start again in early September, Linzy was determined to ignore the heat and enjoy the extra liberty the rest of her summer presented.

1959 was the summer of her twelfth year. It was that pivotal time between elementary school and junior high – between true childhood and the tenuous entry into pre-adulthood. Linzy was excited at the prospect of walking to the end of her block and entering Madison Junior High School in the fall. Oblivious to the reality, just the thought of it made her feel more grown up. However, her thoughts that summer were mainly focused on all the activities awaiting her at the school's annual offering known as "Summer Recreation" at Madison.

Each year, Madison Junior High held summer school classes for those students who had failed required courses. At the same time, multiple activities were available for any other kids who wished to participate. There were art classes with Mr. Catino, beginning band, and competitions of all kinds. There were doll shows and pet shows, track and field, basketball, and other sports with Coach Gorson. Movies were shown weekly in the auditorium, and best of all, for Linzy, there was dancing to rock-n-roll music one day each week.

In the last room on the first wing of classrooms that Linzy would soon learn was Mr. Kliman's seventh-grade science class, the school made rock-n-roll dancing available every Wednesday afternoon. Dancing was Linzy's favorite activity, and though her best friend Trish wasn't so crazy about dancing, she would at least participate, but she was gone for the whole summer. Linzy felt lucky that her older sister Jane loved to dance, too. Jane had initially enlisted Linzy as a handy dance partner when their father wasn't home to stop the music or on the rare occasions when he'd allow their music to be played in the house. Both girls had become pretty good at the bop, the popular dance for rock-n-roll music. It was somewhat similar to the swing dances of the forties without the fancy acrobatic aspects. Unfortunately for Linzy, Jane's friends were always her first choice as dance partners if they were available. The truth was, at fifteen, Jane was outgrowing her younger sister, but Linzy was oblivious to that fact. Jane considered her younger sister a less desirable person to hang out with, but whenever her girlfriends weren't around, Linzy became the next best thing. With so many of their friends away on various vacations, Jane and Linzy had become dance partners out of necessity several times in the Madison classroom that summer.

The science classroom made an adequate dance floor. It had been cleared of desks, so all that remained were a wall of windows on one side and cabinets with countertops below on the opposite side. Most kids used the counters for a sitting area when they weren't dancing. Linzy was often reduced to sitting there because she lacked a dance partner, but her body was still in motion even when sitting. She moved to the beat of the music as if she were a dancer without legs. When Jane told her she looked silly moving around like that, Linzy said she didn't care. Jane had no way of knowing that dancing was so intrinsic to Linzy's being that she couldn't stop herself. She simply had to move to the music.

On dance day, the coach would set up a small record player that the school supplied, and the dancers brought in whatever 45 rpm records they could lay their hands on. All in all, with records in short supply, songs were repeated quite often. No one seemed to care about that, though. For most of them, the desire was for the dance. That little detail made it much easier to accept the fact that only one male dancer ever attended the dance sessions. Some boys dropped by here and there. They might submit to a slow dance with a girl they liked, but they never stayed long. The only boy who *really* danced was Howard.

Howard had freckles and red hair that was greased and slicked back into a ducktail, with the front combed into the style of Elvis Presley. Howard's sideburns completed the look, and that boy could flat-out dance. Undoubtedly, every female in that science classroom wished – with every fiber of her being – to be asked for a dance by Howard. Few ever got the privilege, and it was common practice for most girls to dance with each other. Howard danced most often with Betty Parker, but he always chose the prettiest or the most accomplished dancers if she wasn't there. The girls he preferred for dance partners were always those within his age group, which placed him in ninth grade in the fall. Linzy, who, even in her youthful naiveté, should have known better than to hope for a dance with Howard, nevertheless held out that secret hope all summer long.

Linzy had not missed a Wednesday dance session all through that sweltering summer. Even when Jane found other things to do, and Linzy knew she'd probably sit on the counter without dancing, she still went to the classroom. That had happened more and more often as the summer waned, and it happened again on the next-to-last dance session of the summer. Jane had promised to be there for the first hour of the session, but she didn't show up. Linzy still hoped her sister would walk through the door, although she knew the odds were not good. Despite her difficult home life, the girl was usually more optimistic, but on this day, she was downhearted. It seemed to Linzy that people rarely kept their word, and she felt that breaking a promise was a very wrong thing to do.

Linzy waited. Near the end of the first hour, Cindy, one of Jane's friends, stopped by for a few minutes, and Linzy begged for a dance. By the time the girl agreed, they only managed to dance the last half of "Sweet Little Sixteen." Linzy's heart sank when Cindy grabbed her purse afterward and sing-songed, "Toodle-oo, Linzy. Tell Jane I said to call me if she can get Mrs. Lancaster off the darn party line."

Linzy went back to her place on the countertop and watched. She watched all the dancers and noticed the ones who danced enthusiastically or at least tried and those who did not. It was easy to pick them out, but Linzy spent little time watching them. Mostly – as was often the case – she became drawn to and entranced with every move that Howard and his partner made on the dance floor. Their movements seemed so precise, unlike the haphazard dancers around them. Linzy wondered if they practiced those steps and movements or if they were natural actions. Linzy imagined herself in Betty's position and imagined that she could move so smoothly.

Betty was there as always in her perfectly starched pedal-pushers with a sleeveless button-up shirt tied at her waist. When they danced to "Get a Job," "Splish Splash," and "All Shook Up" – three fast songs in a row – Linzy couldn't figure out how Betty remained nearly sweat-free with every hair perfectly in place. She wondered if that was one of those teenage-girl secrets someone would tell her about when she became a teen herself.

As she continued observing, Linzy marveled at the smooth, easy movements and the fancy footwork that Howard included in his dance routines. She watched how Betty took her cues seemingly, from just the slightest pressure and tiniest movement of Howard's guiding hands. Together, they made it look effortless.

When they transitioned from Elvis right into Sam Cooke's "You Send Me," and Howard pulled Betty into his arms, Linzy sighed. She felt a real longing and pictured Howard pulling her close in that same way. The girl caught herself thinking such and immediately snapped out of that reverie as if someone could know what she was thinking.

Linzy's father often threatened and was adamant that his daughters should have no thoughts of boys until they were sixteen. She often wondered *how, exactly, is a person supposed to not think about boys when they're everywhere?* After twelve years of experiencing her father's harsh, physical discipline, though, Linzy took him fully at his word and, except for a secret love she had for Johnny Crawford on the TV show *The Rifleman,* she did actually make an effort to avoid "thinking" about boys. However, the girl experienced an odd longing for Howard when she watched him dance.

There seemed to be something different about the feelings for Howard, though. She couldn't quite determine if it was like what she felt for Johnny or some unidentifiable but similar feeling more related to the dancing. Essentially, Linzy had nothing with which to compare her feelings. "Love" confounded her. So far in her short life, she'd only felt for Johnny what she thought of as "being in love." She hugged her pillow at night and pretended it was the actor.

Like many young girls, Linzy developed her understanding of love by watching movies and television. When she watched Tammy's longing for Pete in *Tammy and the Bachelor,* she thought she understood what it must feel like. She thought the same thing watching Liz with Nick in *April Love.* Linzy felt a similar heart-tugging sensation when she watched Howard and Betty in a dancer's embrace as Howard swept the pretty girl around the dance floor. Linzy wondered if a real embrace would ever come for her. That's when it suddenly dawned on her that even though Johnny was her secret crush, she might have just a hint of a crush on the red-haired boy. It was an impossible, never-to-be crush. That was undeniable. It hurt in a way, but Linzy understood the reality. Still, she could never share those thoughts and feelings with anyone.

Linzy was disappointed at being stood up by Jane once again. As usual, however, she was the last dancer to leave the classroom that day. She sat on the counter as the others meandered out the door, discussing plans for the next hours and the upcoming weekend. Then, finally, coach Gorson came in to collect the record player.

"Time to close up, Linzy," he said. " You and your little sister coming out for the final track and field events tomorrow?"

"Yes, Sir." Linzy hopped off the counter and produced a weak smile.

The coach sensed her melancholy. "I think you and Shelly have a good shot at taking the girl's broad jumps and, for sure, the high jumps… you two are great jumpers. It'll be a good competition."

Talk of the upcoming events took over Linzy's thoughts as she walked toward the art classroom with the coach.

The following week was to be the last week of summer recreation at Madison, and the new school year would start a week after. Linzy went through the next few days with a sense of imminent loss. While summer recreation allowed her to be away from her home life for hours, more importantly, it gave her a couple of hours of dance and rock-n-roll music. Sadness gripped her heart as she thought of the impending loss of those things. It gave her the same lonely kind of feeling she got when her cousins came to visit, and it was suddenly time for them to go home again. Linzy hated endings and the pain that followed. In that still-childish part of her mind, she vowed that when she was grown up, she'd do something to make sure she didn't have to endure the loss of things that she enjoyed or people she loved. The girl understood very well that children had no control over anything. Her father had always made that abundantly clear. Kids were to be seen and not heard – an old adage he held over his children's heads like a hatchet. All decisions belonged to him. Linzy also understood that as an adult, she'd have more choice in such matters. He wouldn't be able to hold her down anymore. She just knew it. That knowledge, however, did not ease her immediate feelings of loss and sadness.

The following Tuesday night, after her sister's constant barrage of questions and begging, Jane finally assured Linzy that she would go to the dance room the next day. It would be the last dance session of the summer, and Linzy needed to dance. That agreement, at least, gave her hope. If Jane actually did show up, Linzy knew she'd get to dance a lot. With all the broken promises and Jane being so unavailable for weeks, Linzy had not been sure that her sister would even agree to go. Jane had been distant all summer, and Linzy couldn't understand why. She knew Jane loved dancing as much as she did, but her sister had changed. Jane was secretive and preoccupied and had spent hardly any time dancing all summer. Nevertheless, Linzy believed Jane would keep her word, and that eased her mind. The girl fell asleep with thoughts of dancing, rock-n-roll music, and Howard's perfect dance moves while she hugged onto her pillow, embracing it as her secret love, Johnny Crawford.

On Wednesday afternoon, Linzy waited outside the dance classroom in a great mood. Earlier that morning, Jane again assured her sister that she was coming to dance. Linzy was excited at the thought of dancing but still suffered a slight underlying melancholy. It was the final day of dance and the last few days of summer recreation – more of that awful feeling of loss. Regular school sessions would begin soon. Jane would be moving on to high school, and Linzy would be a junior high school student. Starting a whole new grown-up chapter in her life was both exciting and terrifying, and she thought about that as she waited for Jane.

Coach Gorson arrived right on time. He opened up the classroom and plugged in the record player. He told everyone to have fun before he left. Debbie pressed an insert into a 45 rpm record – "Oh Boy" by Buddy Holly. Just entering the doorway, Howard and Betty hurried to the center of the dance floor, and both were in great form.

Linzy was annoyed that Jane hadn't arrived yet. Now, they had missed the first dance. She wondered what was holding her sister up. Twice, the girl went outside to look down the hallway, but there was no Jane in sight. Linzy's heart was quickly sinking.

Next played were "Summertime Blues" and "Wake Up Little Susie." Finally, Jane walked in with some of her friends. The song playing then was "All in the Game," a slow dance. When the fast ones started again, Linzy pleaded with her sister for a dance. "Please, please, please," she begged.

Jane turned from talking with her friends and faced her little sister. She said nothing, but her mouth was pinched tight in her face, and her eyes opened as wide as possible. The facial warning was clear to Linzy, and she held back the "you promised" that was about to come out of her mouth. Sue and Sharon paired up, and Cindy pulled Jane onto the dance floor behind them. Jane continued to dance with her friends, never leaving the dance floor through three more fast songs. Linzy was hurt. Tempted as she was to walk out and be angry, her body danced when the music was playing, and she had to stay. The girl waited and hoped for a turn. Eventually, they played "Searching" by the Coasters. It was one of Linzy's favorite songs, and finally, Jane came over and, with an aggravated attitude, pulled her onto the dance floor.

While the sisters were dancing, Jane told her, "Look... I'm leaving after this one, Linzy. We're all going up to the drugstore to get cherry cokes if you wanna tag along... but we're meetin' those boys who moved into the Copeland's house, so you gotta promise to sit quietly... a few stools away... and promise not to tell Daddy. I'll buy you a Coke. "

"You *said* you were coming to dance," Linzy protested. "You promised, Jane. You promised, and all you've done is dance with them! This is the last day to dance. I don't wanna go for Cokes... I wanna dance!"

"Well... I came, and we're dancing now. Listen, this just came up. I didn't plan it. I'm sorry, ya know? My promise didn't work out. But Sharon really wants to do this, and so does Cindy and Sue. And me, too. Darn it all, Linzy. I really wanna go meet these guys. Drew is so cute. So is Dougie."

"You're only fifteen! You're not supposed to be *thinking* about boys! Remember? Remember what Daddy said?" Linzy flared at her, but the girls kept dancing.

Jane could see the tears rimming Linzy's eyes. She could feel her sister's disappointment. "Listen... I'll be sixteen in four months... you'll see in a couple of years. Daddy doesn't have to know everything. He can't control our thoughts... and... and you'll be doing the same thing I'm doing too. You're gonna start junior high, for Pete's sake. You're gonna start liking boys yourself... so try to understand. I can't do this stuff when Daddy's home. He watches every step I make. Now I'm trusting you on this. So... so... can I count on you? You won't tell?"

Linzy couldn't answer. She couldn't even look at her sister at that moment.

When the song was over, Jane returned to huddle with her friends. Soon, she came back over to Linzy. The girl was sitting alone on the countertop. "Listen, I'll dance three songs with you when we get home this afternoon before Mama and Daddy get home from work... okay? I really promise."

"Okay," Linzy resigned herself to the obvious. "Okay... okay... just go."

The girls left, and Linzy could hear their laughter echo

back from down the hallway. She turned to focus on Howard and Betty. No other potential dance partners had entered the classroom, so Linzy returned to her spot on the counter. She thought she saw Howard look directly at her for one brief second, but ultimately, she knew that could not be. Howard would never notice someone like herself.

The music continued – "Do You Want to Dance," "A Lover's Question," and another round of "Wake up Little Susie," and on and on – and Linzy danced without legs and dreamed of a time when she too would have her own Howard who loved to dance as much as she did.

About fifteen minutes before the dance session was over, Coach Gorson stuck his head in the door.

"Howard... I've got to go reset the volleyball nets... I'm going to be a few minutes late closing up. Will you get everyone out on time so they won't be late for their other sessions? I'll pick up the record player when I get back, so just lock the door behind you."

"Sure thing, Coach." Howard had stopped in the middle of *Love Me Tender* to listen and gave a half salute before continuing the dance.

Betty left a few minutes later, and Howard gave the last dances to one of his stand-bys. The final song played was "Born Too Late," and Linzy felt sure the song was written just for her. It filled her with sadness and that longing feeling again. She wondered if there really would ever be someone like Howard for her. But, she knew for sure that she truly *was* born too late for the Howard she watched.

When that last song ended, Howard ushered everyone out, and as usual, Linzy was the last straggler. She headed toward the door, but just as she was about to step outside, Howard called to her.

"Hey... you... just a minute," he said.

Linzy turned back toward the boy. He stood by the record player, and the bright sunshine coming through the windows behind him made a white light around him. Then, with one hand on his hip, he curled the index finger of his other hand and motioned for her to come back. The girl pointed her own finger to her chest.

"Me?" She asked.

"Yeah... you," he said. "I noticed you didn't get a chance to dance much today, and seeing as how this is the last day of dance... I thought you just might like to get the last dance of summer recreation."

Linzy could find no words but slowly inched toward him.

Howard quickly sorted through his own small stack of vinyl records – not waiting for Linzy to respond. He pulled one from its paper sleeve and popped a yellow plastic insert into the center hole. He placed the record onto the turntable, and Elvis Presley's voice began belting out the lyrics of "Don't Be Cruel."

Howard quickly turned, took Linzy by the hand, and led her to the middle of the dance floor. Though she could find no words to speak, her body, her feet, and her very soul began to respond to the music and to the lead of the boy who was two years beyond her. Linzy found that with each slight movement of Howard's hands, he would easily guide her into the next dance position. When he twirled her underneath his arm, she followed smoothly. Linzy gave no thought to the steps. The two of them just became synchronistic within the natural rhythm of the music. Their ease of movement would have seemed to an observer to be the regular routine of seasoned dance partners rather than the first dance of two unlikely partners.

When the music concluded, Howard retrieved his records and led her to the door.

"What's your name?" He asked.

"Linzy," she whispered.

"Well, Linzy... You followed real good. You're a natural dancer, so don't you ever give it up."

Linzy's cheeks glowed pink, but she could think of nothing to say except thank you for the dance.

"See ya 'round, Linzy," Howard said.

"Ok... see ya..." she'd finally found an easy voice.

Howard stood by the science classroom door as Linzy stepped into the hall, gave a half-wave, and started down the walkway. When she reached the end of the row of classrooms, she turned the corner out of Howard's line of vision. Then, in a kind of delirious joy and oblivious of the child still within her, Linzy twirled around, jumped three times, and skipped the rest of the way down the hall toward Mr. Catino's art class.

As the summer waned, the new school year started. The girl found junior high school a new and exciting experience of changing classes and meeting new friends. In her seventh-grade school year, Linzy often saw Howard, the ninth-grader, around school. If they happened to catch each other's eye in a hallway, they'd wave or say hi, but they never danced again.

After the school year ended, Linzy never saw Howard again. Once he'd graduated ninth grade and was preparing for high school, he didn't attend any more summer dance sessions. Someone said Howard had gotten a job to help out at home, and someone else said his family had moved away. Linzy just assumed that he'd outgrown the idea of summer dancing with junior high kids. Whatever the real story was, Howard had moved on.

Linzy's life moved forward, too. Though she missed watching Howard dance during the two summers following his departure, she stayed too busy to dwell on the loss. Time moved on as time will do, and Linzy became occupied with high school studies, an after-school job, and teenage adventures. Eventually, thoughts of Howard and summer recreation faded gently into the background.

There were still moments in time when Linzy would reminisce about Howard's kind act or those days of summer dancing. In those moments, she would play the scene of her last dance of summer like a 45 record on an old record player. Remembering that dance with Howard and how wonderful it felt to dance with a dancer stayed with her throughout her life as a cherished memory.

Several years later, in December of 1965, Linzy heard more about Howard. She was in her first year at the Community College. She'd just left her car and was walking through the college parking lot, mentally running through her schedule for the day's classes and activities, when she heard someone call her name. Linzy stopped and turned to see Kathy, a girl from the old days at Madison. Kathy told her in a rather matter-of-fact way that Howard had been killed in combat in Vietnam in November. The girl provided no details about how it happened, but Linzy didn't want to hear them anyway – couldn't bear to hear them. She felt a sinking feeling in the pit of her stomach. She listened politely but quickly feigned a forgotten book and returned to her beat-up '54 Chevy.

Linzy was shaken, stunned. She couldn't even say she actually knew Howard, and yet she felt the great weight of loss.

Linzy sat down in the car and opened the windows to the balmy December breeze. She sat there with her eyes closed for a long time, just reflecting on the young Howard. She remembered the feel of his hand as he took her onto the dance floor and the smooth, effortless movements of his body – movements that made him a dancer. Linzy could *see* him dancing with Betty – owning that dance floor. She saw it all again as if it were just yesterday.

Slow tears overflowed Linzy's eyes as all those thoughts of him rushed at her. She began to think about the significance of her dance with him. It was a gift he didn't have to share – a great kindness granted to a young girl who just wanted to dance. A thing he certainly didn't have to do that was such a monumental thing for her as a twelve-year-old. That moment in time had stayed with her all the intervening years, and she was sure it would continue to be an important memory. Linzy had never stopped dancing and was sure, God willing, she never would. Although she'd never thought about it in such a way before, it suddenly hit her how such small, kind acts like the one Howard had bestowed upon her could stay with a person for a lifetime. It was a lesson Linzy would remember and spread to others on her journey through life.

Linzy attended no classes that day. She leaned back in her car, remembering all those things about Howard for a long time that December morning. Finally, she turned the radio on. Tears streamed down her face as she mourned the loss of a red-haired boy who she didn't know but who moved magnificently on a dance floor – a boy who had kindly and graciously given the last dance of the summer in 1959 to a skinny, twelve-year-old girl who loved to dance. Linzy had changed, and the music had changed significantly since that memorable summer. The Byrds' voices now echoed softly from the old Chevy radio – "Turn, Turn, Turn." She thought how true it was, as the Bible verse said, 'To everything, there is a season.' Linzy knew she would never forget the boy who danced at summer recreation, and she hoped that Howard had reveled in many seasons of dance before his last.

- the end -

* The Last Dance – like every other story in this collection – is fiction, and all the characters are fictional. As in most fiction, however, some elements within a story are based on truth. The character, Howard, was inspired by a boy named Howard, as I remember him from years ago. I knew nothing about him except that he was an incredible dancer I had the privilege to watch. He did not die in Vietnam. This story was simply inspired by watching and still remembering that boy – an exceptional dancer attending summer recreation at Madison Junior High School in Miami. I recently learned that Howard is still a talented dancer. He is a winning, competitive dancer admired by many for his excellence on the dance floor.

ALSO BY LINDA MARIE

Beyond the Mangroves tells a tale of trust and betrayal, of love lost and found. It is a story of survival, faith, and understanding in the face overwhelming treachery and deceit within the most unlikely of places—an island hidden deep within the watery expanse of the Everglades.

ROBBED OF HER LIFE...

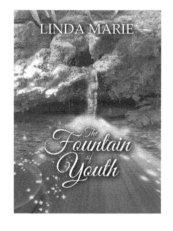

...when 82-year-old Eula is stripped of her home and possessions by a scheming banker and her scoundrel son. Suddenly she is forced to begin a new life in a brutal assisted living facility. Feeling lost and broken, she soon learns that a vicious nurse is determined to make her life far worse than she could have ever imagined. But when Eula discovers that she owns an odd but real 'Fountain of Youth,' she begins to work on a plan to take her life back and rescue an old friend. To succeed, she must deal with a dangerous woman who has the power to not only destroy her plan but to destroy Eula as well.

ABOUT THE AUTHOR

Linda Marie is a native Floridian and grew up in Miami. She retired after a 28-year career in law enforcement forensics, where she worked in crime scene and latent fingerprint identification. Linda was also a member of the U.S. Disaster Mortuary Operational Response Team (DMORT) and the Weapons of Mass Destruction Team (DMORT-WMD). She was a member for almost 20 years. In addition, she has worked with dog rescue groups for many years, and some of her "fosters" have become permanent members of her family. Linda currently lives in North Florida and continues to write.